STORIES
FOR A
WAITING
ROOM
(OR TO READ IN BED)

STORIES
FOR A
WAITING
ROOM
(OR TO READ IN BED)

MAGGIE KRAUS

First published in 2020 by Sixth Element Publishing
on behalf of Maggie Kraus

Sixth Element Publishing
Arthur Robinson House
13-14 The Green
Billingham TS23 1EU
Tel: 01642 360253
www.6epublishing.net

© Maggie Kraus 2020

ISBN 978-1-912218-74-5

British Library Cataloguing in Publication Data. A catalogue record for this
book is available from the British Library.

Printed in Great Britain.

CONTENTS

Foreword 1

The Usual Delays 3

The Weight of Winter 9

Imprisoned by Snow 12

The Wood Hummed 17

Threat 23

At the Museum 27

Time Warp 33

The Dealer at the Door 38

Not Waving but Drowning 39

On Holiday 45

Chip Shop 51

Out of Hand 55

The Discussion Group 61

Moses Carpenter (The Middlesbrough Mohawk) 65

Dressing the Part 66

Garrets 73

Next, Please 76

Give In 81

Holidays are the Only Cake 86

In the Valley Gardens, Saltburn 90

Lionel 91

Lists 98

Forever Amber 104

Funds and Father Luke 111

Me an' the Sarge 117

Melissa 122

Moonwatch 127

Muck 129

Anyone for Tarot? 132

Auntie Gertie and the Frogs..137

Away..141

Better by Train..147

Dog Rose..153

Caught in a Shower..155

Empathy..157

Altruism..162

Coming on Christmas..169

A Battle of Wills..171

Winter Church Sunday..180

Town Twinning Week..181

Under the Bridge..186

Snobs?..189

All the World's a Snowy Stage..193

A Brush with the Law..195

Class..200

Waiting for the Blue Light..205

On the Telly..211

Browing the Hill..213

Why is it that the Poets tell
So little of the Sense of Smell?..214

Ronnie..220

The Chicken that Blinked..225

The East Wind..231

Steel Men..235

The Leg..236

Getting it Wrong..242

The Light from the Candle..247

The Meeting..251

Remembrance Day..255

Isaac..256

Playing with the Professionals..261

FOREWORD

These very short stories and poems have been hanging around for ages, both in my head and lounging around the house, getting in the way. I eventually decided it was time to gather them all together because it struck me that people waiting for the dentist, the hairdressers or an MOT would rather not read the tatty, ancient copies of Bella, Country Life or even car magazines to pass the time, so… here it is.

The stories cover a range of subjects, from cancelled trains to making a will. They look at class, a school staff meeting, and the girl in the chip shop. One or two are a bit spooky. You could even read them in bed if you wish, but be warned, they may not always let you sleep soundly…

MK 2020

THE USUAL DELAYS

Three of us on the platform on a winter's evening. An announcer (who sounds as if he's in the warm) tells us in a smug, barely intelligible voice that the train is cancelled. It will be another forty minutes until the next one, which may or may not turn up, depending on how bad the weather is further down the line. At first we all look around us in the silence that follows the bad news. We do that odd thing that strangers do when they're thrust into unwanted intimacy because of a 'situation', first smiling uncertainly at each other, then, in our case, grumbling about the train company and the lack of service. The initial establishing of contact over, the conversation tails off.

We don't want to take this any further now. We've all calculated how friendly to get, and decided not too much in case we have to sit with each other once the next train arrives. I decide to get into a different carriage when it eventually comes. I fear creating too much intimacy, which could lead to someone telling me their life story all the way to the end of the line. There's an awkward silence, then we stand, uncertainly, awaiting further announcements.

The station has no facilities. No toilets, no cheery little shop-cum-café and no railway staff. There isn't even any shelter or overhead cover. Should it rain, we're banjaxed. In truth, there's a likelihood of snow, going by the earlier forecasts.

I stamp my feet a few times in a rhythmic movement and thrust my hands deeper into my pockets, breath steaming out of my mouth. I notice the woman next to me making her breath-signals too. The man has moved further along the platform with a no-nonsense walk. He's probably decided his blood won't freeze as long as he keeps moving. That coat he's wearing looks warm and stylish. Even from a distance you can see it's

3

well cut and expensive. I think it's called a Crombie, and I start wondering where that name comes from. Crombie. Is it short for something? I'm well into this line of thinking, having established that it's named after a town or a person, when we're shocked out of inertia by a new announcement. All trains are cancelled until the morning.

Crestfallen, the woman looks at me hopefully. "Surely they must send something – a bus or something?" The announcer interrupts her, "A replacement bus service will be available every twenty minutes and will take you as far as…" Silence.

"What's happened?" the woman asks unnecessarily. Does she really expect me to answer? I simply shrug, too fed up to respond.

The man, sensing that some leadership is needed, pipes up, "It's obvious that the tannoy's packed up. I've phoned my son and he's ringing the train company to get some more information."

The two of us heave a sigh of relief. Even though I didn't want him to take charge, now he has, I'm glad and grateful.

"Have you got far to go?" I ask.

"Too far." He is abrupt and short in his response, so I decide not to continue and he carries on walking away to the other end of the platform.

The woman looks as if she's in some difficulty with her breathing. I consider asking her, but then, that might exacerbate her problem and render her even more desperate. I give what I hope is a sympathetic little smile that turns into a downward grimace as if to say, 'poor you' but it's hardly helpful.

This is when I realise that my mobile phone has only one solitary bar of energy left on it. Stung into action, I switch it off, to be opened only in an emergency, so I'm effectively cut off from the outside world now, or so it seems to me. The cold is seeping through to my skin, through the too-thin layers of clothing that are only adequate to protect me in the time it takes to alight from one train and board the next. Luckily I've brought a thick scarf which, if wrapped double round my neck and shoulders, may help. I have a moment of frustration when I recall the conversations

I used to have with my mother about always carrying a top coat after Autumn. Go on, mam, have a gloat.

By now, I don't want to move around much, preferring to hold onto the small amount of heat I've generated just here inside my clothing. No point in wafting.

The woman, in her own attempt to stay warm, is still walking up and down the platform, taking tiny steps probably also avoiding the wafting draught. I notice how thin the soles of her boots are. At first they looked substantial, but the soles are plastic and the kitten heels are impractical and probably useless at keeping out the wet and cold. However, her coat is pretty good – thick and woollen by the look of it. Nice. My back, in contrast, is cold – and being penetrated by the damp night air.

I notice her checking her watch and automatically take out my phone to check the time, having forgotten the lack of charge until too late. Hmm, we've only been here ten minutes. The bus will be another ten. I decide I can cope with that, deluding myself that I can be stoical.

The man has disappeared but he can't have gone far – there's nowhere to go and it has just started to snow and I know it was predictable and I am ill-prepared for it but I am becoming increasingly irritated by this situation. Where's the bloody bus?

Just as I'm getting in a stew, something horrible happens. The woman suddenly screams, "Aagh! A rat!" whilst simultaneously losing her footing and sliding towards the edge of the platform. It's one of those 'slo-mo' moments when time behaves oddly – like in a dream when you're trying to cover your nakedness and running for shelter. I make a dash to help the woman who is hurt and shocked. She is making little sounds of pain and fear and doesn't seem to realise how close she is to the edge of the platform. In an attempt to rescue her, I make a desperate grab for her middle, but only manage to be dragged down myself by her panicking arms.

I imagine our fall is spectacular: the two of us in tandem, clutching at snowy air and platform edges, tearing our nails and fingers as we topple onto the filthy tracks below.

I am first to recover and quickly realise our predicament. I slowly get to my unsteady feet and soon I'm almost upright, stooping slightly to protect my back where it hit the metal rail full-on.

Trying to ignore the spasms of pain, I ask the obvious, "Are you alright?" but the woman is not conscious. I gauge the amount of agility needed to scale the wall to the platform. I might have been able to do it in daylight and dry conditions but my fingers are bleeding from trying to cling on earlier and I realise it's hopeless without a hand up.

'Where's Crombie?' I wonder. He'll have to help us. With a wry smile, I realise that at least we're not in any danger from oncoming trains, cos they're all bloody cancelled.

"Help. We've fallen onto the track!" I yell. "Mr Crombie! We're down here!"

At first there is nothing. The snow is thickening, I am shivering with cold, or fear, or both, and my companion is still comatose.

"Where are you? Help us!"

Suddenly he is there, shining a mobile phone to locate us. He's none too pleased and doesn't seem inclined to do much. "How the hell did you get down there?" he asks – more irritated than compassionate.

"Look, I can't wake this poor woman. She saw a rat on the rails and fell, and I tried to help her. If you have a working phone, ring 999. Now!"

He's exasperated but responds to the urgency in my voice by making the call. "Twenty minutes," he says. Mm, the magic number.

We stare at each other for a minute, until I'm sure he's prepared to make no rescue attempt.

"Can't you do something? If you take my hand, I'll be able to get up and maybe between us, we can lift her onto the platform."

'How did I land myself with this wimp? Where's a farm labourer when you need one?'

I must have said that aloud, because it forces him to spring into action. In a second, the overcoat is off, and he's slid down to join

6

us. Quickly assessing the situation, he checks her pulse and kneels to see if she's breathing.

"Get her arms," he says.

I do as I'm told although I'm not sure I'm capable of lifting her – she's quite hefty. He hoists her legs with ease and we drag and push as best we can until she's half on the platform, then he gives the remaining overhang of torso a shove and, voilà.

I stare at this man with a new-found admiration. Without the coat, he seems pretty well built and up to the job. "Come on," he says and I feel myself being clasped by brawny arms and placed in a sitting position on the cold, wet welcoming platform. In a gesture of belated gratitude, I offer my hand to help him in turn, but, using the swing of a gymnast, he's up beside us both in a matter of seconds. I'm truly impressed.

The woman begins to stir at this point, making, 'where am I' sounds. Mr Crombie is too preoccupied to notice. His once-white shirt is covered in dirt and oil and his trousers are torn. He's looking ruefully at the beautiful coat, unable to touch it with his now-filthy hands. Rather than soil it, he lets it rest on the snowy ground. How odd he is

I'm still kneeling by the woman, who tells me her name is Rose. She's still dazed so we don't talk any more. I turn to the man. "Thank you," I say. What else is there to say?

A bus and an ambulance arrive together. We are both checked for cuts and bruises and then we put Rose in the ambulance to be taken to hospital and when it leaves, we go to board the replacement bus.

The driver gets out of the cab and looks us over – and I realise that we must look a mess, but he astonishes us by refusing to let us board.

"Sorry, mate," he says to Mr Crombie, "I'll be in trouble if you get on in that state. All that oil on yer trousers – this upholstery's only been re-done last month." Looking me up and down, he says, "And you'll get blood everywhere. Nah, it's a health and safety issue."

Mr Crombie pushes past him, negotiates with some of the

passengers and comes back with a couple of copies of The Sun and a big headscarf. He covers a double seat with them and motions me to get on too. Then he sends the driver to pick up his Crombie from the platform.

My whole body begins to unstiffen with the heat of the bus, and we manage to smile at each other.

Did I ever say I like the strong, silent type? Well, from now on, I do.

THE WEIGHT OF WINTER

Browsing idly through the most recent pile of rejection letters, the creator of 'Meryl Bell Designs' was in reflective mood. 'Where do I go from here?' she wondered, holding a particularly galling letter from Marks and Spencer, explaining the lack of demand for a 'Have a great first day at school' card. Apparently, M&S had no plans to expand their range in view of the current financial climate. Hm. *They* **had a problem!** What about hers?

When she was left with a heap of debt by the death of her profligate husband, she had determined to clear it, but after the weight of grief had lifted, the selfish gene had kicked in and the 'good-times' memories gave way to impotent anger at the dead life partner. His debts, victorious, still squatted on her life.

There were many temptations to which you could succumb in a lifetime but gambling with other people's money, she decided, was the least forgivable. Strange then, that she had now chosen to design greetings cards for a living – a massive gamble, considering how she was fixed financially. However, the alternative had been shelf stacking in Lidl.

"They pay really well – being German," her friend Lilian had told her, brandishing the application form. Eh? How did that make sense? The only alternative she could think of was to put her modest talent for drawing to good use. She could also spot a photo opportunity and enjoyed searching for interesting subjects, so she'd kicked Lidl into touch and decided to go it alone.

She stared out of the window, hoping for inspiration. Dull, grey skies and dull, uniform houses glowered back, reflecting her present state of mind.

Her two most recent failures stared resentfully from the cluttered table. The first, 'Ice Queen,' depicting a Freddy Mercury lookalike, covered in glitter and licking a giant choc ice, was considered 'too lascivious' by the card company. That was laughable. She'd seen a lot worse. The expensive 'Freddie' she'd hired from the 'Lookylikees' agency had been a right diva, complaining of the cold all afternoon and claiming to be allergic to the glitter. As if!

Picking up the second card, she smiled to herself. Ah, little Howie, from the Golden Lotus Takeaway had been really great, and wouldn't take any money for the session. She had been really hopeful for a few weeks, but then Roxanne Cards accused her of racism. That had been a shock. All Howie was doing was sitting in a vandalised bus shelter in a thin grey jacket, with the rain tanking down on him. The caption simply read, 'The Bleakest Chink'. As she told the company at the time, it was meant to be poignant, and if Howie didn't consider it racist, why should they? "I think the world has moved on and left me behind," she sighed. "And that's another thing. This talking to myself all the time. I'm on my own too much."

She wished she could come up with a final Christmas Carol caption to complete the set of six commissioned for next July. Number 5 had just been drawn. It depicted a line of choirboys in surplices wearing tinsel haloes. Their hair was slicked down and parted at the side. Their mouths formed tiny 'o's. Once she'd finished printing the caption, it would say, 'Hark, the hair-oiled angels sing'. Surely nobody could object to that?

Of course, if it would only snow, there would be opportunities galore – a series of robins on dustbins perhaps – clichéd, she acknowledged, but best sellers.

'Come on, God, even a bit of a frost will do. I'm not fussy.' The silent prayer drifted around the shabby sitting room, where piles of debris glared malevolently from every surface, willing her to tidy up. Half-finished ideas and jottings upbraided her with the sin of procrastination. She turned away guiltily. The rain continued to fall with a vengeance.

On the wall above the desk was a framed print of her favourite cartoon. She took solace in re-reading it.

A family at the christening font stared out at the reader, each mouth drawn in one straight line, as the vicar asked, 'Is it wise to call your son Orson, Mrs Cart?' Meryl Bell stared gloomily at it. September 2004. Sadly, all the money she'd earned from that one had been spent years ago. No good being morose now though. Work to be done.

Rallying, she set to work on the current non-Christmas drawing. In the wings of a theatre, in the foreground of the drawing, the stage manager leaned forward, hand cupped at his mouth, whispering to a panic-stricken actor on stage. A few deft strokes of the pen made the actor hold a skull. Finally, the pen created a bubble from the prompt's frustrated mouth. The caption said, 'Or not to be!' She smiled, satisfied.

Seconds later, the coat was grabbed, the envelope addressed and she was off to the post office. This was a trusted method – get rid of it before second thoughts crept in. No time for them when money was at stake.

At the post office the queue was out the door and into the winter gloom. The assistant urged and squashed the customers in and locked the door. "You just made it," she told Meryl.

'If this were a film,' Meryl mused,' the first flakes of snow would now appear in a star-filled sky and I'd produce my camera and get some award-winning shots.' As it was, the woman in front was noisily sharing her delight in the all-encompassing chemical-peach smell of pot pourri emanating from a nearby display of Yankee Candles. "Oo, I do love comin' in here. It always smells great!"

Meryl's eyebrows lifted slightly in disbelief.

The Post Office hadn't quite decided what it wanted to be. Wrapping paper and sellotape vied for shelf space with pocket-money toys. A man at the counter reached for two staplers. 'Why two?' Meryl wondered, imagining various scenarios involving stationery.

An ancient, papery-skinned woman at the other counter

coughed loud and long. Suddenly, the air was rent by Cheryl Cole, declaring how she would fight for love. The queue jumped. The old woman answered this unlikely mobile summons. "That you, Dion? We're locked in," she rasped. It was an 80-capstan-a-day voice. "Meet us in the car park, will yer, son?" The phone was put away and silence reasserted itself.

Ten minutes later, business over, Meryl trekked gratefully home.

"I need a new subject," she sighed, switching the television on and settling down with a cup of coffee and a chocolate biscuit. The words to Christmas carols whirled around her head. "Only one more, then I can relax." She flicked idly through the TV channels with the remote.

"O little town of Bethlehem," hummed Meryl. There must be a joke in there somewhere. She remembered a photo she had of a camel staring at the signpost on the Redcar/Guisborough roundabout during the visit of the circus earlier in the year. Could it be asking, 'How far is it to Bethlehem?' No, that's pushing it a bit too far. She stretched and sighed.

On the telly, Dirk Bogarde was snogging a redhead, using that strange, lip-flattening, shoulder-grabbing technique that fifties-style actors used to denote urgency of passion. Dirk was wearing a neatly pressed plaid lumberjack shirt with rolled-up sleeves, meant to denote machismo. The woman didn't know Dirk was gay as she was responding passionately. Was there any card mileage in this? 'I must stop this and get on with my project,' Meryl thought, turning Dirk off.

"While shepherds watched..." she sang, staring through the greying net curtains hopefully, and trying to ignore the irritating label of her jumper which prickled her neck. No snow yet. 'What is a cartoon?' she wondered, then strode around, playing with ideas. 'It's a frozen moment, where you encapsulate the essence of wit in a few well-chosen words, twisting the situation from the expected to the improbable.'

'That'll do for my 'how to' manual.' She scribbled down the pompous sentence, feeling smug.

Hours passed, then, 'Of course!' It was a Poirot moment. She half-expected the great man to walk in, hit his forehead with the palm of his hand and declare, 'Mon Dieu, of course! Quel idiot!'

Dashing to the table, and knocking over her coffee cup, she began to work furiously.

Meryl's cartoon showed a starry night. Rounded, green hills and fields lay all around. In the foreground, a shepherd sat sporting a regulation stripey-teatowel-and-robe combo, and looking bored. The curly-coated sheep beside him also looked a bit fed up. The shepherd was holding a mobile phone to his ear. The caption read: 'Nowt much really. I'm just abiding in the fields at the moment.'

The snow outside began to fall as Meryl drew some cartoon snowflakes around her shepherd.

IMPRISONED BY SNOW

I'm imprisoned by snow,
Freshly fallen, it hides the brown earth,
And garden grass.
Replacing all with white beauty
where once
the dead residue of Autumn lay.
Weak midday sunlight melts the snowquilt to slush
Which freezes as night falls.
We hibernate.

At daybreak, snow falls on snow,
Hiding the glistening treachery of black ice beneath,
On the tarmac'd, ungritted surface of a minor road.
Scenic but deathly, the hushed earth muffles sound.
A five-barred gate, supports with ease, the weight
of each snow-covered post.
Three feet deep; immovable now, it bars the way.
So that, unable to shift it,
I must wait.
The car must wait.
My journey must wait.
For snow is my gaoler.

I'm imprisoned by spring.
Blue of the sky entices at my window.
Smell of new-wakened growth in the earth, beckons and seduces.
Buds, cautious at first, become aware
Of lengthening days and tempt me.
'Come, treat your winter-worn senses!'

Almost bewitched, I succumb momentarily,
But,
midges swarm at the garden fence.
Horseflies hide in the apple-tree hedges.
Before emerging from the chrysalis, I must
Take cover.
Spoil the scents of spring.
Protect my body with chemical sprays
Add an extra layer to spring-like, cotton clothing,
'Just in case.'
Yet, still, the sharp residue of winter winds
Pierce too-thin clothing.
Spring betrays me.

Glorious, the summer elbows through, claiming precedence.
Now, all will be well.
Promise of azure skies, lighter nights, gentler breezes,
seductive in its abundance, opens the prison door and beckons.
How sweet the air with honey scents,
how kind the temptress roses
Swaying on heavy branches! A loaded and fragrant paradise,
Yet, how thickly the pollen floats, unseen,
To choke the lungs and redden streaming eyes.
And prickly heat makes tiny stabs of pain on pale, tender bodies,
How skin itches and burns in the sun's rays.
We grope for tissues, stem sneezes and cover noses.
Hurry indoors and, closing windows, seek respite.
We can only watch the summer pass us by,
and marvel at its beauty
from the windows of our prison house.

Autumn, brimming with abundance, supplies
A feast for the senses.
Still, the greedy earth steals summer's warmth.
Fruits, already- ripening,
Await the harvest

And are gathered and preserved.
Delicious scents of pickles, jams and pies,
waft from warm kitchens,
to lull and cajole us into well-being.
Insects, replete and drunk with nectar
Buzz around frantic, taken off guard by their own death-throes.
We are quiescent, idle and happy.
Cosseted by the still-mild sunshine
Until the first stirrings from the east announce,
with a fanfare of wind and rain,
The Coming of Winter – again.
Summer things are stored away, gardening tools, paddling pools.
Gathering in the last, late- ripening crops, we head indoors.
Once more
imprisoned by the weather.

THE WOOD HUMMED

'The wood hummed and the rain was a cold weight but he observed this rather than felt it. The water ran down inside his clothes and squelched in his shoes as he eased his way carefully over the bedded twigs and leaves. At every instant he expected to see the prick-eared black head looking down at him from the hedge above.'

The rain was not torrential. It was heavy but steady. Nevertheless, the car headlights reflecting on the wet roads did not help with visibility. Joyce, wisely, had not said much apart from the occasional, "Left here," or, "This is a sharp bend," for which I was grateful. I gripped the steering wheel and took the roads slowly. When we reached the A171 we began to relax a little. Phew, a proper road that I recognised. It wasn't far now.

I'd realised early on that such a trip, under these conditions, was folly, but I am nothing if not dutiful and, having made a commitment, was determined to see it through. A quick look outside confirmed my worst fears. It had been raining non-stop all week and although there had been what the weather forecasters annoyingly referred to as 'spits and spots' that morning, the big guns had rolled in about lunchtime and the outlook was bleak.

I had agreed to drive to Commondale that Monday – alone, and in the dark in this driving rain and with very shaky knowledge of the route. "Sheer folly," I'd said to the cat, who gave me a deadpan stare. "Oh, did I say that out loud?"

He'd walked away, dismissing me.

As I say, it was an ill-advised trip from the start. Floods had disrupted travel for weeks now and our journey was not what you'd call 'essential', but neither was it a jaunt. I used Google to find the best route but it was no help. It would've sent me onto something called 'Potter's Side Lane' and thence onto a 'partial restricted usage' road. What did that mean? There'd be no nice rustic signpost saying Potters Side Lane, that's for sure.

A phone call to Joyce saved me. She would come along for the ride, give directions and bring her knitting in case of boredom. Wonderful!

So, here we were: bound for Commondale Village Hall, to rehearse for a concert. We'd be singing Wassailing songs, dressed in some sort of odd get-up involving mob caps and cloaks... the details were rather sketchy at present but I'd been looking in my, 'things-I wouldn't-be-seen-dead-in' box in the loft and felt reasonably sure I could cobble something together.

That optimistic sigh of relief we'd allowed ourselves on leaving the main road was premature. I knew from experience that as soon as anyone lets their guard down, things happen and I was about to be proved right.

The street lights were left behind now and we had only the car headlights to show the way; beautiful in daylight whatever the season, heather-clad and dotted with sheep at random intervals on the vast expanse of moorland but now a sheet of nothingness.

"Isn't there a cattle grid around here somewhere?"

Full beam on now, because the blackness was as dazzling as the light and eyes needed adjusting. Just as well, or I might never have seen the black bulk of him as we drove across the cattle grid, the familiar brammm of the tyres drowning out conversation momentarily.

"What was that?"

Joyce was perplexed when I slowed down, still willing my eyes to work in the unaccustomed darkness. "Sorry?"

"Did you see that thing on the cattle grid?"

I felt, rather than saw her move to look back, but of course it was too black to see. Besides, the rain was still pelting down, making visibility minimal.

"Might be a sheep caught in the grid. We'll have to check."

Joyce sighed. She'd been dragged out of her lovely, comfortable home to teararse round the countryside on such a night – simply to ensure that I got to Commondale safely – and was in no mood for further colder adventures. There are plenty of tales – superstitions mostly – about strange creatures on the moors; but nowadays few people believe them.

"Do a U-ee' and use the headlights to see by," she suggested, still reluctant to venture into the chill wetness.

Since we were the only fools on the road, it was an easy manoeuvre, but involved backing onto the verge and risking getting stuck. I chanced it.

He was now clearly visible from the car. A man. Bent double and obviously stuck; his boot trapped in the transverse bars of the grid. When the headlights hit him he flinched somewhat, shielding his eyes with his forearm but still tugging at the trapped heel.

We didn't ask him why or where he was going along that desolate stretch of road. We just added our heft to the task in hand. Ever practical, Joyce ran back to the car to rootle around for scissors in her bag. His boot was inexorably stuck and she planned to cut the laces to free his foot.

"Better lose your boot than your life, eh," she crooned cheerily, chopping at what passed for laces on his strange footwear. He remained silent throughout this operation. The rags holding the boot together were discarded on the roadside

"You can come back for your shoe in the daylight." Having noticed the poor state of his clothing I guessed it might be a greater loss than we'd first thought.

Once freed, we helped him into the back seat and wrapped his swollen foot in my old tartan picnic rug.

"At least it'll be warm." Joyce smiled, nodding at him but looking at me. She'd probably noticed that he smelled strangely of the woods and bracken. She sounded patronising and I cringed. She could patronise for England could Joyce.

We continued on to Commondale where he would be able to phone for help at the village hall, then we could carry on with our wassailing. I still wasn't sure what wassailing was, having only attended one rehearsal, but it involved singing old Christmas carols and I love to sing. And besides, there would be kind people there to help our wounded soldier.

There's a steep dip on the Commondale road, just before you enter the village, and I checked in the rear view mirror, fearing that our invalid might roll forward. "Hang onto your hats!" I counselled as we plunged through a shallow stream of floodwater at the bottom.

Staring back at me in the mirror were a pair of cat-green eyes, so startlingly close that I swerved a little and stalled the car, freewheeling for the last few hundred yards. "Oops. Sorry about that." I'd used a hearty tone but it unnerved me that I'd felt a curious current of connection to those eyes.

Joyce lurched forwards with the sudden impact but the passenger didn't flinch. The eyes in the mirror smiled forgivingly at me.

"You okay?"

He nodded.

Now we were under the street lights I could see him better. The clothing was truly shocking: thin and worn, but the face, though weather-worn was pleasant and calm. However, I noticed that a curious livid wound, like the bite of a wild creature, still bled from his forearm where the sleeve had been torn away. He withdrew it from view, so I thought it best to say nothing for the time being, but he'd need a doctor that was sure.

We busied ourselves with the usual stuff. Joyce opened the boot to retrieve her knitting and a spare scarf which she gave to him. I collected a bag of tabards, lately made, to kit out the children's sword dance team.

"Why don't you stay in the warm while we take these in and I'll ask if anyone can get you some dry clothes? Won't be a sec."

Warmth and well-being flooded into us as we entered the village hall where soup was being ladled out to all-comers. I thought of our wounded guest and asked for a bowl then went to collect him.

The car was empty when I returned. All traces of our passenger had vanished. Joyce fretted about his welfare most of the evening but I just felt quite empty, and, if I'm honest, I was a bit resentful that he'd gone off without even acknowledging our help. I suppose we all like to believe our good deeds are truly altruistic, but my reaction does me no favours. He had been silent, so social skills were probably not his strong point, but my disappointment was disproportionate.

An odd incident distracted me when one of the soup ladlers caught me by the arm. "You shouldn't ha' let him in," she said in an urgent whisper.

"What? What else was I supposed to do? Leave him to die of the cold?"

"No," she said, nodding at me, "YOU shouldn't ha' let him in."

We were called to order then so I didn't get to question her further, but the conversation unsettled me.

We wassailed cheerfully until we could sing no more, then ventured out into the drear of the night. Joyce talked again of the mystery man and his injuries.

"I just hope he's not on the front pages of tomorrow's Gazette."

She could sometimes be a bit of a pessimist.

"Well, it didn't look life-threatening to me. Anyway, we did our best."

"Ah, but what if our best wasn't good enough?"

I began to feel uneasy about him so I distracted her with a chorus of, "A soul cake, a soul cake, please good missus a soul cake," and the subject was dropped.

Soon, Joyce's bungalow hove into view and we said goodbye. Collecting all her belongings, she scoured the back seat of the car for any clues the man might have left, but drew a blank. I was becoming tired of the whole subject and rather rudely revved up as she was closing the car doors.

"We all have free will," I said, trying to sound convincing. "We're all responsible for our choices." I heard my words echo hollowly around me.

I was pulling in to the driveway, turning off the engine and anticipating hot tea and late night snacks, when a familiar current took hold of my body once more. I felt compelled to be still and

21

wait for it to subside. Deathly cold penetrated all my clothing. Against my will, I looked in the rear view mirror, where a familiar pair of feline-green eyes stared into my mind and crept in.

•

THREAT

A bulky silhouette blocked out most of the light coming through the semi-glazed front door of the neat little bungalow. Seconds later, Radio 4 was rudely interrupted by a loud, persistent knocking. Mrs Hodgkins, in mid-bite, put down her piece of toast and, leaving her cup of tea rapidly cooling on the kitchen table, padded out to the hallway to answer it. She assumed, wrongly, that it was yet another salesman offering bargain block paving, "Seeing as we're in the area, love."

The man was standing on the topmost step, virtually spilling into the house as she opened the door. They usually stepped back to ground level after knocking. This one, big and grubby, extended no such courtesy. She saw after the initial shock of him that he was only of average height but his bulk and proximity belied the fact.

He nodded, but it was an upside-down kind of nod. First the head raised slightly, then swiftly dropped back into position on the thick neck, as if a question had been asked. He didn't smile.

"Tony," he said.

Mrs Hodgkins was flustered, but instinctively, politeness reasserted itself.

"Oh, you're Bob's friend. Come to do the jobs?"

She backed into the hallway and stood to one side. Tony silently crossed the threshold. He didn't seem to have much in the way of tools with him. In fact, he had nothing.

"Right, what needs doing?"

"Oh, didn't Bob say?"

"Bit of carpentry an' drillin?"

"Erm, well, there's quite a few bits and pieces – curtain tie-backs?"

She led him into the living room. "I need hooks here and the curtain pole putting up."

Again that upward nod.

"There's some replacement skirting board to do in the hall, where I had a door blocked up and the bathroom light fitting's broken. Oh, and shelves."

Tony had taken out a small, dirty notebook and half a pencil from his grease-stained trouser pocket and was making a list.

"Have you got the wood?"

"Sorry?"

"The wood – for the shelves."

They were standing by the kitchen table. The half-eaten toast, now curling at the corners somehow exposed her vulnerability. She stood in front of it, half-ashamed, feeling an overwhelming urge to explain herself. "I was in the middle of breakfast, sorry." No response or acknowledgement. Embarrassed, she answered his question. "The wood? No, not yet."

He looked from the table to her then back down. The tea, now lukewarm, had developed a thin darker surface layer and would have to be thrown away.

"Oh, would you like a hot drink? I'm going to have another one."

"No, you're alright." He scanned the room, poker-faced; knowing.

"Anything else?" he asked, pencil poised.

"What? Oh, jobs. No. I don't know offhand. I had a list somewhere."

She walked over to a bureau where various bits of paper, bills and letters sat in messy piles, when she suddenly noticed a £20 note in full view and some pound coins beside it. In a sudden, inexplicable panic, she moved papers at random in a clumsy effort to conceal the money in the process. He watched impassively as she grabbed the list and offered it to him.

"Well now, Tony, where do you want to start? "

There was about him a fug redolent of a dirty mouse cage,

that she had chosen to ignore at first but that was now becoming insistently unpleasant. She smiled uncertainly. There was no response.

"I'll leave you to it then, shall I?"

She was making a fresh cup of tea in the kitchen when another loud knock startled her.

"That'll be our Andrew." He inclined his head in the direction of the knocking.

"Sorry?"

"Andrew. Me son."

"Oh, right!"

Mrs Hodgkins scuttled back to the front door where a plump young man – who was no stranger to a meat pie – filled the doorway. He grinned – whether this was at her or the anonymous person on the end of his mobile phone was unclear.

"In here, son," the gruff voice summoned.

As Andrew wafted past Mrs Hodgkins, his scent – already familiar to her – augmented Tony's, laying claim to the very air she was breathing.

Andrew was happy to have coffee. "Strong, three sugars."

With no further communication between father and son, Tony drifted out of view. Anxious now, Mrs Hodgkins went after him.

"Oh yes, the light pull. Do you need the new one? It's on the shelf here."

She had joined Tony for a second but he backed her out and closed the bathroom door, indicating with his head, saying only, "I'll just…"

Mrs Hodgkins stood for a few seconds, flushed slightly then scurried back to the boy in the kitchen, feeling as if she had committed a faux pas of some sort. She handed a plate of biscuits to Andrew.

Fifteen minutes passed, in which Mrs Hodgkins and Andrew stared impassively into space clutching their cups, waiting.

"Shall I take that?"

She removed the cup from his grubby hands and headed to the kitchen to wash up. Andrew hadn't said a word of thanks.

She was surprised to feel a tensing up in her neck muscles which could only be resentment. She was being made to feel out of place in her own home. The outward expression of her anger was not discernable to an outsider, but the loud clattering of the cups and slamming down of plates onto the draining board was a very satisfying change from the generally placid person she was. She glanced round at the young man now semi-recumbent on her sofa.

"Is there anything *you* could be making a start on?" She wondered whether she'd be charged for having him loitering, and what his hourly rate would be.

He shifted slightly, trying to get more comfortable. "Better wait for me dad."

Finally, the bathroom door opened to the sound of flushing water. "Andrew!"

The boy stirred up the dirty air around him and walked to the door, wreathed in his distinctive pot pourri of odours.

"Come on. We gotta get these." Tony handed him a half-page list of materials.

An abrupt, "Won't be long, love," and the front door slammed shut.

Mrs Hodgkins listened. Blessed silence.

After a few minutes of uncertainty, she flung open all the windows and collapsed into an armchair, where the lingering smell was beginning to mingle with the fresh air. After ten minutes or so, she would close them again. She would get the Marigolds out and clean the bathroom, thoroughly. She would spray the new herbal air freshener around a bit. She would get her coat, put the alarm on, lock all the doors and go to see her friend, Bob. Indignation was building slowly inside her. Her sanctuary had been invaded by aliens. Bob would be castigated.

He would be told to keep the men away from her house.

She expected the visit to be of some duration.

AT THE MUSEUM

It was a rare treat, being taken to York Castle Museum. The two cousins were full of eager anticipation and – if truth be told – a chance to cause some mischief. The adults, however, were determined that this was to be an educational trip.

Annoyingly, they began pointing out all the worthy things that could be seen; adding to them a sparse and misleading amount of half-remembered facts and exclaiming over the exhibits in raptures.

"Eee, look, Granny Murphy used to have a flat iron just like that!"

These bursts of enthusiasm were echoed by other families, overlaying the same reminiscences. "Look, mother, Oxydol!" and, "When we lived in Gurney Street, we used to have a poss-tub just like that! Remember wringing the sheets out, Jean?" as, grasping the mangle and pushing with all their might, the women got stuck into the household tasks of their youth with more vigour than they'd shown when it was compulsory.

Rob secretly thought it would be tragic if all the stuff in his life was stuck on shelves at a museum. It was tantamount to admitting that your life was almost over. How must that feel, he wondered. He couldn't talk to Billy about such a subject. His own mother, Jennifer, and Billy's mother, Pauline, were sisters. Then two years ago, Auntie Pauline went into hospital and died. None of them had really recovered and Rob just sort of pretended it hadn't happened. Neither of them acknowledged Billy's loss nor his grief. Since then the boys had spent most of the holidays with Rob's family who had never been able to say anything about his mother's death to either of the children.

He was brought up short when he found some replicas of his

older toys in the 'Present Day' children's section and felt quite unnerved.

Billy had no such sensitivities. "Phwoa, it stinks in here," he said, looking at the ash privy, complete with fake faeces, just before they entered the magnificent Victorian Street. Rob grabbed his collar and pulled him away, anxious to see everything.

The visit was meant to be planned and orderly but that idea fell at the first fence. The children had moved away from the adults; not deliberately, more by a clash of interests. Things they found worthy of further study were polar opposites to those which fascinated the rest of the family. Each breakaway group had gone their separate ways and assumed they'd meet up at the café, once they'd seen everything. The grown-ups thought this would be the best place to eat their packed lunches, foolishly distributed a full fifteen minutes earlier; but, once free from adult constraint, Bill said he was desperate for 'just something little to tide us over' and Rob knew better than to stop him.

He opened a Tupperware of sandwiches and began to chomp, wedging the box under his arm and pausing only to say, "Ooh corned beef," spitting out a few globules of bread and filling as he walked, when they reached the full sized Victorian Street, complete with shops, houses and sound effects.

The cousins were awestruck at first and stood still, trying to take it all in. Lights dimmed, and day turned to night before their eyes. Sounds of skirmishes between alley cats and the loud crashes of goods being loaded onto carts made them stare in wonderment as the sound effects began, then, as a storm rattled and thundered all around them, and fake rain and thunder enveloped them, the boys were both confused and enthused. They thought momentarily of running for shelter until Rob, the brighter of the two said, "Nah, Bill, it's not real." They both smiled as Billy said, still clutching his food, "This is brill."

The bells of numerous churches pealed almost in unison and horses hooves on cobbles struck an incongruous note which jarred with the flashings of 21st century cameras as the lightning struck.

The boys looked for a seat so they could finish their lunches. They spotted a green wooden bench outside a shop, where a woman in a purple puffa jacket sat, busily filing her nails, oblivious to the magical scene unfolding before her. The boys shuffled along and jostled just enough to irritate her. The final blow came when Billy opened a packet of cheese and onion crisps and offered her one. When she'd gone, they looked at the shop properly.

A rocking horse sat proudly in the front window. They checked the name swinging to and fro on the wooden sign directly above. 'W. Hendrikson Toy Dealer and Fancy Repository'.

"What does that mean?" asked Billy.

Rob really wanted to have a clever answer but eventually gave up and looked back blankly at his cousin. 'Fancy' he knew but 'Repository'? "It's just where they sell useless stuff," he said, accidentally getting it right.

"Aw yeah, what mam calls 'dust gatherers'." Billy was satisfied.

Food finished, Billy 'accidentally' left the empty containers on the bench and bounded along to the end of the street.

"Look, Rob," he shouted, staring into the face of the life-sized stuffed horse attached to a carriage, which stood in the centre of the road. He put his finger up to the horse's eye and gave it a poke. He wasn't sure what he expected, but had hoped that it might be moist.

"Puh, glass," he complained, his disgust almost palpable as he rubbed his grubby fingers together and wiped them on his jumper.

The lads managed to drag themselves out of the street scene, where a woman was shouting, "Ted, get one of me and Jean getting into the carriage, will you?"

They looked back to see the fatter of the two women perched precariously on the tiny steps leading into the vehicle. They exchanged grimaces and hurried on.

A later room was also dominated by another full size horse,

only this one was pulling a glass-panelled hearse. Two mourners, a father and his daughter walked behind, dressed in black. The child, head bowed, held her father's hand.

Billy turned away quickly and went across to the display around the walls. In one, he saw some pictures of men working in the wire-drawing sheds of a steelworks. Next to it was a group photo which named the people who stood smiling into the camera. A stylish middle-aged woman was presenting a silver cup to the leader whose hand she was shaking. Billy examined this for some time, before calling Rob, an urgent tone in his voice, continuing to stare at the photos.

"What?" The irritation in Rob's voice was clear.

"The photos." Not taking his eyes off the crowd, Bill pointed to the man in the picture whose features were exactly like their grandad's. Of course, that was impossible. Grandad Phillips was very much alive and active, and too young anyway. Also, the newspaper cutting was faded and fuzzy but there was something about the way he held himself – the angle at which his head was turned, quizzically, to the camera lens that was deliciously recognisable to the cousins. They stared until their eyes watered trying to focus, then they looked away, blinked, and stared again searching for more familiar faces in the crowd.

Rob spoke first. "He must be related to us." The picture had been folded over to fit into the display case and the boys wondered if they could get someone to open up and show them the caption. "It'll have some of the names on, I bet," said Rob. "Let's ask."

He looked at his watch. When was closing time? It couldn't be long now.

He wanted to show the family his amazing discovery, but they were probably waiting impatiently at the café.

"You stay here. I won't be long," he shouted to Billy as he made a dash for the stairs.

Almost as soon as he'd left, Billy was aware of a slight darkening of the lights in the room. He wasn't alarmed – he knew how the staff set the lighting to create a mood – but nobody was around and he didn't dare look at the funeral procession in the centre of the room. He'd always refused to think about death.

He walked along to the display at the other end. A collection of babies – well, baby clothes padded out to look real – were suspended at an angle; the finely embroidered christening clothes hanging palely down. When he'd entered this part of the museum, Billy, full of bravado, had jeered at many of the exhibits and made jokes at their expense. Now, alone in the fading lights, the featureless faces of the infants hanging in mid-air looked very spooky. They reminded him of tiny corpses, laid gently to rest in a glass case. A small row of Snow Whites in their glass coffins.

It was then that he realised the exhibits were more than just entertainment for a rainy afternoon. People had lived the real lives being displayed here. He forced himself to look at the mourners in the central display. The pretend little girl, head bowed in grief, clutched her father's hand as she walked behind what Billy imagined to be her mother's funeral bier. Billy stood for what seemed an age, clutching his stomach, not knowing how to react. He felt the child's sorrow acutely, and shuddered. Turning away, for it was more than he could bear, he surveyed the room again.

That case, where his ancestor's photo waited for recognition, goaded him into action. Why hadn't Rob at least tried to slide the glass panel over? That way, they didn't need to involve anyone else. Not being as hidebound as Rob about rules, Billy had a go. It was very stiff but he managed to get one hand half in and was wriggling it around when an assistant and a flurry of adults rounded the corner, encroaching on his solitude and espying his lawlessness.

Plenty of fussing and scolding ensued. Bill was pushed to the back whilst the grown-ups investigated. The man in the picture was identified as a William Phillips of Middlesbrough, who was indeed the boys' great-granddad. He was being presented with a football trophy by some minor dignitary. The curator offered to send the family a copy of the photo for their 'archive' and everyone but Billy was ridiculously excited. Rob mouthed, "What's an archive?" at him, but he just shrugged. The group moved to the stairs as the staff had directed. The museum was officially closed.

Billy was the last to leave the room. Rob walked on ahead, still preoccupied with the excitement. He was having praises heaped on his head by the mothers when Billy was turning round and looking again at the mourners. He sneaked back to the little girl. "Sorry," he whispered, "but it will get easier," and kissed her cold, waxen cheek before he left.

TIME WARP

She looked excited. "I start with a quotation, okay?

'One day tells its tale to another,
And one night imparts knowledge to another.
Although they have no words or language,
And their voices are not heard,
Their sound has gone out into all lands
And their message to the ends of the world.'

Then I go straight into the stuff from the war. Tell me honestly what you think and what needs explaining. I need a second opinion."

Throat cleared, she shuffled papers and began to read.

'SCENE 1: Ext. Night. Virtual blackout. 1943. In the moonlight, the back kitchen window of a street house can be seen. There is no street lighting. SOUND of rain tapping on a window.

SCENE 2: Int. Night.1943. Through a tiny chink in blackout curtains can be seen a young woman in a pink slip, washing her face and neck by the light of a single candle.

SCENE 3: Ext. Night. 1943. Rain is splashing heavily on some kind of grey tarpaulin, under which a young man is sheltering. He leans in, putting his eye to the light and watches the woman through the window intently.

SCENE 4: Ext. Night 1943. A torch clicks on. SOUND of heavy rain on tarpaulin, beneath which, the young man is reading a piece of crumpled paper by its dim light. He is shivering. Switching off the light, he hurries down the now-moonless street and bumps into someone coming from the opposite direction. Both mumble apologetically.

SCENE 5: Ext. A Clifftop. Day. 1943. Dawn of a clear day. The young man is standing on a clifftop looking out to sea. There is a concrete bunker beside him. He puts down his rucksack and sits on the grassy edge of the cliff. Leaning against one of the bunker's walls, he unlaces his heavy boots. He undoes the rucksack and brings out a pair of brogues and an envelope. He puts on the shoes, then, carefully taking something from the envelope, he unlaces one of the boots and relaces them; bypassing one hole.

Removing something tiny from the envelope, he inserts it into the now-empty lacehole. He places the boots into the rucksack which he hides carefully in a clump of nearby gorse bushes, before setting off along the clifftop to Saltburn.

"And that's as far as I've got." She sighed, fanning out the few pages of completed script she'd brought for her friend's approval.

"Have you made it up?" Mary demanded, looking puzzled.

"Er, yeah. Well, sort of." She checked her watch and walked slowly to the door. "If I'm going to get this walk in before dark, I'd better go now. See you tomorrow."

She adjusted the rucksack and was about to walk away when Mary asked,

"But who are these people? I don't get it." She managed to sound light-hearted and smiled, tentatively but was rewarded only with, "Ah, all will be revealed soon!"

"Okay. Good luck with it then."

As she walked away she heard the disappointment as Mary's words trailed off.

Overwhelmed with relief at having escaped without saying too much, she set off on her usual route. Five miles every day had been the target and she found it easier as the time passed. The weight wasn't dropping off but she felt more comfortable in her body lately and it allowed her some precious thinking time to develop plot ideas. This screenwriting idea was becoming an obsession lately. Was the psalm at the beginning a bit too religious?

Looking to her right she saw the familiar line of balsam poplars almost shimmering in the heavy calm of the summer air. Beneath her confident exterior however, there was a sense of dread. What if it happened again?

She was a woman who liked a sense of order and control, but this… thing… that kept happening was weird and she felt helpless against it because she couldn't understand what it was.

After checking all around once more, she breathed deeply and relaxed her body. Everything was as it should be. There was the local pub, where it should be, and in the distance the church sat, fat and squat as usual in its tree-lined lawns.

These 'episodes' had been unnervingly frequent lately. Was it simply the unusual heat of the summer this year? People got restless, didn't they – they rioted and set cars on fire during city heat waves – perhaps this was a rural equivalent?

Three miles further on, she checked the landscape again. Removing her jacket, she tied the sleeves about her waist and carried on at a slower pace. She took out a water bottle and gulped down half of it at once to quell the dryness in her throat. There was plenty of time. Just take it easy.

Your mind wanders if you let it. That image of the man on the clifftop was probably just that: imaginary. How familiar he seemed though. He just blended in with the sky and sea so well – as if that was the only place he would ever be. He had been very clear at first-she could easily see the handsome face, the colour of his eyes and hair. How strange, then, that the closer she got to him, the vaguer his features became.

Pay attention to where you are! All these visions are just silly ideas for a film. She began to think about that. 'It needs finishing – and soon.' Why couldn't she be done with it instead of being frozen by… what was it called? Writer's block? She couldn't decide what would happen next in the story. Still pondering on the option, she continued with the fat-busting walk.

Maybe in the next scene she should have another agent come to pick up the boots and remove the microfilm from the lacehole? Or would that be best left until later? Should she include the story she'd read in a local history book about the German captain in the war who left his ship and went to the cinema in Redcar, keeping his ticket as proof that he'd actually done it? That was a cracking story. Well worth using, that one.

She swiftly checked her whereabouts again and was relieved to see the familiar landmarks all around. Chiding herself, she shook away the idea of a time warp as illogical. 'That's not the way I think!' she told herself.

Ah, there was the white house on the left, so she'd soon reach Sandy's place, after the bridge.

The dusky air outside the church smelled of mushrooms and leaf-mould. Autumn was in it, along with the end of the summer's dreams. A chilly breeze caused her to shiver. How suddenly the weather had changed! And how could there be so many fallen leaves here? It was as if the seasons were changing as she walked, like that scene in Notting Hill in the market, with Hugh Grant.

She glanced around, uneasily. 'It feels like someone's watching me – just a shadow at the corner of my eye – an unpleasant feeling, but familiar.' She dismissed it as just lack of sleep and continued musing. That psalm she'd used in the film script talks about interconnection – 'one day tells its tale to another' – and something about their sound going out into all lands. Could that mean time and space too?

Then came the realisation. She checked around her again.

'Hang on a minute. The trees should be on my right.' They were behind her now, yet she didn't turn. She walked straight ahead. She was walking towards the cliff again, where she knew he was waiting. He would speak in a foreign tongue yet she would understand him.

"Jede nacht," he would say, "jede nacht traume ich von dir," and when she looked down, the walking gear would be gone and she would be barefoot, wearing the same pink slip again – the slip from the chest in granny's loft – and the German sea captain would take her to see the bunker, now half buried on the beach. In the war it had been a lookout post, but as the cliffs had crumbled in the intervening years, it had tumbled and was now half-submerged in the soft caress of the sand on the beach below.

When they reached it, he would show her the inscription he had stencilled on the roof over half a century ago – hidden until the last storm had sunk it even further into the sand. 'Jede nacht träume ich von dir,' it said. 'Every night I dream of you.' She would see his face clearly again... and it would be enough.

THE DEALER AT THE DOOR

The big woman places herself at the open doorway.
Suspicious.
Aggressive and hard-faced.
Shoves the skinny boy back inside
To hover on the threshold, behind her,
And shiver, in the dirty passageway,
barefoot.
Bends behind her bulk,
bruised and helpless head peeping
through the fleshly crook of
arms, akimbo.

Chins raised, quivering with rage
and eyes glittering, she spits out;
"Keep away."
The doorway spiv retreats.

The boy, with his half-broken voice
echoing the uncertainty of
half-realised ideas,
Breathes again.
"Sorry, mam.'"

NOT WAVING
BUT DROWNING

The first time I met Beth we were just eleven and beginning secondary school. We were the baby boomers – born after the war and just starting out on the path to adulthood. She was up to her ankles in water even then, what with passing the eleven plus and being sent, with the rest of us, into an alien environment that would see us crossing the line from working to middle class – and being offered the precious chance of a good education.

Of course, we were all in the same boat – or so I thought at the time. We came from the council estates and our parents were proud that we'd been given an opportunity that they had been denied. If I look back now, I thought we were blending in with the daughters of doctors, solicitors and all the other professional people the teachers were used to working with.

We were the first four-form intake; doubling the usual quota of first year pupils and we must have been quite a culture shock to the genteel women who were to be our tormentors and our salvation in equal measure in the ensuing years.

I say we 'blended in' but that was only on the surface. The school uniforms mostly blended in because we'd been sent a list of exactly what to buy and where to buy it – from the only two shops in town that were officially recognised. It had been a bit of a palaver getting my uniform because I specifically wanted a scarf from Lockeys – the very posh shop – as opposed to the coarser woollen item stocked by Newhouses. Otherwise, I looked okay at the start, allowing for the usual 'two sizes too big' syndrome of all the first years.

Beth, however, couldn't blend in anywhere because she was the only mixed-race girl in the school. She was destined to stick out among the pale, middle class faces of the older girls and the white roughneck renegades of the new intake.

Our uniforms emulated those of minor public schools, being bottle green and grey. The blazer was a forerunner of the Thatcher wardrobe, having silver braid edging all around and on the badge pocket. The beret was a marvel of four triangles – green, grey, green, grey with the school badge and logo – KSGS – proudly displayed in the centre position. It was forbidden to be seen in school uniform without your beret and eating in public was punishable with detention.

However, if you lived on a council estate, you were pretty safe from the eyes of the teachers, night or day and could run with your dog to the fish shop with impunity, still wearing your blazer. (I had to, as it was the only jacket I had. Beth was more fortunate. Her wardrobe was less sparse.)

The water level began to rise around her when the summer term began. We had a special summer uniform of red or green striped dresses, modelled on prison garb by the look of them. The green and red were muted and teamed with a dun-coloured contrast stripe. They had a high square neck, sleeves to the elbow and a skirt with a few meagre gathers below a thin waistband. The details are important; because fitting in was important. Everyone wore regulation dresses, with one exception.

Beth's mam, wanting the best – or the most exuberant – frocks, asked a neighbour to make her dresses. Without telling Beth, she chose really bright candy-striped cotton and insisted on very full gathered skirts. The style was more or less the same, but not workhouse chic, like the rest of us. The water was creeping up to calf level now. She was a sore thumb.

Luckily, she seemed able to shrug it off. A tall girl with an explosive personality, she became the leader of our little group from the outset. Being Beth's best- friend-of-the-week was our aim and we vied with each other to gain favour.

One way you knew you were in the running was if you went shopping together on Saturday and both bought the same outfit.

She was big on dressing you as if you were her twin. My dad and sister used to be irritated by it.

"You look daft walking round the streets like that – in the same dresses."

"No we don't. We both liked them at the same time. I think we look nice."

"Well, nobody'll take you for twins, that's for sure."

"Oh Dad, that's horrible. You're just a racist!" And I'd flounce off.

I didn't know at the time that he knew Beth's father from the workmen's club and thought he was 'a nice fella', because he wouldn't tell me. He told my sister to mention it once I'd 'cooled down'.

From this gap of time, I can see it was a desperate attempt to fit in. She probably thought if we wore the same clothes at least *some* part of her would be the same. At the time I just thought it was a great honour to be the 'best mate'.

The darker side of this coin was when she'd suddenly decide for some spurious reason that you were this week's outcast. If Beth fell out with you, the other girls ganged up and you were left to wander friendless during the hour and a half dinner time.

You had no choice but to sit at your designated place at the same dinner table, where cruel comments were directed *about* you, but not exactly *at* you. It was a crude but most effective form of bullying which helped me understand those sad adolescents who consider suicide because of it.

Clever, clever Beth always highlighted your weakness and publicly exploited it. I hated her. Then the spotlight would turn on someone else and you were welcomed back to the fold, like Mary Warren in The Crucible, running to Abigail's arms; forgiving her tormentor and turning on those who'd befriended her in her misery.

Although we had been close friends at school, we went our separate ways once we'd left. Beth's new best friend was Christine, another member of our school gang – I saw them in their 'twinny' outfits a few times, but we only renewed our friendship many years later, after a chance meeting at a shopping centre.

Wholeheartedly embracing me, she would tell Christine later, "I have a new best friend – Guess who!!" Christine and I sighed together at our subsequent meetings – it was an embarrassingly childish expression to use. Had she changed at all?

Married to a charming German and with three lovely children, she seemed content and settled in a beautiful house in the most expensive suburb of town. Dieter had done well and was working for half the year in Mali. Our families met up a few times and liked each other. We had nights out and lazy Sundays at each other's houses, and all was well until a year later when I told her my marriage was over, after seventeen years.

I was unprepared for her reaction. She burst into spontaneous tears – the only time I'd ever seen real emotion or any loss of control. Apologising profusely, the water waist-high around her, she explained, "Of all my friends, you were the happiest." I didn't know how to react to this alien version of her and simply muttered incoherently. It was all too raw.

The friendship faded on her side after that revelation and for a couple of years we didn't see each other, until one summer's day I was half watching the local news when she intruded on my life in a most terrible way.

A reporter was telling viewers of a tragic accident. The film showed a local woman being wheeled to an ambulance. The words didn't make sense to me at first, in the impersonal 'television' tones of the newsreader. Nobody I know is ever in the news so when I heard the details, it was as if I'd been dowsed with cold water.

I phoned my ex-husband, Martin, still in shock. "Beth's tried to kill herself and the children," I told him. "They're saying she'll be tried for murder. The two youngest are dead." Once he'd recovered his senses he rang me back and told me he'd seen her in town a few days earlier. He'd waved and she'd hurried across to greet him.

"She was her usual self – you know, talkative, cheery. She said Dieter was away and that she didn't have any money – but you say you haven't got any money when you only have a few quid till the end of the week, don't you? If I'd known she *really was* at rock bottom, I could have helped her. Oh God, those poor kids."

I took some freesias, her favourite flowers, to the hospital. I'd waited a week before I went and I wrote the card in my maiden name but I don't know why. I left them with the ward sister, with my love.

So, with the water lapping about her chin, she'd taken the car exhaust pipe, fed it into the bedroom window of her luxurious bungalow and, with all her children around her, had gone to sleep. The eldest girl survived, and so did Beth, thanks to a neighbour – an ex-classmate, who had noticed the pipe and gone to investigate.

Apparently, Dieter had left her with nothing – no food in the house, no money in the bank, no hope. I wonder how long she'd been flailing around in the deep end with nobody watching.

After years of incarceration and therapy, Beth managed to cobble a life together, for the sake of her daughter. She began working as a midwife, her former profession, and volunteered as a Relate counsellor. The press got wind of it and was cruel, dubbing her 'the angel of death' and grubbing around in the dirt for old detail, but she set her face against them and lived from day to day. The beautiful bungalow in Northumberland Road would not sell because of its history so she rented a tiny terraced house in the town centre.

Eventually we took up the threads of our friendship again. I realised that she used a variety of distractions to get her through life: fad diets, not buying clothes for a year, sending money to Africa to help orphans of war and believing resolutely in reincarnation and in 'choosing a script to live out in each of our lives'. She admired Myra Hindley, she told me. "Imagine having the nerve to live out that script."

One day, I plucked up the courage to ask how she managed to live with those terrible memories and, with surprising candour, she told me.

"I go back to the house sometimes. It's empty now but I remember how it used to be. Most of the time I can block out what's happened, but sometimes, I just pretend they're upstairs and I call up to them. 'Stevie, John, your dinner's ready'."

ON HOLIDAY

It was decided early on, before we even set off on holiday, that one of the 'must see' attractions of the Amalfi coast would be a trip to Pompeii. We only had a few days, so sacrificed the joys of Capri, and with neither of us being big Gracie Fields fans, that wasn't too much of a deprivation. We also declined the heat of Vesuvius, which could be seen from the hotel terrace, and was near enough to entice us, but the scorching weather put paid to that idea too. Pompeii, however, was a big attraction and not to be missed.

We went to the Tourist Information Office at the station. This was a misnomer. There was no 'information' available, but a man who thought himself much more charming than he was, tried hard to sell us a trip to Capri for 80 euros and another taking in the ruins of Pompeii for yet another 80. We rustled up false smiles, thanked him and said we'd think about it.

My daughter, meanwhile, had been researching the attractions yet again, and had changed her mind about Pompeii.

"Let's do Herculaneum instead. That's where the ordinary people lived and the ruins are not that far by train. If we go early, we'll beat the heat and we'll pass Pompeii on the way there. We can get off the train on the way back, when the crowds have left, and have a tour then," she said, optimistically.

It sounded like a plan and one which had an irresistible appeal to my socialist heart. Accordingly, the alarms were set for 7am – although the alarm clocks were superfluous to requirements because, at around 4.30 every morning we were treated to what I dubbed, 'the cocks' chorus' which consisted of at least the whole tenor section of the cockerel choir, a fair selection of the basses and a few castrati for good measure. These discordant sounds came from a chicken farm within spitting distance of the rear of the hotel.

The sound was layered, each voice trying to outdo the rest. I assume they were calling out for a mate, so eager were they to stand out in the crowd. Despite the three parts, there was no harmony, only overlaid screeching.

At first, one would try to ignore this cock-cophany, and try to keep as still as possible in an attempt to stay cool and recapture sleep, which even in the stifling morning heat was hard enough; but every day, they won. Six o'clock would see us padding around the bedroom in search of water, eye sockets ever deepening; or splashing our faces, pre-shower, with semi-warm water from the bathroom taps.

With breakfast from 7am and no tea-making facilities, we were compelled to wait, with different degrees of patience, until then.

Much could be said about the shortcomings of the hotel. It was meant to be four star but that meant nothing. In short, food bad, 'balcony' a tiny space for smokers to stand and have a fag and stare at the peeling paint, and at breakfast the waiters, in their cheap polyester tuxedos, growing more supercilious and unfriendly by the day as they proffered their tinned fruit. That is, *tinned* fruit in a country where orange and lemon trees were growing in abundance in the hotel grounds.

On the plus side, the view of the bay of Naples, Capri and Vesuvius, spread out in all its magnificence before us on the terrace. We decided to be philosophical. "Ah well, some you win, some you lose," said my tired daughter, trying to drink the semi-hot tea before it cooled.

On our 'tour' day, armed with train timetables and huge bottles of water, we headed for the railway station in Sorrento. Using my 'O' level Italian, I felt triumphant as I bought two 8 euro tickets to Herculaneum and we boarded the comfortable train along with the locals and a few American tourists. We did feel smug, I must confess. We'd only paid a tenth of the price the trip organiser had wanted and we felt wise and happy.

A French family sat next to us about half way there. The

mother was very organised and sorted the various children, aunts and daughters out into seats, then sat opposite to me, then two stops later, a very big, bearded American got on and sat in the seat across the aisle from us. By this time, the Frenchwoman and I had exchanged pleasantries in French (I was on a roll by then) and we were smiling at each other a lot. My daughter was less happy because as I heard later, the woman was 'a bit sweaty', so she turned away to avoid the armpits.

We journeyed on, past non-tourist towns, all of which looked enchanting, with the blue, blue of the sea and the silver boughs of overhanging trees. By this time the train had standing room only.

Ever one to see an injustice, I drew my daughter's attention to the American's bag, which he'd carelessly flung into the window seat as he sat down.

Now there were a couple of old people, as well as an assortment of different shapes and sizes, standing in the carriages, I'd expected him to have the grace to put his bag on his knee, but no. Oblivious to everyone else in the train, he took up both seats unencumbered by conscience.

When I said as much to Emma, the Frenchwoman said, "Oui, c'est vrais." We sat there agreeing in a spirit of 'entente cordiale' for a few minutes, at which point she pulled herself up out of the seat, and went across to the opposite one.

"Excuse me," she said to the startled Yank, "I would like to sit here. Thank you."

He looked confused for a few seconds then moved his bag onto his knee, and a few nods and smiles were exchanged by everyone in the carriage. Justice had been done.

Emma had been reading about the town of Herculaneum, as I mentioned, and she drew my attention to the possibility of thieves and pickpockets who, apparently, (and her probable source was Google) were lying in wait to fleece the unsuspecting tourist. With this thought uppermost in her mind, when a young man spoke to us seconds after we'd emerged from the station, she gave him short shrift.

"No, no," she said, dragging me by the sleeve.

I turned to listen to him, having a more open mind.

In turn, he said, "No, no. Here. Take this. Come back for food later."

It was a map of the town and directions to the ruins. She stopped panicking and looked suitably embarrassed and grateful. Crisis over, she/we turned on the gracious smiles and nodded vigorously, and all was well. There were no pirates, cut-throats or gypsies in Herculaneum. Take heart, all you future adventurers and don't believe everything you read on Google.

The ruins themselves were fascinating. We got an audio guide and tried to make sense of the numbered commentary. A couple of times we were looking at a house when it should have been a public place, but we got the gist most of the time.

Apparently 43 feet of volcanic ash fell on the town in minutes. It was near enough to Vesuvius to have covered the town at the same time as Pompeii. There was a moving account of a survivor, sent away by his mother just before the second ash fall covered the place, killing most of the citizens. The archaeologists had painstakingly unearthed all the houses, and in the square was a marble statue erected by a freed slave to his master, which was particularly moving. It must once have been a pleasant, reasonable place to live.

Had we been able to stand the noonday heat, we might have gleaned more of the history, but with no shade and 34 degrees C bearing down on us, we felt the need to find some shade and, inevitably, a cup of tea.

Accordingly, we meandered away from the site to find some refreshment. I suggested returning to the café by the station where the lad had given us the town map, so we sat in the sweltering inner shade and ordered tea.

Half way through our tea break, I noticed something strange.

"Em," I muttered surreptitiously, "I think that man in the corner has just taken a photo of me."

She wasn't convinced. "No! He's just looking at his messages, surely?"

And yet, there had been something about the way he held his phone and the tiny clicking sound which bothered me.

"Why would he take a photo of *you* anyway? You're no spring chicken you know."

Hmm, lovely!

Anyway, we were rather uncomfortable after that, so we drank up and left. As we approached the station steps, I half-turned and there was the man from the café. He was following us, and as I turned he spoke, "Signora, Scusi."

I assumed we'd left something at the table, but no. My daughter began tugging at my arm. "Come on! Hurry up! Don't stop."

"Would you have dinner with me tonight?" he asked. This was in Italian.

Emma was panicking. "Come on, Mam. Don't talk to him."

I turned and said, "No, thank you. We're going for the train."

"Where are you staying?"

"In Sorrento."

"Mam, Mam, don't encourage him. Come on."

"Then I will come to Sorrento and we can have dinner together."

"Keep your dignity and let's just go," said my anxious daughter.

I thought I'd just say one other word, "Impossibile," and that would be that.

But no. "Ma perche? Perche?" he asked.

By this time we were up the station steps and at the ticket collecting machine. Having fumbled for the tickets Emma thrust one into my hand and said, "Here, let's go!"

The man, whom Emma had by now decided was part of a mafia gang, stood at the top of the steps by this time, still looking genuinely confused and asking, "Why not?"

I pushed the ticket in the machine and waited for the barrier to open. It didn't.

"Try the other way!" she shouted.

We both tried. And we tried again. No use. I went to the window and asked the man there what was wrong with the barrier. My would-be suitor stood and watched. The station master looked at the ticket. Then he looked at me.

In a very patient voice he said, in slow Italian, "Signora, this is a ticket for the ruins of Herculaneum."

The man was still there, watching.

Feeling incredibly foolish, I fished in my bag, found the real train ticket, pushed it through the machine and we dashed up some more steps to the platform.

Once there, the heat of my embarrassment, mingled with the heat of the day, was tempered by a certain relief but I still blush, whenever I think about it. I feel that I behaved ungraciously and my daughter should have counselling.

To all the Googlers, I have a message. Forget pickpockets and thieves. My advice is: Beware the British abroad. We're all idiots.

However, I do have one remaining niggle. Will my picture be on some dubious website long after this holiday is a distant memory? If any of you visit dubious websites and come across it, would you delete it, please?

CHIP SHOP

Mari doesn't notice the letter anymore. It's just there, stuck in time in the dull, greasy landscape of the chippy.

Sometimes, when trade is slack – which it increasingly is these days – Mari will stand for a few minutes and read the 'Dogs for Adoption' notices on the far wall. She's already got a dog but is thinking of adopting a little Jack Russell for her gran, just as a bit of company.

"Big Jackie been in?" shouts a voice at the open door.

"Not yet, no," and the voice moves on.

Mari looks at her watch. Half eight. He's a bit late.

Edna shakes the chips around in their squared-off wire holders and watches Mari rewriting new signs for the wall onto star-shapes. The shapes are day-glo orange, green and pink. Mari writes, 'Cod Bites and chips £3.50' and blu-taks it on the wall behind her, near the letter.

"Have you mentioned the dog to your gran yet?"

Mari messes up the sign she's writing. It now reads, 'Gaelic' instead of 'garlic sauce'. Surreptitiously, she slides the spoilt paper to the bottom of the pile, a faint blush rising on her cheek. Edna, ever vigilant, has noticed but says nothing.

Edna's trying to update the image of the shop since the Chinese takeaway opened across the road. Mari chose the coloured stars 'to brighten the place up a bit'. She bought them at the new shopping mall in the town centre.

A customer comes in, backside first up the two steps, and hangs half out of the shop, shouting at someone in the street. "Not if you do that again, I won't," he laughs, as he turns round and leans against the heat of the counter, pressing his face to the metal and glass of the display cabinet, where freshly-fried cod offer themselves for selection. He sighs with pleasure at the heat, addressing Mari.

"Hiya, give us that big one at the end, will you... and a sausage... and a large chips."

Edna steps up to serve him, leaving Mari to continue her task.

"Where's your Jackie tonight, Tom?" she asks him as she loads the chips into a bag, allowing them to spill out, golden and still sizzling, onto the wrapping paper.

"Dunno. Hasn't he been in yet?"

Mari sighs. 'Obviously not', she wants to say, 'or she wouldn't be asking.'

Tom takes the package, loading it with salt and vinegar and eats one of the too-hot chips as he goes, slamming the door shut. 'Now the heat will become unbearable', thinks Mari, lifting the steel hatch to escape from the business end of the shop and re-open the door.

Whilst she's there, she takes a moment to peer out along both ends of the street, and breathes in lungfuls of non-chip shop air. Now she's in the street, she can smell the greasy scent of her hair and clothes. He's not there. Reluctantly, she shuffles back to work.

She's wearing her new pinny today, white with a strawberry motif. She knows it looks nice on her. She's hoping he'll come in again.

"You know what he is, don't you?" says Edna, casting an old-fashioned look at Mari.

"A travelling salesman." She pauses, dipping the fish in batter. "And we all know what they're like."

She's shouting now, over the racket of the fryer, as she slips another portion of cod into the hot fat.

"We all know what they're like."

Mari doesn't. She's thinking about his eyes.

The fish is fried to order, so you have to wait, your senses buoyed up with anticipation as you stand in the greasy heat.

The melt-in-the-mouth batter, Edna's secret recipe, is reputed to be the best in the area. The secret, Mari knows, is the pinch of bicarb Edna puts in at the last minute. Her fish and chips are fried in the best beef dripping – the traditional way, as Edna constantly boasts.

If it were up to her, Mari would use oil. "It's healthier," she tells her friends, "but Edna's stuck in the dark ages."

They serve a few more customers. There are only a couple of sausages now sitting in the display cupboard so Edna makes them both a cup of tea.

She sees his eyes first, looking through the glass panel at the top of the door. He takes his time up the steps into the shop and stands, with his head slightly cocked to the right, looking straight into Mari's face.

Something primeval stirs in Mari's soul.

This is the third time he's been here. Three weeks. How long, how long will he stay in the area, she longs to ask, but doesn't.

Under Edna's critical gaze she greets the stranger. "Hello again." It sounds unnecessary and foolish. He smiles slightly with one side of his mouth, gives her his order, then, as is the custom, he moves to the end of the counter to wait, reading the signs, and the letter, on the wall.

When Big Jackie finally enters the room, he fills it with menace.

"Bit late tonight, Jackie." Edna puts a special into the fish fryer.

"Aye. Trouble at t'mill." It's a joke but nobody's laughing. "Give us whatever's ready, love. I'm in a herry."

The stranger looks at Jackie in a detached way, noting the strongly-accented 'herry', then turns to finish reading the letter – the letter of praise that was written by Jackie's mother.

Mari smoothes down her new apron and spots a chance to talk. "It'll be another five minutes," she tells the stranger. "Is that okay?"

The ludicrous p.s. in the letter makes him laugh aloud. "God, your scraps are beautiful!" he reads aloud, still chuckling.

Mari is anxious.

"Is that okay? Cos Jackie's in a hurry." Mari's repetition hangs in the air.

The silence is palpable as the two men look at each other.

Jackie, who has no fear of physical violence, senses that he's in the presence of a man of unusual force, even perhaps of occult powers. The stranger finally breaks his long silence, looks Jackie in the eye without flickering or blinking and says, "No, let him wait his turn."

Mari's knees have turned to jelly.

Edna steps in.

"We look after our regulars here," she says, handing a package to Jackie. She has a smile on her face that Mari has never seen before.

Almost simultaneously, Mari proffers another fish and chip supper to the stranger, holding tight to his hand until Jackie has left.

"This one's yours," she says, as the heat from the food permeates their clasped hands.

He stiffens momentarily, then winks at Mari. "Right. See you next week then."

He gives her a nod, and is gone, into the dark of the night and the fresh sea air, leaving Mari to dry her palms and finish clearing up.

OUT OF HAND

I thought, 'This is getting out of hand.' And Glen agreed with me. In fact, she pointed it out in the first place, but I ignored her, because she can sometimes be a bit melodramatic.

I only realised this morning that I was obsessed when I spent my break, not with my feet up in the staff canteen, warming my hands on a cup of the usual, horribly stewed, orange-tinted tea, but hiding in my place behind the piano with a crick in my neck and fantasising – as usual – about Kamal.

Meanwhile, Glen was at the main till, making a few disparaging comments about me in a stage whisper to Lee, the cashier. I knew because I could see her worried eyes flick across to my hiding place from time to time.

'They all know and they think me a fool.' And it was true – the bit about me being a fool. In the words of the song, 'How long has this been going on?' It was a question I could've answered but chose not to think about too much.

He was there, of course. Whenever he wasn't there, I began to panic. What had happened? Was he ill? Or worse still, dead? Had he found a girl he wanted to stay with for longer than a couple of weeks this time? It was no less agonising for being pointless and foolish. And if all or any of these tragedies came to pass, I would never know and there was nothing I could do about it.

An arm reached slowly round and I was grabbed by the waist and edged out of the crevasse in which I had wedged myself, between the wall and the piano. It was Mrs Bentley, the supervisor.

"My room, now," she threatened. Her eyebrows clamped together in a seagull shape across her forehead, a sure sign that I was in big trouble.

Kamal sat at his usual table being served by June, his usual waitress. He had no idea about the small personal dramas evolving around him as he ate a slightly overcooked croissant and poured a large cup of strong coffee from an old-fashioned coffee pot, feeling the familiar satisfaction.

This place was so handy and nobody disturbed you. Tranquil. Yes, that was it – old-fashioned, but calming. No background music; waitresses in black wearing spotless white aprons and serving quietly and discreetly. He hated being asked if, "everything was alright" or whether he needed anything else. He could live with the almost burnt croissant as long as they all kept their distance. There was a tendency with some cafés to offer you other stuff… "Would you like a scone with that, sir? Or we have muffins on special this week?" Once, he'd protested and was told it was the new policy, and "Nobody has ever complained before". The half-finished coffee had been left to go cold and he hadn't returned for six long months.

Scanning this place now, however, he noted the demeanour of the staff was straight out of the 1950s – or how he imagined the 1950s would have been. Was it a good thing for people to know their place? With his family history, should he even be entertaining such thoughts? He recalled how proud his father had been to work as a servant in India all those years ago. It was considered an honour at that time to work in the British Consulate. Then, when the consul was posted back to Britain, Kamal's grandfather was doubly honoured when invited to accompany him. A little snort of disgust escaped from Kamal, sending flakes of croissant pastry across the table, onto his lap and onto the floor beneath. Quickly wiping the sides of his mouth he tried to contain the flakes into a little pile by his plate, surreptitiously checking to see if anyone had witnessed his tiny faux pas. The family influence was firmly in place – etiquette was still of paramount importance as it had been for his whole life.

Mrs Bentley's room was very pretty – more like a boudoir than a place of business. She had what I believe are called 'café curtains' – sort of half way up the window, snowy nets on a brass bar.

Above them, I could see pretty purple crocuses randomly planted in the lawns, and decided to focus on them whilst spleen was being vented all around. Mrs B soon ran out of steam like a kettle that's just been switched off, but although short-lived, the anger was ferocious.

Me: Sorry Mrs B, I thought nobody would mind if I just looked out at the customers for a bit.

Her: OH, is that right? And how might you enjoy ME gawping at YOU while you're trying to eat?

Me: Well, I probably wouldn't mind.

Her: Don't be so daft. Anyway – what were you looking at? Anything in particular?

I knew then that Glen had told her everything, despite my urging secrecy, so I thought I'd better tell her a bit of the truth. I held my head down and examined the corner of my apron – a very smart little apron; I'll give her that – Mrs Bentley made sure we looked good at work. I slowly met her eyes.

Me: You know the man who comes every Monday and has a croissant?

How stupid was that? She stayed silent, looking at me as if I was mad. The facts of the case are these, m'lud.

Her: Hmmm...

Me: Many years ago, when I was fifteen, I joined the Drama Club at school on the advice of the social worker, cos I was getting picked on for being shy. Well, I was terrified at first but then I got into the swing of things. I was a bit too good actually cos I found myself being given a leading role in the school's production of Romeo and Juliet – mainly because I was the best reader and I put the stresses in the right places. (I didn't know what that meant but the producer did).

Vicky Quinn had been the first choice, cos she was going out with Kamal, the class heart-throb, but she shot herself in the foot one day when she asked the head a daft question.

I could see by now that I had Mrs Bentley hooked. "What question?"

I explained how Vicky had put on this portentous, head-on-

one-side expression and leaned forward, addressing the room in general. "Whorr I don't get Miss, is, if Romeo and Juliet were the first people on earth, where did the Nurse come from?" The triumph in her voice was short-lived as she heard the teacher say kindly, "I think you're getting them mixed up with Adam and Eve, Vicky."

Mrs Bentley almost laughed. "What's that got to do with any of this?"

I tried again. The sun was slowly disappearing behind a cloud on the crocus-lawn, and the wind was beginning to strengthen. 'Kamal will be gone by now,' I thought.

Me: Can't you see? As Juliet, I had to kiss Kamal!

Her: So?

How could she not see the impossibility of kissing a boy I'd worshipped for four years – in public – and not because he *wanted* me to but because he *had* to. The embarrassment and humiliation became palpable all over again and I could feel the colour climbing up my neck and into my cheeks at the memory.

After the 'croissant incident' Kamal felt it incumbent upon him to explain and apologise to the waitress who brought his bill. He told her that one of the pastry flakes had caught in his windpipe and he'd "made rather a mess". She didn't care. She knew he tipped well, so she smiled and said some platitude or other – "not a problem" etc. He ordered a second coffee that he didn't really want – as some kind of penance – and scolding himself inwardly for lack of resolution, he sat back in his chair as she wiped the table with a grey bleach-tainted cloth.

'What a wimp,' he thought, castigating himself for lack of a backbone. 'Who cares, except me? I am paying. She's not doing me a favour, she's doing a job.'

He sent a text to his secretary. At least he was on solid ground there.

"So, what happened?" Mrs Bentley was dying to hear.

I continued. The dress rehearsal was considered time enough

for the kissing business. I was terrified yet excited. I persuaded myself that it would be up to him to do the kissing. I'd just be on the receiving end, so to speak. But when it came to it, I turned my head at the last second so his lips just brushed my cheek. I was in such big trouble. I was threatened with a week's detention if I did the same on performance night. The stupid thing was, I'd found even the cheek kiss exhilarating. I danced home, thrilled to bits and knew I'd manage the full-on lips next time.

"So that's him – Mr Croissant – the customer you were gawping at for – how long?"

"Six years," I whispered.

Her eyes opened even wider in disbelief.

"Does he even know who you are?"

With glowing cheeks I had to admit that I'd never spoken to him or even looked at him properly in all that time. What I *didn't* tell her was that I was stealing his napkins from the table after he'd left – but only if he'd used them on his lips. That wasn't really awful, was it? What I wanted to do more than anything now was to put things right between us.

Kamal should have been at work by now. There had been appointments to keep and he'd just dreamt an hour away in the warmth of the café. The rain had begun to fall and he had forgotten his raincoat and umbrella. 'Seize the day, man!' he urged, using his mantra to gain some sense of purpose, but then he fell back into his reverie and once more dreamt of the warm Indian sun on his face...

Mrs B couldn't end the interview without asking about the performance of Romeo and Juliet. Was it alright?

Of course it wasn't. My shyness crippled me on all three nights. First night he kissed half my nose, as I was turning away, second he got a mouthful of hair and on the final night I lifted my chin and butted his nose causing the whole audience to fall about. It was a disaster. Blood everywhere – although it looked worse than it was.

Mrs Bentley and I faced each other. I should have apologised for stalking a customer, but I didn't. I thought she'd understand. She muttered something about "unacceptable behaviour" and told me that Glen, my so-called friend had told her about the napkin collecting. I think we both realised then that my days were numbered. I turned and walked out of the office defiantly as she spat out the dreaded words.

In the café, Kamal still sat at his usual table, looking pensively gorgeous. I walked over to him boldly and without stopping to think, I touched his shoulder and said, "Remember me?"

I put out my hand to his cheek, turned it towards me and gave him a real smacker on the lips. I remember his skin was smooth and brown. The lips were warm and full. My face was scarlet and tingling with triumph as I turned and walked out into the spring rain.

It was a great day, that day I got the sack, and it was definitely worth it!

THE DISCUSSION GROUP

The conversation had turned nasty and all because Mary, who usually played devil's advocate, had said one word. The word was 'fascist'. Of course, everyone had an opinion and everyone jumped in at once, metaphorical fists flying. I checked my watch. They'd been at it for about an hour and a half now and the verbal missiles were still humming around the room.

Phil caught my eye. He was sitting at the table, out of harm's way. He shrugged slightly as if to step back from the whole scenario and I gave him an understanding smile.

As a rule, our discussions petered out as soon as the refreshments were ushered in. It's quite hard, I find, to maintain momentum when hampered by a mouthful of corned beef pie, so most of us give in and begin to mellow at that point. Not Kay, though. Someone had cast aspersions on her latest man and she was not to be placated – not even by the huge platter of ham and mustard sandwiches currently being demolished by the rest of us.

I took my drink and moved from the heated discussion to the unheated conservatory for a breather. Who had introduced this topic in the first place?

Of course, it was Mary. The subject had begun as 'relationships' and several of those present had taken the opportunity to either praise or abuse their various partners or exes: simultaneously portraying *themselves* as paragons of patience, loyalty and virtue in the face of massive unreason.

I happened to notice Mary's posture seconds before she spoke. She was sitting on the floor, hugging her knees in an artistic pose – one shapely bare foot protruding from a flowing plum-coloured skirt. The foot, along with the rest of her body, pointed directly at Clive, Elaine's husband. Now, I'm no expert on body language – haven't got time for all that rubbish – but this seemed like a blatant come-on to me.

I took stock of the situation. Mary fancies Clive, I thought, wonderingly. Clive the bigot. Clive the closet racist. Clive, tall, strong, red-faced and good-looking (if you liked that sort of square-jawed faded-film-star type; which I did not). This was very worrying because Mary usually got what – or who – she wanted.

Perhaps I should leave early.

If I had any sense, I would leave early but then Kay burst in, knocking over a mother-in-law's-tongue which lived behind the door of the conservatory. She was furious about some imaginary slight and I was forced to listen.

As soon as I could, I drifted slowly back into the melee, feeling somewhat miffed at the loss of my solitude.

'Time to give these gatherings the heave-ho,' I told myself; conveniently forgetting that I had been the instigator of the currently-opened can of worms.

Mine was a perfectly innocent remark and I stand by it even now. I merely used a quotation to challenge the group. It was from Dorothy Parker – to whit: 'Every woman loves a fascist.'

Their responses had been instant and unvaried. They were universally appalled. The women who were married to bullies were the most vociferous in their denials. I noticed clever Mary, arch seductress, glimmering girlishly at Clive. "I would never settle for a domineering partner – that is, unless he was very good looking." The toe advanced an inch or two.

Poor Elaine. As Clive's downtrodden wife she was in an impossible position. I thought, 'How can she react and keep her dignity in such a situation? She simply can't win.' That was when I decided to step in.

"It's true," I claimed. "Parker was nobody's fool, but even she became entangled with unsuitable men – stupid, handsome and ruthless; to use her description."

A few of us turned our eyes momentarily to Clive and then to

Elaine. To refocus them, I began to list, off the top of my head, all those fictional heroes who might fit the bill.

"Well, there's Heathcliff for starters," I claimed. "Loads of women fancy him although I can't for the life of me see why. He had no redeeming features. He was a violent thug."

A couple of them murmured assent, so I continued. "And what about the early Mr Darcy – before we knew he was capable of feelings? Be honest. An arrogant snob?"

Again, a mumbling concurrence.

"The new Sherlock? Doc Martin? Not handsome, not caring, they wouldn't bring you flowers, they have poor social skills and don't suffer fools gladly? And yet they have an attraction for huge numbers of women."

They were warming to the theme now and were making suggestions of their own.

"That mill-owner in North and South!" one shouted.

"Hannibal Lecter," another one said.

We all stared at her.

"That's outrageous," Kay responded, and the proposer had the grace to look shamefaced.

We were really getting somewhere now.

"I think it's cos I like Antony Hopkins," the Lecter fancier said by way of apology.

Up until this point the men had mostly been silent, not knowing what they thought of this very novel idea. Their wives – who, by and large, demanded that they be 'new men', nurturing and nappy changing, cooks and cleaners, respectful of their wives' ambitions and opinions – were all the while secretly lusting after strong, silent, brutish heroes.

Before they could do anything but make affronted noises, I declared my position.

"Steerforth." They stared at me. "Steerforth," I repeated. "In Dickens. David Copperfield? He is David's hero who saves him from the school bullies, even though he mocks him gently for the rest of the novel by calling him 'Daisy'."

They demanded further explanation.

"When David takes him to meet Peggoty's family, Little Emily is dazzled by him, so without a thought of how many lives he's destroying, he runs off with her. The only outcome Dickens finds acceptable for him is to drown him at sea. Well, I always had a tremendous crush on him despite his arrogance. Does he come into the category, do you think?"

They went quiet. I think I'd gone down in their estimation. Mary broke the silence with her own agenda. "Fascist," she purred at Clive, whose eyebrows lifted in surprised but hopeful anticipation.

I decided to get out of there as soon as possible. I signalled to Philip who grabbed our coats and we left before things got out of hand.

Philip Welsh, who had been listening intently to everything thus far, decided to respond to my confession in the car on the way home. "I suppose these men control women like a strict father might," he began. Phil, my dearest friend, and one-time lover, was a man of the world, reserved, perhaps a little suspicious, but in my company he knew he could be frank and enjoy that frankness. After much deliberation, he broke the silence once again.

"Sergeant Troy," he said. "He was my particular weakness. He was the man Bathsheba Everdene fell for in Far from the Madding Crowd despite having that honourable farmer and the practical shepherd both wild to marry her. Again, dazzling, handsome, cruel and careless with hearts. Yet that swordplay..." He sighed, with something akin to longing. "I always thought he was wonderful." He smiled apologetically, his long-delayed confession hanging between us.

For once, I was lost for words.

MOSES CARPENTER
(THE MIDDLESBROUGH MOHAWK)

That ancient, tribal heart,
Transplanted; now rests beneath alien earth
A rootless hybrid in the steel-grey landscape.
His given name, spanning the Testaments,
a poor fit.
'Giver of Laws? 'King of the Jews?'

Embraced in death by men of steel
United in their humanity…

Memories of the ancestral homeland
deep-rooted in his soul,
Now
Buried deep in Linthorpe clay.

Only a greystone monument
to mark his passing.

Passed on
And by-passed.

I wonder,
Do the haunting drum-rhythms of warrior blood
Still beat in that stilled breast?

DRESSING THE PART

"Oh and we'll probably do a bit of riding, so bring the appropriate stuff."

Entry 1

The words were spoken with nary a second thought of what it might mean for 'the likes of me'; and I go into that particular Victorian idiom advisedly because truly they threw me into a panic. What was it? This 'appropriate stuff'? Surely they wouldn't expect me to be decked out like a member of the Berkshire hunt – red coat and stuff? No, hang on, those coats; blatantly red though they are; are always referred to as 'hunting pink'. Why? Does the fox have pink blood? I felt nauseous at the prospect.

Surely I'd only have to wear something approximating to outdoor posh – green wellies and a waxed jacket? All the same though, it would save embarrassment if I checked at that tack shop in Guisborough?

It must seem that I was going to an awful lot of trouble over a casual remark, but I have always had a dread of looking out of place. As a child I went to a grammar school but my version of the uniform wasn't quite correct and I was bullied mercilessly because of it. I don't do myself any favours either, because I get so hung up about what to wear, I get it wildly wrong and either dress down too much or dress up for Cinderella's big moment. In both instances, I end up looking odd.

'Let's examine the wording of the invitation,' I told myself. '*Why don't you come to us for Easter?*' Hmm, why don't I go to them for Easter? I have no idea where to begin. How long do they want me to be there, for a start? Does 'Easter' mean the day itself, or the weekend, or a few days either side? I couldn't bear to be thought of as someone who stays too long. They could be wanting rid of me by the Monday. They'll probably have stuff to do with rich rellies – parties, dinners and – here we are again – riding around the countryside, looking the part and killing things.

Then I felt a glimmer of hope. Maybe I wouldn't have to ride at all. I could hide in their library. (Do they have a library, I wonder?) Also, it's not as if I know how to ride. Well, I can get on a horse and joggle around a bit with my toes pointing upwards and my heels pointing down but that's about it.

Mary Kelly and I used to help out with grooming the horses at a stables when I was a kid. As payment we'd get to trot around the yard for ten minutes, and Andrea, the owner, would teach us the correct posture. So, at least I'd know how to sit and how to get the horse to walk with me on its back. But that was it. I am having serious doubts as to whether it's enough.

Entry 2

On the internet now, looking up 'riding outfits'. Lots of photos of posh blonde kids in black hard hats and fitted black jackets.

I don't get how this is appropriate for riding. I'd've expected padded things to be more suitable – especially if you're not certain how to move on a horse. Oh, and I have it on good authority that it's called having 'a seat'. If you can ride well, you have 'a good seat'. I don't know any more than that, though. I just hope my seat's up to the occasion.

Lucy, the girl who's invited me to her country retreat, is the poshest person I know. She's the only posh person I know, actually. It's odd that she and I became friends but we met at night school where she was trying to learn Italian. I was brushing up on my O Level skills because I'd just been offered a job in Lanciano teaching English, and we bonded because the rest of the class was so dire. She looked up to me because I have a very good accent, although I fudge my way through the grammar. Not that it mattered in our group. Half of them had signed up on a whim and were regretting it because they thought it was only a matter of using the same word order as in English. The others had holiday romances left over and were determined to pick it up in a month when their Giovannis and Mariannas were coming.

Anyway, Lucy suggested the pub after one of the early lessons when I'd just explained to her about adjectival agreements.

"Excellent idea!"

She laughed when I made it a rule that we try to converse in Italian the whole night, just to make it interesting.

After that it became a regular occurrence. She got better at pronunciation and her parents insisted on meeting me because I 'must be a good influence'. Then I got the fateful invitation.

I'd been expecting to be invited for coffee, if I'm honest. That's the way most of my mates do things. You don't just have strangers to stay for a few days the first time you meet them, in my world. I suppose it's a class thing but it seemed mighty odd. I felt absurdly privileged, to be honest and found it hard – being me – not to be grovelling about it. It was all perfectly normal to Lucy, I suppose, as she took it in her stride.

Lucy's in her late twenties, just a bit younger than me, but in some ways she's more sophisticated. I mean she seems to know the rules more than I do. How to behave and how to treat people according to their position in life. They're very good at this, the posh people.

Generally, the upper classes still think they're better than us, believe you me. They are incredibly polite to your face, but you're not supposed to know what they're thinking cos the impeccable manners kick in – and I'm not saying they're cleverer than us, because they're not. They just know how to tug your chain and make you feel subservient, even if they're thick themselves. Beware the confident thickie – that's all I'm saying.

I realise that there is no basis for saying any of that. I have no knowledge or understanding of anyone who's attended public school or owns stables and land. Hence my feeling of inadequacy over this 'riding weekend' as I'm now calling it.

Entry 3

My mobile says 4.48am and I'm suddenly wide awake, with one question... *Will I have to wear jodhpurs??*

Now, I've never tried jodhpurs on, but a pair of thick stretchy trousers that have been created with deliberate puffed out empty thigh bags for some esoteric reason, wouldn't be a good look for most women. In fact, it would be a stretch for a skinny supermodel, let alone me. Sliding reluctantly out of my cosy bed, I turned on the computer and googled them.

Of course, I expect some of the riding women will be bigger than I am, and thick-thighed and hearty. I'm only a size 12, after all. However, after looking at a few photos, I realise something. Get your leg across a horse and you're bound to look slimmer, compared with the giant, polished horse-buttocks you're sitting on. Even so...

Giving it up for the time being, I creep back to bed with a shiver. I now knew that jodhpurs would be costly, like everything else to do with riding and this was strictly a one-off – and an outrageously expensive one.

Entry 4

In the last few weeks I've tried every charity shop in a ten mile radius, looking for a waxed jacket and a pair of jodhpurs. No joy.

My last resort, the tack shop, did prove helpful though and I was talked into buying two pairs of their most expensive jods (I was getting into the swing of things now –using the slang) – by a terribly clever saleswoman called Camilla. Apparently I needed a spare in case I fell off the horse.

I wouldn't look too awful in them, actually, if I put the wax thing on too, as it covers my bum completely. I was beginning to feel as if this mini-break might just be a triumph. No, don't stop me from calling it a mini-break – the terminology was urban enough to be comforting, and on the eve of the adventure, I needed comfort.

Entry 5

It's tomorrow. The Easter break starts tomorrow, and despite the success of jodhpurgate, I still feel insecure because: what am I wearing for the rest of the time, when I'm *not* on a bloody horse? That is, most of the time. I haven't thought about any other outfits I might need. A decent dress, for example.

I did a short survey of my friends and their wardrobes to see what I could cobble together last night. Our Italian teacher came up trumps and dropped off a very sparkly bronze dress. As she gave it to me she leaned in, twinkled and said, like it was a big secret, "C'era una volta…" with the implied three dots at the end.

C'era una volta – once upon a time! I got it now. Cinderella. "Yeah, but if they're all wearing jeans I'm gonna look stupid."

"Ma no! You will be stylish, more than them."

I tried the dress on after she'd left. It was outrageous. I could only wear it in a panto. The words 'laughing stock' came to mind.

You know what, I'm so worn out with the stress of it all I might not bother going.

Entry 6

It's my final day in Lucy's house. In twenty minutes we're going riding and I couldn't care less. Her brother Giles has been very nice to me but Lucy herself has been a real cow. She has no respect for anyone's privacy.

She said it would be 'fun' to sleep in the same room so I just said okay, although I wasn't keen. The room's massive and very nice – that's not the problem. Lucy's the problem. She keeps going through my stuff and trying it on. It's really cheeky.

She's just walked out of our room wearing my new jodhpurs – the nicer lovat green ones. Didn't ask. Didn't even tell me. Just paraded about a bit and walked out with them.

It's just one thing in a series of mini-invasions of my boundaries. The reason I'm even madder is because I can't bring myself to say anything about it. Pathetic. She just takes it for granted that it's okay and I just let it happen. If it was my other mates, I'd go spare, honestly. So why am I being a doormat?

"Come on, Jenny. We're leaving."

I'm in the beige jodhpurs and I couldn't be more tongue-tied if I were trussed up in a scold's bridle. Lucy's a confident horsewoman who knows I'm useless. She's been whispering to her boyfriend Matthew and the brother Giles, all the time I was struggling to get on this flaming horse. The groom spent a good ten minutes hoiking me up until I managed to get feet and stirrups to work together temporarily.

They all went off and I brought up the rear with an ancient uncle who kept making off-colour remarks. I couldn't shake him off or I would have shaken myself off at the same time.

Half way through the ride, just as I was feeling better about my performance, Lucy hung back to ride with me.

"Hey, ciao cara. Come stai?"

I was taken aback by this. First Italian she'd tried for ages. Then I noticed a huge rip in my jodhpurs. It went lengthwise along her right thigh and looked as if a thorn had caught them.

"Oh no. What happened?" I must've looked horrified. We had slowed down and were entering a wooded area overhung with trees and I had to bend double to get through.

She looked unconcerned, as if it were the most normal thing in the world to wreck someone's clothes. No apology necessary.

"Ah yes, that. I always think they're better for being worn in, don't you?" an easy smile, then she continued. "Now listen, if Giles asks you out, you're not to go. Mother doesn't like the idea."

"What?"

"Oh, it's just that you don't seem comfortable with the family, that's all," she shrugged.

Somehow the feelings aroused once we were in the canopy of foliage, freed my tongue.

"Get them jodhpurs off now." The grammar had slipped, matching the anger.

Lucy froze, staring uncomprehendingly.

"Now. They are mine, they are new and you stole them from my luggage. I want them back."

I couldn't believe this was my voice. Something inside me had finally snapped.

"But Cara, I have nothing else to wear."

The silence was thick with resentment from both of us. Eventually, she slid gracefully off the horse and stripped down to her expensive underwear.

I took the still-warm jodhpurs, and examined them, then, realising immediately that they were beyond repair, threw them deep into the thicket amongst the nettles and rode off.

Back at the house, already packed and waiting for the backlash, I spotted Giles coming in through the kitchen. "Here," I smiled, handing over my details. "Let's leave the horses behind next time." His fine aristocratic eyebrows rose and a hint of a blush spread across his features, as if it were a dream come true.

Well, why not? He's quite fit, revenge is sweet and I quite fancy being somebody's bit of rough for a change.

It's called 'hunting pink' because the tailor who originally used the red cloth was a Mr Pink.

GARRETS

Garrets and attics are not for the likes of us. We are the modest middle who neither starve in the former (for the sake of our art – singing rather beautifully as we burn our poetry to keep warm) nor inherit huge houses where unknown, cobwebbed treasures lie, ready to thrill and repulse us in equal measure.

Not for us, this mystery and excitement. No appearances on the Antiques Roadshow, claiming our priceless objects belonged to an old aunt. We have settled for the humble loft; a repository for semi-useful, 'come in handy one day' stuff. On closer examination, our stuff echoes everyone else's stuff. We recall father squeezing into unfeasibly small loft openings to grope around in the torch-lit blackness for the treasures of Christmas Past each December; carefully skirting round the once-prized collection of 78rpm records we knew would never emerge again once the old wooden radiogram was sent to Oxfam.

The only other treasures in the loft are a collection of old clothes, bedding and chipped vases; all viewed with distain by the antiques experts on 'Cash in the Attic' as fit only for the skip. "Oh for a proper, interesting attic," we sigh, chasing the usual rainbows.

My fantasy attic has dust in it, of course, but clean dust; the sort that doesn't make your hands dry out and doesn't contain mouse droppings or insects. It smells of promise. There, look, in the far corner, there's a dapple-grey rocking horse with red bridle and a splendid, real horse-hair mane with nary a crack or a split in its wood. The proud angle of the head suggests a readiness to take off and escape the red-painted rockers at a moment's notice.

To the left of Dobbin – the name is scratched on his neck – a set of discarded hats spanning different eras are thrown together in a designer-like tumble atop a wicker basket, out of which peep feather boas and silken nightwear; impossibly glamorous; and dresses, gossamer-fine, discarded, I imagine, after some past theatrical endeavours but somehow expectant... the show is not quite over yet..

A child's compendium of games sits on the floor beside a wooden top and whip; the whip tightly wound and ready to spin exuberantly across the darkened floorboards once again at the drop of an old penny.

Jewellery boxes abound in the fantasy attic – one tantalisingly spilling out pearls and Victorian gewgaws; insubstantial and fascinating. A smaller box, once the holder of fully-fashioned stockings (it says so on the front) reveals when opened a set of lace bobbins, each one a different work of miniature art; crowned with tiny beads and crystals, the heartbreaking, unfinished lace collar still attached and waiting for some dextrous hands to finish it – alas too late now... Who are these people?

Clues obligingly offer themselves in the dingiest corner. Leaning against the slatted wall are several paintings of – who knows? A youngish man with a kindly face stares out from a heavy wooden frame. He looks familiar; like someone we know – could it be us? Perhaps around the eyes...? We pull him forward impatiently - dissatisfied, needing more clues. *Are* there any more? Disappointingly, we discover only a few dull-looking landscapes. We return to Great Uncle Basil – for such we have named him. We like him. We examine his face again, closely. A very attractive man. Twinkling intelligent eyes and good cheekbones.

Ah, but he is Great Uncle Basil, sadly passed away long ago. The attraction recedes and is replaced by a warm feeling of belonging. We linger over his features for several minutes, noting the well-cut clothes and arrangement of facial whiskers around the sensitive mouth before reluctantly putting him away beneath his dusty cloth again.

Like covering the canary each evening, Basil no longer speaks to us once he's under wraps.

The main feature of the attic – the inevitable sea-chest – sits

74

patiently, centre-stage. It has no need to raise its skirts one iota to tempt us. It is like a beautifully wrapped gift, promising everything impossible.

'What does it contain?' we ask ourselves. As this is a fantasy, there must be something intriguing, bewitching and ultimately life-transforming in there. Should we look or speculate? Our imaginations run amok. A long lost will. The deeds to a castle? Pirate gold? A missing manuscript or an original first edition of Shakespeare's sonnets? As long as we do not look, we may allow ourselves to enjoy.

Back in reality-world, we teeter on a ladder, fingers tentatively skirting over shapes in the impenetrable nether regions of the loft. Maybe there is something more of our past to be found here? A small cardboard box with several oddly-shaped packages wrapped in tissue might be worth a look?

They will turn out to be small tin cars and a ragged teddy bear. Initially downhearted, we quickly rally and rethink. It may not be what we'd hoped, but it's *somebody's* past, after all.

It is then we make the decision. Our photograph collection in its variously neglected states, lying around the house in drawers and plastic bags, is a good place to start. We will preserve and label every one for future generations to discover. Perhaps a hundred years hence, those who come after may regard our photographs of childhood seaside outings, that first Spanish holiday, the disastrous trip in the old Ford Anglia and a very fetching new bikini caught on camera in the back garden, as important 'treasure trove'. We might be *almost* as fascinating as Great Uncle Basil. We'll never know. We can but hope.

NEXT, PLEASE

Jean shifts the shelving out of her way. Stopping for a moment to reflect, she asks, "Don't you hate it when people say, 'You remind me of someone,' and, half flattered, you compose your features to accept the compliment graciously and it turns out to be – ooh I dunno – Miss Marple or some other old biddy."

We are moving Frank at the time so there isn't much possibility of a response as we heft him into the corner. "Once we've got all three bodies shifted," Jean says, "we should have a cup of tea before we do anything else," so we nip up to the office and take the chance to get our breath back. There is a rather jolly atmosphere, now the hardest part is done. I think Chloe even cracks open a packet of chocolate biscuits.

"Who told you that, then?" Dougie asks.

What?

"That you looked like Miss Marple?"

The others have a good laugh at that one, but Jean seems confused. "Eh? Did someone say I looked like Miss Marple?"

I can't help sensing the note of indignation in her voice.

"Do I?"

"Of course you don't!" Andrea protests. "That's ridiculous." She picks up the thread.

"This bloke once said I looked like that woman off the OXO advert. He followed me around B&Q for ages so he could say it. It was the one who cuts your wood to size while you wait. Yeah. Followed me and left his station to do it." There's a pause. "Still… better than Miss Marple, eh?" Slipping a fresh piece of chewing gum into her already full mouth, she moves a shopping trolley full of brown boxes to the top of the stairwell to be shifted later, enjoying the effect the dig's had on Jean.

As they wend their way downstairs, Jean still has a pensive look on her face. I mistake it for the Miss Marple business still being on her mind but then she asks, "Are we going to put the woolly hats on these or not? Better stick one on him, don't you think, especially if we're taking them in the van tomorrow, and he's got no hair to speak of?"

Chloe chips in, "You mean Gavin?"

Dougie perks up at this. "The bald one? He's not Gavin. The one with the surfer hair's Gavin. Baldy's called Barry, I think. At least he was when I first started working here." He looks critically to where the bodies have been left in an untidy heap. Limbs have been thrown at random and Gavin's bum's in Frank's face.

"Look over there!" He addresses them all, pointing in disgust. "Honestly, there's no respect from youse lot. They deserve a bit of dignity as well, you know."

He gently manoeuvres them so they will look – well – alive, to anyone passing by.

Jean tuts and says, "No such word as 'youse', Dougie," giving him one of her looks at the same time.

Everyone ignores her.

Tony observes this concern, smiling wryly. "You're a right softie, you Douglarse. Anyway Baldy is called Stefan. He's Polish."

The others look at one another with deadpan faces, only their eyes moving to see each others' reactions – and Tony realises he'd said too much. It made no sense to let yourself get carried away with their histories, but he has. Stefan/Barry was a particular favourite. He doesn't know why. Perhaps because he looks like a hard man – something about the angle of the head – always at an aggressive tilt.

He begins to wonder if anyone noticed how he caressed the limbs as he moved them, but then Jean breaks the mood, reminding them that they still have tons more to do before it gets dark and the moment passes.

"We'll dismember them after dinner," she decides. "You all have plenty to do for now, sorting their clothes out and cleaning up the mess on the floor. And remember; we're getting a new brown one tomorrow – ethnic minority and all that. Have to keep up with trends."

The sound of the midnight clock chimes in the town centre. It sounds a bit like Big Ben, but then, the old Gothic town hall was built at a time of prosperity so it might have had ideas above its station.

In the silence of the corner where the bodies were dumped, there is a stirring. Tony puts the keys down, feeling his way in the semi-dark to the heap they hadn't managed to sort out earlier. He's doing a favour for Jean, who has promised him a bonus if he gets it done, but he doesn't know how much: probably less than he wants.

He sets to work, picking out arms and legs at random, trying to match them, like pairing up socks after laundry day.

"Come on, lads," he says, in his 'hearty' voice which belies his feelings, for he's a bit spooked to be honest. This somewhat grisly job and the atmosphere created by the half-light and emptiness of the store isn't as much fun as he'd expected. He tries to make short work of it, not even speaking to Stefan, his favourite, until he's finished.

"Here, Stef. I'll stand you next to the wall so you can see what's going on. Right, Gavin, you can surf across to look at the stairs – watch all the lasses as they go up to the top floor, eh? And Frank can have a chat with Stef. Good."

He piles up the shelves and boxes, hemming them in on all sides. "I'm off lads. See you tomorrow." And he leaves, picking up the keys, and whistling, to hide the little wave of anxiety as he switches the alarm on and the remaining light off.

It takes a while, but eventually 'Stef' breaks the silence. "Well, thanks very much, Tony. Look at the state of me! Didn't even have the courtesy to stick a pair of boxers on us."

"Yeah but at least you've got me stuck in front of you, hiding the private bits. I mean, I know we're not exactly well-endowed but my bum's exposed to the whole store – whoever walks past can look and laugh – and before you say anything, I know it's a nice one but I'm still naked in public, for heaven's sake. It's just wrong."

"Oh, poor you." This sarcastic response from Gavin is unexpected. He's normally quite confident and cheerful. "Look where I am. I'm certain when we're on show nobody realises we're eunuchs!" He looks down sadly to where his genitals should be. "In the morning I'll be a laughing stock, unless they hurry up and get some clothes on us."

Then, with just a hint of malice he addresses Stefan. "Oh, and I'm sure you'll look really butch in that bobble hat."

Disconsolate, Stefan goes quiet as Gavin continues, "And it won't be a Boro one either."

The knife twists.

In an attempt to deflect the conversation, Frank becomes peacemaker. "So, I wonder who the new boy will be? He'd better not upstage us."

"Oh, nothing surer! That's the whole point. Fresh faces. I reckon we're for the scrap heap." Gavin is in a 'we're all doomed' mode and the others daren't contradict him.

Stefan is thinking of the factory where he was churned out; a factory of Stefans all identical. He'd overheard one of the customers commenting on their standard proportions and the 'sameness' of them all. "Hardly Michelangelo standard," the man had commented.

"Apparently," his companion had said, "when people asked how come his statues were so perfect, he explained that all he had to do to sculpt David was to chip away all the parts that weren't David."

In the silence that follows, Stefan realises he's said it aloud. "Clever sod!" mutters Gavin. Everyone goes quiet.

"What did you think of Jean's new hairstyle, then?" asks Frank, deflecting again. The others have obviously not taken any notice so can't comment. "Have a look tomorrow. It's a right mess. She reminds me of someone – an actress I think."

By noon next day, the window display has to be up and running. Fully clothed now and striking various poses, Gavin, Stef and Frank look down at their public, in a selection of the trendiest outfits from the new season collection.

Gavin subtly turns his plastic head a couple of degrees to the left.

"You were right about Jean's hair," he mutters to Frank. "And I know who she reminds me of – that old TV detective – the one who's always knitting?"

The others chorus, "Oh, Miss Marple?"

"No," Gavin says, correcting himself, "the other woman. Her off the old OXO ad."

And I have to smile.

GIVE IN

As I remember it, I was practising 'delayed gratification' just before the incident occurred. Well, when I say 'I', I mean 'we' – that is, me and the dog. No; best be honest; *I* was trying delayed gratification, using the dog as a sounding board. He was getting pretty good at it actually. Oh, you don't know what it is? Let me explain.

'Delayed gratification' is about not allowing yourself to enjoy something until you're so fed up with waiting for it that you don't want it anymore. Apparently, it's good for your 'emotional intelligence' which is something I didn't even know I had until I read it in a magazine.

The dog was doing fine. I'd managed to perch a dog biscuit on the end of his nose and make him wait for it to the count of ten. So far he'd managed six but I could see the apologetic look in his brown doggy eyes as he slunk away – knowing he was a failure – eating the ill-gotten gains in a dark corner of the kitchen. It wouldn't be long though, I thought, optimistically, before our goal was reached. The only fly in the ointment as far as I could see was this – I couldn't ask him if he'd enjoyed the biscuit any more than usual because he'd waited for it.

Perhaps it was time to test myself. I'd never had much willpower. 'Lead us not into temptation' was my favourite line in the Lord's Prayer. I mean, if you've never been tempted, you need never succumb. For example: all those plain people who were never invited to sin, could smugly look down on the nice looking ones who were fending 'em off left right and centre. So, I was testing myself – a bit like they do in Lent really, but I already knew I was rubbish at giving stuff up.

"Right," I said determinedly, choosing my first object of

desire... one of those big, soft, American biscuits. Well...we'd call it a biscuit, but *they* call it a 'cookie'. Cookies are just stale British biscuits really. You know, when you've left the packet open for a couple of days. I know a lot of people who throw the top one of a half-eaten packet away, in case it's gone soft, but the Yanks just make them twice the size and call them 'cookies' so they can charge more for them. Sometimes, I annoy the woman on the bakery counter at Asda by asking for 'a couple of them big, stale biscuits please'. Childish, I know, but gratifying.

Anyway, I took out the white chocolate chip *biscuit* (you didn't think I'd pander to that Asda woman did you?), placed it on a dainty 'Old English Roses' china plate and made a cup of tea. The test was to finish the tea with the biscuit still intact. I know it wasn't much of a test but I'd decided to start small.

It did look tasty though, as I sat and stared at it whilst sipping slowly from the steaming cuppa. I *was* tempted, but I thought 'deliver me from evil' – that is, the evil of swigging the brew down in seconds and chomping on the biscuit.

Do you know, it almost scintillated on the plate, that forbidden biscuit. The sugar shone and the embedded creaminess of the chocolate pieces seemed to beckon. 'Just hold me for a second...' it whispered seductively from its blossomy china refuge. 'You don't *have* to eat me: a simple caress of my textured top will do.' I checked my watch. A minute and a half. Near enough.

Just as I was about to surrender, I heard the doorbell. Nooo. Grabbing at the biscuit I walked slowly to the door, cramming my mouth with sugary badness.

They were very early, and Mr Wilkins wasn't with them. He was doing good works at the church centre and they were in an excitable state as a consequence.

Alison was the first to speak. She held a paper bag aloft shouting, "I've brought cookies!"

The others cheered and I arranged my face into some semblance of pleasure then muttered the word "biscuits" under my breath. The other two, Marie and Peter, shared the upstairs flat. I knew not what their arrangements were up there, nor did

I care. It turned out that it was Alison's birthday – hence the resplendent feast before us.

I opened a bottle of wine – disallowed by Mr Wilkins at our first meeting – but today they made the most of his absence and necked the lot within minutes of pouring. I left mine untouched for the sake of DG. If it was good enough for Sting it was good enough for me. Well, I'm assuming here that that's all tantric sex is… sort of hanging about for ages waiting for the good bit.

The second bottle, a nice Chenin Blanc, went down a tad slower but was still much appreciated. When Alison produced a bottle of Schloer, we half-heartedly filled the glasses once more.

"So, have you made any worthwhile decisions yet?" I asked, looking at everyone in turn. Everyone gazed blankly back.

That was when the doorbell rang, to everyone's relief. We expected Mr Wilkins, but when I opened the door there was no one in sight. There was, however, a package at my feet. Small, brown, official and a bit smug-looking, if you ask me. As I bent to read the small printed label, they almost mowed me down, jostling to see – which was pointless actually as there was no name or address on the label. It simply said, 'At last I've found you', written in a fancy font.

"Hooray!" screeched Alison. "Another birthday present!"

I'd shifted myself out of the inner circle by now and was watching; enjoying the interaction.

They were all staring at each other after Alison's confident assumption, when Peter piped up.

"Actually, I was expecting something through the post today – and I do live here, you know, which makes it more plausible that it's for me, when you think about it." He was always too wordy, was Peter.

That was when they all tried to claim in unison that *they* must be the 'found' person; urgently offering rationales for their reasoning. We had now managed to return inside – Marie having felt too cold to stay on the step without her poncho. Peter brought in the precious package and placed it on the table. I was desperate to rive and rip at the thing until its secrets were revealed, but I calmed myself and stroked the dog slowly, which helped.

Mr Wilkins chose this moment to make his grand entrance – hoping to catch us in some act of wrongdoing, I suppose. 'Too late, matey,' I thought, enjoying his disappointment, and kicking one of the empty wine bottles under the sideboard.

Our dilemma was shared with the poker-faced cleric. He spoke at last. Or should I say he pontificated. He enjoyed a good pontificate did Mr Wilkins.

"As I see it," he frowned – pomposity pouring out of every pore, "we have no right to open this until it can be shown to belong to one of us."

So, he saw himself as one of the prospective recipients too. What a cheek!

It was at this point that I made a suggestion. "How about leaving it here for now, and getting on with the meeting? It'll be quite safe until next week. In the meantime I can make some inquiries – neighbours and so on – and hopefully someone will have seen who left it in the first place. After all," I said, craftily, "it might be something horrible."

A change crept over their countenances at this. Everyone had assumed there was to be some material gain from this box of tricks. How sad they all looked as they nodded agreement. We returned to the business in hand and put the box out of sight. On leaving, each one looked longingly at the cupboard where it lay, but I remained steadfast. The dog, sensing victory, lay its head across my feet. I felt almost masterful.

Alison lasted a couple of hours. Sheepishly tapping on my window later that day, she said she couldn't bear it a moment longer. She *must* have the package. I passed it through the window to her and she left, delighted that it had been so easy.

Mr Wilkins was next. He blustered on the doorstep for a while then said he'd decided it would be better to keep it in his safe. I gave him the package and he left, gleefully hugging it to his little pigeon chest.

The most impressive were Marie and Peter. It took them until the fourth day to challenge me. "You see, Marie's certain that it couldn't be for anyone else." There was a pause. "It's her birthday in a fortnight." "Congratulations," I smiled, giving them the package.

Well, not the real package, obviously. That was still in the cupboard, but I had managed to make some reasonably accurate copies of the original. Sadly, I'd filled the duplicates with the bubble wrap I'd saved when I bought the new telly. I'd pondered on wrapping gifts or little messages but I couldn't see the point of causing further intrigue.

At our next meeting, they were all strangely subdued – nobody wanted to confess their duplicity and weakness. Naturally, I said nothing and the subject was never alluded to again.

So, you ask, what was in the original package and who left it? The truth is, I don't know. I haven't opened it yet. Delayed gratification is working really well for me. I'm not bothered any more.

But come round next week and we could look together. I could make you tea, and I'm sure I still have some of those biscuits left.

HOLIDAYS ARE
THE ONLY CAKE

"Holidays are the only cake that makes bread taste better after."

A world-weary me would wholeheartedly agree with this quotation. I could go on ad infinitum about having your first proper cup of tea and sleeping in your own bed the night you return from a couple of weeks away from home. And it's all true – your whole body sighs with pleasure and relief that you're once again back with the familiar, everyday life you once longed to escape. Even looking in the usual mirror to check how the carefully cultivated tan looks in the grey light of the bathroom doesn't faze you. It's still good to be back.

But, the proof of this one depends on your age.

Around dawn on a Saturday morning in the last week of July, a taxi drew up outside my house. It was the first time this had ever happened. Ironically, this was also the one week in the year when the town smelt cleaner and the air was fresher; but our family was never there to 'feel the benefit' because we were off on our annual jaunt to the seaside. It was known as 'the works shut-down' week when the blast furnaces were cooled and cleaned out and all the workers had a week's paid holiday. How wonderful it was from beginning to end.

I would dearly love to recapture even the smallest fraction of that childhood excitement: waiting on the street with my sister in the greyish morning light and watching anxiously until the taxi finally rounded the corner and stopped outside our house. I remember the driver as he hopped out and opened up the heavy, shining black boot of the cab, smiling at us as our old, battered suitcases were respectfully placed inside – honoured for the precious cargo they were. The rear door was held open and our mam and dad herded us in, to sit in the beautifully upholstered interior. Inside, the smell was rich – a warm mixture of leather, tobacco and scented women. To me, aged five, inhaling deeply, it was the most thrilling atmosphere I'd ever known. The world was doing fine inside that taxi.

My parents in turn, were accorded the same degree of deference as they too were ushered in and took their seats beside us. I desperately wanted to bounce up and down with excitement, but instinct told me not to move, as the grown-ups were unusually tense and best behaviour was called for on this most momentous of journeys. Our destination – the railway station.

A quick glance at the view from the taxi windows might explain my excitement. Across the road from our house was the bombed-out shell of an old neighbour's home; some of the rubble still in situ. A series of chalk marks denoted where various children's games had been played out on the tarmacked road. Directly opposite our front window, on Derby Street, was another bomb site, euphemistically called 'the common', where at least three houses had been destroyed; and to the right was a huge gas tank flanked by tightly-packed terraces of tiny houses just like ours – the lucky ones that had escaped the worst of the wartime raids. The only hint of green came from a few weeds scattered here and there amongst the half-bricks and bits of bike tyre; and they were hanging on for dear life against the daily onslaught of kids' games and bonfires.

This was the only time I'd ever been in a car, so who can wonder at my pleasure?

Where were we going after the station? Directly to heaven of course.

Our destination was Scarborough, a resort on the North East Coast. It had everything I'd ever wanted. There were pleasure cruises, sandcastles, sea bathing, donkeys, Gala Land (of which, more later) waffles with jam and cream and knickerbocker glories awaiting us as soon as we had unpacked and settled in at my Auntie Betty's Boarding House.

Auntie Betty was not a real aunt. She was related by marriage to my mother. The link was so tenuous as to be a mystery to my sister and me, but we embraced the 'auntie' title enthusiastically.

To us, used to the greyness of the streets and the presence of war damage all around, Auntie Betty's house was beautiful. There were lovely gardens on every side, where stone gnomes hid near clumps of lilies. Summer-flower-smells hung heavily in the air, in contrast to the dirty river and industrial wastelands thick with chemical smells, that we lived with all year.

Auntie Betty had opulent, top quality carpets on her stairs and snowy linen and silver cruets on her tables. As a child, I was a connoisseur of smells, and sometimes I can relive the warm-toast-and-breakfast aromas exuding from the very pores of that house and I am immediately enchanted, and feel the urge to shout, 'Auntie Betty's!' aloud.

However, wondrous as all these treats were, the jewel in our holiday crown was Peasholm Park. It was only the most wonderful park in the world – or so it seemed to me in the early '50s. There were pedal boats on the lake, a floating bandstand and a water chute, shaped like a giant tin bath, whose one function was to make its passengers scream with fear and pleasure as they hit the green lakewater causing a giant spray. Of course, we would try to avoid the inevitable soaking and my dad was always ready with his plastic raincoat shielding my shoulders, making me think I'd escaped the worst, then to my delight, as we soggily disembarked, he'd shake droplets of water from his hair onto mine saying, in mock horror, "Look at me, I'm drownded."

There were also naval battles on the park lake, fought by miniature grey model boats. At the time I didn't understand their appeal but I now know they played out famous sea battles from WW2: still very fresh in the adult consciousness of the '50s. It wasn't interesting to me though. Even through the fires, smoke and loud explosions, I would find my attention wandering as the grown-ups discussed the technical skills of the operators and the accuracy of the battles. It was the only low point of the week however, and I endured it with as good a grace as I could muster.

Towards the end of the week, we were allowed to stay up until it was dark, and go on 'The Tree Walk' in Peasholm, where various plastic squirrels and woodland creatures would light up as we meandered through the trees. Such simple magic to give such pleasure.

My parents saved the final treat for Friday. It was held in abeyance just in case it rained, but if the weather had been kind – and it usually was – Friday meant Gala Land – a huge subterranean fairground.

Scarborough was once a spa town where people could take the waters, but as the masses were given paid holidays, the nature of the town changed and incredibly, in those pre-theme park days, the Gala Land cave-like complex boasted dodgem cars, fairground rides and, as I remember, an all-female band, complete with palm court. I believe they were called The Ivy Benson Band, but all I remember are the cream and blue uniforms and an oldish woman with startlingly red hair and harsh make-up, banging the cymbals enthusiastically in time to the Trish Trash Polka.

At the end of our week in Scarborough, we headed reluctantly for the station, taking many last looks back and waving sadly at Auntie Betty who stood on the porch, still wearing her apron and smiling back until we were out of sight.

In a lifetime of holidays, from the mundane to the exotic, there is no recapturing the sense of joy I felt in those early years. Certainly, the contrast between home and away has never been more marked than my first experience of the seaside. I think I've spent my life trying unsuccessfully to recapture the long-lost halcyon days when cake tasted better than bread.

IN THE VALLEY GARDENS, SALTBURN

In the valley gardens, I feel like Eve
On a mission to sin.

It's the Tree of Knowledge
Versus the miniature railway...
The knowledge, offered freely and generously.

So what, if he's a serpent?
The fruit looks delicious
(and it's organic).
Why wouldn't you?

But – when Adam has tasted:
proffered the apple
Smiled, knowingly,

You will lick the inner whiteness; where the flesh is exposed
Slide your lips along the teeth marks
Slip the tongue's tip across
the outer edges of the white wound
taste the sharp, sweet juice.
Knowing
you will *not* be delivered from evil.
Ah – then,
Divine
temptation.

LIONEL

Ruby was to blame for Lionel's present predicament. There was no doubt about that.

When Thelma died, and they assembled for the will reading, he was surprised that she hadn't been more precise about her wishes. There were certain codicils and charitable bequests that lacked clarity, and Lionel, who was a stickler for clarity, found himself increasingly irritated by the muddle that had always been his wife's mind. Ruby had had a hand in it though. Of that he was sure.

There had only been four of them at the funeral apart from him, and they all assembled – after the obligatory sherry and sandwiches, of course – at the solicitor's office, to be told whether or not good fortune, in the form of a legacy, had smiled on them. Thelma's younger sister Marion kept a sombre silence throughout, and he never doubted for a minute that her grief was sincere and deeply felt. Thelma had left most of her mother's jewellery to Marion, who allowed herself a hint of a smile when the details were revealed. She was not an avaricious woman and had no designs on any more of Thelma's estate. When he looked at her, Lionel felt a frisson of warmth toward his sister-in-law and her simplicity of spirit. He took her hand and squeezed it. 'Good old Marion,' he thought.

Trevor, Thelma's older brother, who was in the early stages of Alzheimer's, looked bemused throughout the proceedings. She'd left him some money and their father's train set – a Hornby, complete and quite rare; 'so that it could be sold to pay some of his future nursing home costs,' mused Lionel, who felt as if he were floating slightly above everything – so unreal did it seem to him that Thelma had gone first.

He had always been the sickly one. He'd had no end of chest infections, both as a youngster and an adult, brought on by a lifetime of Players Untipped Navy Cut, and his risky job in the castings department of Smith's Foundry – an environment hardly likely to promote optimal health. His lungs were shot to pieces, with the cumulative effect of forty years worth of microscopic iron filings, dust and pollution floating around in them in a cocktail of fag ash with an ever-present sprinkling of tar and bacteria, (shaken, not stirred).

Thelma, in contrast, had, like so many women of her generation, enjoyed rude health and had never worked. Well, not at what Lionel would consider a proper job. In later life she had driven the school bus for the local primary school. This had brought in a small amount of money which she didn't need anyway. Lionel never asked what she did with her wages. He suspected she'd given most of it to Ruby, Trevor's spoiled daughter, but it was of no consequence now. Thelma had gone and that was that.

He couldn't resist a small inner smile to think that now, Ruby would have nobody to sponge off, but as soon as the thought was out he began to feel sad again. He looked across at Ruby, who was wearing a most unsuitable hat, and assumed she'd seen someone on an American film wearing something similar – flamboyant and inappropriately big. Typical of Ruby's need to show off. She was a girl who always seemed to be asking the question, 'What about me?' even when she wasn't speaking.

The fourth person at the table was a stranger to all of them. Nobody but Ruby had any idea who he was. She now stood up – well, she'd have to make a meal of it – and introduced him as Richard.

'Richard,' mused Lionel, 'Richard. Thelma didn't know a Richard, did she?' He did a mental count of all their friends' offspring but no, he couldn't place this young man. Very good looking, but with a scarred upper lip, he wore a beautifully cut suit – 'expensive', thought Lionel, the expert. It was the kind of suit that Thelma used to buy for *him* in the early days of their marriage.

Thelma's first marriage had been to a wealthy man, but Lionel had never wanted to know anything about him. Jealousy had raised its ugly head and they would end up rowing whenever she brought up the subject. He'd gathered that the husband, John, had died in less than transparent circumstances and he, Lionel, preferred, 'not to hear the details, thank you, Thelma.' Something about gambling was inferred, which was a world that terrified him. Consequently, he had barred Thelma from ever spending any of her inheritance from John on him. He knew it was old-fashioned but he would provide for his family thank you, without the underworld having a hand in it.

'Pity about the suits, though,' he thought at his wife's funeral. 'Too late now, for regrets, Li,' said his inner voice.

Richard smiled benignly at him. Who was he and what was he up to? Reluctantly, Lionel managed a one-sided grimace in Richard's direction.

The solicitor coughed discreetly and everyone perked up again.

"To Lionel, my dear husband, I leave the sum of one thousand pounds, being the monies saved from my job as a bus driver. Since he disapproved so strongly of my inherited wealth and land, I will not insult him or cause distress by leaving him anything else. The title deeds of our house will be signed over to him, of course, and the remaining mortgage paid in full by the insurance company."

The solicitor droned on but Lionel was incapable of listening. Unworthy thoughts whirled around his head. A grand? Only a grand? The daft thing was that it wasn't greed that was upsetting him. It was the question, 'Who's she left it to then?' And of course, 'Who is Richard and what's he up to?'

He didn't need to wait long for the answer. Forcing himself to focus again on proceedings, he heard the following sentence, "To my son Richard and his fiancée Ruby I leave the rest of my estate in its entirety, in the hope that they will look after my husband, Lionel, until his death, at which time our house will be theirs."

WHAT? What? SON?

Thelma couldn't have children. Where had this so-called 'son' sprung from? When? Who was this woman he'd been married to for thirty years? His brain was utterly incapable of making sense of anything. He lunged out of his seat and clawed his way to the exit, coughing and spluttering as he opened the heavy oak door. As he stumbled, he had a flashback to the words, *'His fiancée, Ruby?'*

Once he reached the relatively fresh air of the tiny garden outside, he found a bench and sat gratefully on it. The muddle in his mind was like a skein of tangled wool – threads of logic and unaccountable nonsense knotting themselves together. Taking a few deep breaths of his inhaler, he also tried a yoga breathing technique he'd been taught by the physiotherapist at the doctor's surgery. "Now, think," he said aloud. "Thelma must have had a son, this Richard, and yet had never even hinted at it all this time? Is that possible? Have I been so implacable; so unbending a husband and so blind? Why was she unable to confide in me?"

However, he did recall a time in their marriage when Thelma had left him, temporarily, having accused him of not caring about her. They were apart for about six months. Where did she go? Was it Majorca? Well, that's what she'd told him, anyway. He'd responded to the postcard she'd sent, with one of his own. It had a picture of the Iron Foundry in Dock Street and simply said, 'Majorca? Using your ill-gotten gains, no doubt. Enjoy the sunshine.' There was no address so he sent it to the hotel pictured on the front of hers. Did she even get it?

When she had eventually returned, neither of them was willing to discuss any of the issues or problems that had caused the rift. All swept under the carpet, which was the pattern of their marriage.

This reverie was broken when Richard appeared at his side. It had been so smoothly and easily done that he hadn't even heard the door open. He was certainly a specimen. Lionel supposed that women fell at his feet. Thelma's Spanish Adventure, made flesh. Phew. Maybe it was time for some answers.

"Hi, Lionel." A confident voice, pleasant and unfazed by any of the recent drama.

'I suppose he can afford to be magnanimous,' thought Lionel.

'After all, he's a rich man now.' It was only at this point that Lionel recalled what the solicitor had said, 'To my son Richard and *his fiancée Ruby.*' But, his 'fiancée, Ruby' would be related to him. How had she managed to get engaged to him? In fact, wasn't that illegal? What would they be to each other? First cousins?'

Lionel recalled flicking through the Book of Common Prayer as a choirboy, to find the pages at the back (this done out of sheer boredom as the vicar gave his sermon) where it said: 'A man may not marry his....' And there followed a list of close connections which Lionel would try to work out – such as 'his sister's son's cousin,' well – something like that, anyway. Surely, *surely, first* cousins were in there somewhere? Now, he reckoned, he could afford to be kind.

"Richard, congratulations," he said, "on your good fortune and your forthcoming marriage. So sorry about earlier. I didn't know, you see, that Thelma had a son. Always thought she was unable to conceive." There was an awkward silence before he continued, half to himself, "and the problem was *me* all the time."

The young man put a firm hand on his shoulder. "I'm really sorry, Lionel. I didn't know about *you* either. My mother didn't come to see me often in Cornwall, then when I was ten, she told me you were dead."

Oh, the betrayal! Thelma was a *monster.* He could scarcely respond. "Well, as you can see, I'm not – yet," he gasped, pulling out the inhaler once more. He was desperate for a strong coffee at this point.

"Shall we go somewhere for coffee?" asked Richard. "We probably have a lot to discuss."

Lionel nodded.

A mean-spirited thought had just popped into his head. 'Not least your illegal liaison with my niece.' He resisted. That could wait for another day.

"When you left, I don't think we got to the conditions of my inheritance." Richard felt he had to explain the small details. He liked clarity in all his dealings with everyone. He was very like Lionel in that respect.

"My mother wants me to live with my father for a year before I come into any of the money, or estate. Trouble is, I don't know who he is."

"Oh, that'll be easy." Lionel tried to be blasé about it, pretend everything was known to him whilst frantically trying to make sense of the muddle in his head. "I have a postcard I can let you have. It's of an hotel in Majorca where he worked. Probably called Fernando or something. Spanish lad, I believe."

He noticed that Richard was wearing a pair of cufflinks that exactly matched his own. He also realised that they both used the same after-shave. Did Thelma duplicate all her gifts then?

Richard frowned. "I didn't know my mother had ever been to Spain. She once told me she didn't have a passport."

Trying to be patient, and taking the tone of an elder statesman, Lionel smiled benignly.

"Well, I was married to Thelma for decades, so I think I'd know if she'd ever been abroad. We spent several happy years holidaying in South West France in the 70s actually."

"Oh."

It was then that Ruby burst into the cafe in a flurry of 'Rubiness'. She grabbed Richard and kissed him full on the mouth. It seemed to go on for ages. Lionel was tempted to rive them apart and declare something – in the manner of a Witchfinder General. He settled for a discreet cough instead.

"How exciting this is!" she squealed. "Good old Auntie Thelma." Then she carelessly thrust an envelope into Lionel's hand. "Oh, and the solicitor asked me to give you this."

When he'd had time to catch his breath and had looked up at her, he noticed she had lipstick on her teeth, which Lionel found repugnant. He instinctively put his hand to his mouth as if to rub it off his own teeth, only to see Richard shadowing his movements yet again.

That was when he decided not to open the letter. He knew what it contained.

This was Thelma's punishment. She had denied both father and son access to each other for more than twenty years. How had he, or indeed they, deserved this? He'd always longed for a child. He was never unkind or unfaithful, never denied Thelma anything – just insisted they live within his means. And all the time, she'd lived this double life. His lungs tightened in another fit of breathlessness caused by this new knowledge of his wife's duplicity.

He looked at Richard. At least now the truth about the sham engagement must come out. Before he could speak, the hated Ruby leaned gleefully across to whisper something in his ear. She came too close, invading his personal space, as usual.

"Clear out the front bedroom, Uncle Lionel, so we can move *our* stuff in. We're going to look after you very well for Auntie Thelma. You could remodel the back room so you can get some privacy. Oh, and you *did* remember I was adopted, didn't you?" Lionel's neck and collar were smeared with her lipstick. It was a shade called, 'Ruby Red' and it perfectly matched the colour of his face.

LISTS

Everyone has a list of priorities – either in their heads, hearts, on paper somewhere, or saved in a computer. Most people would put, 'keeping those I love safe' at the top of that list – apart from those sad souls who love no one, of course. Popular songs maintain that 'everybody loves somebody, sometime' or some such mawkish sentiments but what about people who don't care about anyone?

Stephen considered himself one such man, although close colleagues in his computer company would beg to differ. To them, he was 'good ol' Stephen' – a kind boss and generous about time off to everyone who worked for him; although he himself rarely left his office before eight each evening and had never been known to go on holiday – not even at Christmas.

Interestingly, although he was a good employer, none of his workers ever called him 'Steve' and nobody ever patted him on the back or said, "Alright, mate?" or "Fancy a pint?" at the end of a working week. There was some sort of animal defence around him – a barrier set up to exclude intimacy of even the smallest kind. So he lived his life in almost total physical isolation.

Stephen's priority list was not itemised because it only contained one word. The word was work. It was his reason for living and it wrapped him in its arms each evening as he ate dinner and when he went to bed each night. Even his dreams were about work.

Until the night Susan crept into his head and he did not dismiss her. She'd swanned around in a knee-length shift dress of indeterminate colour, but of soft, floaty fabric – and she'd touched his things.

"Glass of red?" the dream Susan had suggested, waving an

enormous bottle of Bordeaux seductively in his direction, only to break it deliberately on the side of the porcelain sink when he accepted, ignoring his reaction and putting on another layer of lipstick instead of caring about the mess.

His semi-conscious self emerged from the sleep quite aroused but shocked. How dare she? And anyway, he never drank red wine – well, any wine.

His conscious self didn't like this new secretary in the least. She was one of those women who try to be well-groomed but never quite get it right. He'd noticed only yesterday that she had some traces of lipstick on her front teeth and no matter how even and white those teeth were, Stephen had begun to look disdainfully on Susan and her sloppy ways. Why, just last Wednesday, half the hem was hanging down on a rather bright red skirt she was wearing.

"Get out of my head!" he shouted at the wall, and threw a duplicate accounts ledger at it, knocking over a glass of water with his elbow in the process.

Susan disappeared, but the whole thing was quite disturbing. Unable to sleep, he worked until the sun rose when there would be no more danger of floaty damsels swanning in without a 'by your leave'.

The die was cast, however, and she'd already burrowed into a tiny part of his brain. Indeed, he was worried about how to behave when he faced her at work. It almost felt as if she were 'in on' that sexy dream encounter. Aghast, he dressed quickly and set off to work.

En route he wondered vaguely whether the dream was a warning. He was too much alone. Perhaps he should get himself a dog? Hmm, a huge guard dog might be the very thing to deter subconscious distractions, and give him his space again. It could sleep on the bed – why not? He was warming to the idea. Any signs of unwelcome visitors and Fido (he was too busy to start fussing about what to call the thing) would see them off in record time. He'd call the RSPCA some time today and ask them to send round a selection.

Although he was unaware of the fact, Stephen was adding to his list. Another sentient being to care about? An extra priority?

In the event, it didn't happen like that. The man at the RSPCA told him that "even Prince Charles couldn't simply order a dog selection box!"

"What kind of person *are* you?" he'd asked indignantly when Stephen had made the request.

Stephen couldn't understand. He replied, in a genuinely baffled tone, "The sort of person who needs a dog," and the RSPCA man had hung up in disgust.

That afternoon, Stephen asked Fat Janice on reception to find him a dog on the internet.

Susan was already at her desk when Stephen brisked his way to his office after lunch. She failed to notice as he tried too hard to avoid looking at her and tripped over the tea trolley. Luckily, there was not to be an encounter. She was too busy to notice his embarrassment because she was searching on, 'Muttz are Uz', a rather downmarket website where reject almost-pedigree-but-not-quite dogs had a forum. It was run by a man who obviously had quite a long list of priorities – and all of them canine. The computer screen showed a picture of a dog only its mother could love. Susan was smitten. Even though Fat Janice, who'd delegated the task to Susan, "just till I finish me nails. I'm on a promise tonight," had specified a tidy, pedigree dog, already house-trained and not too much hair, she was about to disobey spectacularly. The animal's eyes were different colours and the mini-video showed a mongrel who was oblivious to discipline. "One word from me and he does as he likes," grinned the hapless trainer on the screen.

"Aw, look at this," Susan cooed.

Fat Janice was just finishing the third coat of 'purple passion' on the nails of her left hand.

"You'll do 'is 'ead in wi' that thing!" she screeched when she saw the apology for a dog on the screen. "If you get it, I'm not putting me head above the pulpit for a week!"

"Parapet," Susan muttered as she clicked 'yes'. She arranged payment on Paypal and the transaction was complete. "Is this legal, Janice?" she asked as an afterthought. After all, it was a living creature. Probably, because it was a charity, they were allowed. Putting it out of her mind, she returned to her own work.

Susan's priorities were many and her list was long. Family, friends, pets, her home, her hobbies and the environment. One of the hobbies was singing. She practiced in church with the organist every week for a couple of hours, but he thought her so scatterbrained that he doubted her ability to work professionally. She simply lacked discipline. On the other hand, at work and with the conservation volunteers she was meticulous and capable.

Tonight was singing practice and she was longing to escape from the office. Little irritations had provoked her all afternoon.

To add to her frustrations, Mr Thompson had been behaving erratically all day. And it wasn't because of Jumble (she'd already named the dog), since nobody had dared tell Stephen about *that* can of worms yet.

Stephen had been working harder than usual all day, banishing uncomfortable images of Susan to the corner of his head and successfully gaining new business for the company. However, now it was almost time for the workforce to leave, a sort of creeping dread came over him. What if it should happen again tonight? He could not allow that. Clicking into Janice's email he asked, 'Where's Fido?'

She clicked a rapid, purple-nailed response, 'Susan is sorting it.'

Seeing the name in print took him aback. He shook Susan out of his brain.

'I asked YOU to deal with it. Has she found one yet?'

Janice boldly replied, 'Maybe you need to speak to her. I'll send her in,' then she grabbed her coat and bag and dashed off, anticipating a great night out.

Unaware of any difficulties around her heart's choice of dog, Susan mailed a picture of Jumble to her boss. She wondered if he was sickening for something. He'd seemed a bit tense all day, but she was sure the stress would vanish when he met Jumble.

She had tried to arrange delivery direct to Stephen's house but that was a problem for the website owner. Stephen worked so late that she was loath to disturb him at home. After the usual possibilities had been explored, Susan suggested delivering the dog to the church that evening. She could have her lesson, take the dog to her place, bath it and look after it overnight. A bath would doubly endear it to Stephen, she decided – and *she* would have the fun of it until morning.

Excitement bubbled up in Susan's chest. How lovely to have a dog – and not just any dog; a sweet, unloved scruff of a dog – so endearingly vulnerable. She couldn't wait a minute longer. Off she went to burst in on his solitary, ordered, office life with the wonderful news.

A hasty rendezvous was organised at the churchyard. Stephen didn't want the dog washed. He wanted it today. He would meet the owner – she needn't be involved any further, thank you.

A crestfallen Susan went to the meeting place early – just to get a glance of Jumble/Fido in person and pet it before it was handed on. She was also dying to see Stephen's reaction.

However, when she met the owner, he looked anxious. He told her how sorry he was; he'd made a mistake. The dog was female. Was that alright? Susan gaily waved him away – no problem at all she smiled, "Cos she's so adorable who wouldn't fall for her on sight?"

When Stephen arrived, he discovered the distant light in the churchyard to have its source at a point very near the ground, but a closer look showed two figures immediately under the wall, within the mouth of the archway. He could now hear voices and he realised it must be Susan talking to the new dog.

"Oh, Mr Thompson, *he's* a *she*!" Susan exclaimed, galloping up to him in a very ungainly fashion. The creature beside her, panting wildly, looked to be of the same untamed stock.

"I'm really sorry. It was the owner's mistake. He's just apologised." She turned to indicate the errant owner, who seemed to have dissolved into the mist.

All three of them stared at each other. The dog sat down, his head hanging low. Stephen noticed a smudge of mud on Susan's cheek. Her hair was almost wild after the mad churchyard dash.

He then looked at her interpretation of the butch, tidy guard dog he'd envisaged and his heart sank.

"I knew you'd like him. I said to Janice; he's so endearingly vulnerable – I mean 'she'."

She proffered the bit of frayed rope that held the animal. He had no choice but to take it.

Turning on his heel, he slowly made his way back through the churchyard, Susan's voice echoing through the mist, "She's called Jumble!"

Patting the dog's head as he led her away, he said, "Come on, Susan."

FOREVER AMBER

Our eyes met briefly. I had no idea about the protocol for this particular occasion and did not move nor speak.

This sounds awful but it's always easier when she's not well. That way I don't have to listen to her all the time, or talk. Don't get me wrong, it's never easy, it just takes the pressure off a bit. Means I get time with me own thoughts – like when she's sleeping. Believe me, that's a luxury. Mental space.

John, that's the son, says I'm an angel. That's a laugh. Just as well he doesn't know what's going on in my head, eh?

"You're an angel, Angela," he says. I just smile. No point protesting, is there?

He's not a bad bloke, as blokes go. Slips me an extra tenner every now and then. Well, he can afford it, working on the rigs. They get well paid, you know.

I keep meaning to ask him if he can get our Colin a start. It must be a year now since he lost his job and he doesn't seem inclined to get another one. It's like all the fight's gone out of him, you know.

"How's your Chantelle doing?" That's her grand-daughter, the Saint. I ask her every time I come. Well, she loves telling me, bless her, all about the college course and how good she is at designing. "Doing a business studies course at the same time, you know, Angie. She wants to sell her own stuff you see, cut out the middle man."

"Very sensible, Mrs P," I say. I do a good 'automatic response', even if I do say so meself.

"I don't know where she gets it from Angie. Not from me, that's for sure."

Then I have to do the automatic disagreement, and it's all smiley between us.

What I really want to say is, Oh, tell her not to bother Mrs P. She'll just end up like me getting peanuts for cleaning up bodily fluids from some rich old biddy for the minimum wage.

Is that cruel? Eee, listen to me. I sound so bitter and miserable, don't I? I'm not usually this negative, am I, Carol?

We're in the coffee house on Tranter Street. We always meet here on a Wednesday lunchtime, me and Carol. They do nice soup and it saves me cooking. I'm always shattered on a Wednesday after a full morning with Mrs P, then I've got Ted in the flats straight after.

Carol's on about what she calls her 'quest' again. She's searching for a man. The ideal man, she says. "Good luck with that," I tell her. And she wants me to write her one of those adverts for the paper. I'm supposed to, 'write something clever and witty that will weed out all the boring ones.' She's a good laugh Carol. She goes to something called the 'knit and natter', and she's always full of gossip about the women in the group. I mainly tell her about Colin being a lazy so-and-so and Mrs P's health problems. Dead interesting, me.

Except, this time I was. Interesting that is. I was telling her about Mrs P's jewellery. How we were having our elevenses, when she suddenly says, "Go and get me that black leather bag, Angie," and when I find it on a hook in the spare bedroom, supposedly 'hidden' on the back of the bedhead, she gets really excited. "Give me the carved box!" she squeaks. "Calm down, Mrs P," I say. "Your blood pressure will be sky high."

She's surprisingly strong for such a little bird-like thing, wrenching the bag out of my hands and making a big deal of rummaging around till she finds this fancy box- and it's full of stuff. She tips it up, letting the contents tumble out onto the bedspread.

There's bits of paper and fluff mixed in with diamond brooches and an opal and sapphire ring, but I'm not looking at them. I'm looking at the most beautiful amber necklace, all tangled up with everything else.

Now I'm not interested in bling. I ask her if the diamonds are real, but I don't care. I've got my eye on that amber necklace. It's smooth and transparent as toffee, in a gold setting and it's really classy. What you'd call understated. And I love it. Then I notice there's a matching bracelet half-hidden in the folds of the bedspread.

She goes straight to it and asks me to undo the clasp and put it on her bony old wrist, and even as I'm doing it, I want to rescue it and slip it over my own smooth, young hand instead. I just know, you know, that it'll look good.

"This is the first time I've worn it since May 1947," she says, puffing her little chest out. Then, minutes later, I have to put it all away again. For another decade, no doubt.

But you know, I can still see that honey gleam on the pale cream of the coverlet whenever I close my eyes.

"Why don't you ask her if you can borrow it for next Friday?" Carol suggests.

"How good would it look with your new green dress?"

And you know what? Suddenly I've got a plan. I *know* I won't ask. Too much hassle. Too many questions and objections. There's nowt spontaneous about old people, you know. They need to be at the bus stop half an hour before the bus, if you get what I mean. Chapter and verse, before they can make a decision. Even picturing it now, irritates me. All that suspicion and… "Oo, I don't know about that, Angie," stuff. I've been working here for twelve years – can't she trust me yet?

"Nah, what I'll do is just *borrow* it for a couple of days. As long as it's back by Monday, it won't be missed. I bet she'll never wear it again anyway. She doesn't go anywhere."

Carol has her 'cautious' face on but only says, "Have you done me an ad yet? I never know what to say about meself." I just pull my mouth into a grimace. 'Don't make me do this,' I think, but I say, "Not yet. Next week." And know I'd better just sort it or I'll end up hating Carol for being stupid over men. She's too desperate, that's her trouble. Always picks the wrong'uns and always on the lookout for the next one.

When I got home, I came up with the advert *I* would put in, but it doesn't describe Carol at all. Is that unfair? Whoever she gets won't last five minutes anyway, so it doesn't matter.

I was thinking about Mrs P's jewellery again. My dress is dark green and I have pale skin so that transparent, marmalade colour will look perfect.

Next Wednesday, I confessed all to Carol. "I was a bit of a 'smooth operator' last week," I tell her. 'Plan Amber' couldn't have gone better.'

Carol tipped her head to one side (her 'practising flirting' look.) I pointed at her to put a stop to it; then smiled and boasted. "To sum up the evening – looked gorgeous – got complements – got tipsy – got hangover BUT – nothing bad happened to the necklace or bracelet."

(Oh yeah, I took 'em *both*). Scandalised look from Carol.

Sadly, I'm returning them this morning. John'll be bringing me my pittance and then I'll be cleaning out Mrs P's toilet and kitchen for two hours again – and slipping the stuff into the box in the bedroom first chance I get. Talk about Cinderella.

I felt really good. "What's all that rubbish about 'best laid plans'?" I asked myself, being cocky.

All was quiet and a bit cold at the house when I got there. I knocked but it took ages for anyone to answer. Then, as I'm getting a bit jittery, here's John at the door and he has this expression on his face, like, doom and gloom.

My poor old heart is beating ten to the dozen – and I don't even know what that means – too fast or too slow? Anyway, irregular, and beating into my throat. He's deffo discovered what will now look like a theft. I'm wondering about my options when he says, "Oh, Angela, she's gone. My mam's gone." I was being a bit thick, to be honest. "Sorry, John. Where?"

Turns out Mrs P has had a stroke during the night. She's gone to the hospital but there isn't much hope. I feel a pang of sadness and pity, and – I'm not proud of this – but there's also a grain of relief in there somewhere. A set of amber jewellery is branding itself into my conscience, and burning a hole in my cardigan pocket as I twist and turn looking for an apt phrase.

"Where is she now, John? Can we go and see her?"

He nodded with relief.

"If you wouldn't mind, Angie, I was wondering if you could get a few of her things together – toiletries and such – and we can go together? I'll still pay you, of course."

I brush this aside – genuinely. Why would I let him pay me for that?

Telling him to make some tea, I collect some of Mrs P's newer nightdresses and underwear. Grabbing an armful of toiletries, I take a small case from the airing cupboard, and listen for the kettle boiling downstairs as I slip the amber stuff safely back in its box. As an afterthought I collect the photo of Mr and Mrs P on their wedding day from the bedside cabinet and wrap it in a bedjacket before snapping the case shut.

"Cuppa's ready," I hear from the stairwell and dash guiltily down.

We sat there for ages together that day watching the semi-rigid body of Mrs P. Doctors bustled about but nothing much happened. I had no idea how to cheer John up. We were going to be hanging about for some time, and in complete silence, unless I tried a bit harder. I glanced at Mrs P. again. "Let's get you settled in, then," I suggested, uselessly, to the shape in the bed as I unpacked her few possessions.

"Aw, that was kind of you," John said, picking up the photo. "Doesn't she look happy?"

I've never been sentimental, but I agreed, then looked more closely. Around the neck of the younger Mrs P in the black and white picture, was a fine amber necklace. My necklace. My *stolen* necklace. I coloured up and he looked quizzically at me.

"See what she's wearing?"

I nodded slightly through burning cheeks. 'He knows,' was my first thought, then, 'He's going to call the police.'

Suddenly, the nurse was beckoning us out of the room. There was no need for words as this time, the old lady had definitely gone. Our eyes met briefly. I had no idea about the protocol for this particular occasion, and did not move nor speak. I was about to make a clean breast of it, you know, stop myself from feeling so crap about everything, when he touched my hand. For the first time I *really* looked into those clear grey eyes, and I liked what I saw there.

"When you go back to the house," he said quietly, "I want you to go into the box behind my mother's bed. You'll find that necklace. I believe there's a matching bracelet as well. She used to have the earrings once but I think they were lost years ago."

"*I* didn't take them if that's what you're thinking," I said too quickly.

He raised an eyebrow. "Why would I think such a thing? No, those were the pieces she said you would probably like to have, you know, in the event of…" His voice wobbled a bit and I instinctively threw an arm about him, then, feeling daft, quickly moved it again.

"Maybe you should wait a while before you give away any of her stuff." I paused, "Maybe Chantelle would like them?" I thought that was a bit noble of me, but guilt does wondrous things, eh?

John looked at me. "Oh, Chantelle's raised her ugly head again has she?" Then, on seeing my shocked expression, he gave a half smile. "She doesn't exist. She's just my mother's imaginary grand-daughter. All her friends have big families, so she felt a bit left out."

Ah, I smiled at that. Poor old lady. So, all my resentment was for nothing.

I reached in my pocket for a tissue and the rough draft of the ad fluttered onto the floor. "Oh, that's for my friend – looking for a man." (I wanted to die).

He read it aloud in a puzzled voice, glancing at me all the while:

'What I'm not. 'A bubbly blonde' (thick and irritating) 'Rubenesque' (fat) and I don't like 'most things in life' (country and western music? UKIP? Peach air fresheners? Coach trips?). What I am…'

By the time he got to this bit my stomach had shrivelled to the size of a pea. I'd listed Carol's imaginary qualities: *Chic, stylish, cultured, sophisticated and attractive.* Finally,

'Please rescue me from Bland.'

"Hmm, intriguing. I'd very much like to meet your friend," he said, smiling at the possibilities…

And that was when I decided to accept the amber jewellery.

FUNDS AND
FATHER LUKE

Father Luke fixed his astounded eyes on me. "Is this true?"

"Well someone has to be the pragmatist here, Father. Obviously that's not you, with your defence of tradition and holding on to the past no matter what." I faced him square on, knowing that fifty years of humbling himself to his congregation would make it impossible for him to withstand a direct confrontation. The ancient face looked defeated before we'd even begun, and I felt truly sorry for the old man in spite of myself.

"How long is it since *you* came to the village, Malcolm?" he asked, a tremble around the edges of his frail voice. "About six years, isn't it?"

I felt a pang of remorse, at this, knowing what was coming next.

"Half a century, Malcolm. Half a century I've been at St. Paul's. A *lifetime.*" There was one of the Father's long pauses as he stared into my wicked soul, at this point.

"And I hope I haven't been found lacking in that time. I've bullied and cajoled where necessary and I've guided and gently suggested when needed. I think I've been a good friend to you all this time – especially with the researching of your book about church histories. Why do you hate me so, Malcolm, I wonder?"

'You wily old bugger!' I thought, all sympathy flying out through the broken stained glass of the windows.

"Oh come now, Father," I half smiled at his stooped figure. "That's a bit melodramatic, isn't it? I have no reason to hate you. I just don't think you can stand in the way of progress… of the future. If we are to save the church, we need to take more drastic steps."

There was an awkward pause.

"I don't know about you," I smiled, trying to inject some lightness into the moment, "but there *is* a limit to the number of cakes I can eat in aid of church funds. We're talking about three quarters of a million pounds here, not just the piddling amounts collected at the services each week and monthly jumble sales. Much as I admire the energy of our fundraisers, we're not Children in Need are we? Nobody's gonna drop the cash in our laps one night and say, 'There you go lads! Sorted'."

Oooh, that hit the spot. The rheumy old eyes flashed at me and he seemed at once older and younger than he was. He spat out, "Well, wouldn't *that* be nice. And wouldn't I be the auld fool if I imagined it would ever happen?"

He turned his back on me. "And before you offer any more of your patronising nonsense, Malcolm, I'm not waitin' on a miracle neither. No nice young lad fresh out of angel college will be paying me a visit on the night of the next full moon and magicking the repairs back to working order. We *do* need a miracle, but one that doesn't rely on selling off church grounds or selling our precious plate. And imagine how it would affect the congregation if there was yet another housing project sitting cheek by jowl with this beautiful building."

The communion wine would turn sour in our mouths at such a sinful use of the churchyard. Well, not in my lifetime.'

The edge of the folder I'd been picking at, which contained the architect's plans for just such a project, slipped from my hands at this point, and fanned out across the cold, stone flags of the narthex, causing me to scrabble around on hands and knees in a horribly undignified manner.

I'll give him his due though, he didn't just flounce out, enjoying his temporary victory. He did a bit of desultory picking-up, deposited the papers in a pew beside me and *then* flounced out. I could've throttled him.

There are so many churches around these parts that have fallen into ruin and disrepair lately. Some of the smaller ones have been used as dwellings – you can see them on the telly from time to time. It gives the spoiled middle classes something they describe as a 'character' property to live in.

Have you noticed, none of them simply live in 'homes', these well-off couples in their 40s? It's always, 'Property number 3 is the mystery house – a converted Methodist chapel in rural Wiltshire which is well within the couple's budget of 450,000. It comes complete with blah blah blah.' (Here, you can substitute any unnecessary stuff; such as an old well or built-in bread oven). And they're never sure, these people, whether rooms are *big* enough. 'It's a nice size but we need somewhere to keep our collection of ludicrous dust-gatherers, Alistair, so it's not doing it for us, I'm afraid.' And they troop out of a beautiful house with the hapless presenter trailing crestfallen, in their wake.

But we digress. After the fruitless discussion with Father Luke, I didn't contact any of the building contractors or the auction houses that were prepared to get us out of our financial hole. It was all too depressing and pointless. I've always been a 'fixer' all my life. If I can't solve a problem, I get a bit depressed, and that's how I felt now.

I did watch a lot of rubbishy television in the days that followed – daytime quizzes and such, when I had the brilliant idea, which I blamed – if that's the right word – on my brain's lack of activity or stimulation over the past weeks. It was a really exciting plan, but risky and I needed someone slightly immoral to share it with. All the parish worthies were discounted one by one. I could imagine the sucking-in of teeth and the disapproving lowering of brows should I mention it to the more publicly upright ones. I had a laugh actually, at their imagined reactions.

Finally, having kept a lid on it until I was about to burst, I mentioned it to Peter Galloway, carpenter of this parish and irregular attender at church. It seemed fitting somehow that he should be a carpenter. 'Just like Jesus,' I told myself – as if that made it any easier. We met in the pub at my request – I knew Peter wouldn't turn down a pint – and I softened him up before getting to the nitty gritty of it.

"Here's the thing, Pete," I said in my man-to-man back-slapping voice. "The church is about to fall down and we can't afford the repairs. Well, not legally. I've looked into it in great detail and we'll never be able to do it. Father Luke refuses to request the sale of the land for redevelopment, which might raise the money, and he won't sell the church's silver and stuff, so we're stuffed. But...."

Well, I picked the right bloke. Not only was Peter up for it, he found us a getaway driver as well. Some cousin or other, who'd had a couple of spells in borstal as a youth, would do it 'for a few bob' to quote Peter.

"No names," I insisted. If I don't know what he's called, I can't get him into trouble should anything go wrong.' Between them they organised the tools for the job with some enthusiasm and I began to feel a bit better.

Trouble is, since then, I've been having that old trouble. You'll know what I mean if you're a Catholic. Years of youthful brainwashing will have simmered nicely into an almighty guilt. A stewpot of anxiety gurgles in every Catholic stomach – constantly questioning, 'Was that a mortal sin or a venial one? Is kissing a girl or any other natural human desire going to send me to purgatory?' Even when you grow out of the terror of the confessional, it lingers like a limpet. I'm sure that's why my marriage failed. Catherine – a Methodist – was too good at turning my 'guilt screw'. She made me feel worthless whenever the occasion arose.

"Have *you* been to the *pub*?" (sniffing the air around me) *Crank*. "So, *did* you take the dog for a walk or not?" *Crank*. "Are you having an affair with that ginger haired trollop in the choir?" *Double crank*. Looking back, our separation was inevitable.

Except that this time it was different. This time we were planning to do something *almost* dishonest, but for the greater good. But was that just an excuse? I didn't sleep well – and I prayed – a habit I'd lost lately. Logic versus faith. Not a race I'd care to back.

On the evening of what Peter had called 'our saviour's

114

plan', which was too bizarre to contemplate – we all met in Middlesbrough, under the Albert Bridge.

Pete had the metal detector and was dressed, as were we all, in black hoodies and dark trousers. The driver carried three shovels and a couple of trowels tied up in a strong bin liner.

"Is this it?" I was dubious about the equipment from the start but Pete made reassuring noises as he held up a hessian sack.

"Oh, so this is to be our salvation then… a sack?"

Pete looked crestfallen, and I relented. "Come on, it's gonna be okay." I pictured the headline, 'CHURCH TREASURER IN CRIME SPREE' then quickly expunged it from my brain. Guilt would only hold me back at this point, just when we were on the brink of victory as well.

The old Cathedral once marked the centre of the town, in the area that is now referred to as 'over the border'. When the town was a thriving port, steel was exported all over the world from these docks and where there are sailors, there are women looking to relieve them of their wages. Alas, the cathedral had to be demolished when it was partially destroyed by fire, but when I was researching in the archives, I found that the majority of the gold and silver; chalices, the plate and suchlike had been removed to – nobody knew where.

But I did.

I did.

I bloody did! Accidentally, I must add. When I was researching my book about local churches, I found an old tatty piece of paper with a hand-drawn map on the unofficial side. I managed to decipher the scrawl and restore it using a computer programme then I made a photocopy. It marked where someone – priest probably – had buried this holy treasure at the east end, where the altar had once stood.

We set to work straight away with the metal detector and a rather inadequate torch, carrying on through the night. It was hard work but we'd got a strong signal which seemed a pretty positive sign that we were onto something. My fingers were aching and bleeding but just before first light, all we'd uncovered was one tiny silver crucifix and a couple of old pennies. The others were hopeful of finding more but I decided we should call it a day before someone discovered us. It was when we were arguing that Peter shouted, "Hey, look at that." He was pointing at nothing – well at the first glimmer of daylight. We stood still, and stared.

"So, what are we looking at?" asked the perplexed driver.

"The sun," Pete told us as he packed our tools away.

"So?"

I enlightened him. It was the hardest sentence I'd ever had to utter.

"It rises in the east," I said. "We've been working at the west end all night."

We must've been standing there for about thirty minutes, trying to get our heads round our stupidity. The driver (I later found out his name was Jess) was all for having another go that night but Pete and me hadn't the stomach for it. We wearied our way home and slept the morning away.

A month later, I was summoned to Father Luke's once more. 'What now,' I wondered. 'Am I getting a sermon because he hasn't seen me at church lately? Let him dare start...'

"Ah, Malcolm: Thanks for coming. I just wanted to show you this. Something I've been working on for a few months." He was smiling that serpent smile again.

I read the letter. It was on thick expensive vellum with an embossed letter-heading in the centre. I glanced uncomprehendingly at Father Luke as he, unable to contain his triumph any longer, shouted, "Yes! I wrote to Sir Cliff Richard outlining our fiscal problems and, being a good Christian, he has sent us this..." (waving a cheque in the air), "which should ameliorate our fiscal worries far into the future."

The picture of that nightmare night swam before my eyes, and I believe I let out a despairing groan, then looked down at my still-scarred hands, muttering, "Dear God."

"Exactly," said he, smiling, beatifically back at me.

ME AN' THE SARGE

Well, how daft am I? What's the first rule of working life? That's right. Never volunteer. And what did I do? Jumped in with me size tens right up to me armpits. So, in a way it was me own fault, really.

Don't get me wrong, being in the army's usually okay. You get to be a big kid playing with grown-up toys and the pay's pretty good – or that's what I used to think when we were on manoeuvres. But these voluntary gigs drag you down. It does my head in, being stuck in a bloody kitchen for – what – eight hours all told – and it was only the first day.

I blame the Sarge. It's the third time he's done this to us, and I fall for it every time.

It starts with him getting an earful from one of the officers about 'civic duties' and, 'givin' something back to the community' and he's off on one. As I said to Keeney... I wouldn't mind givin something back if I'd got something to start with.

Last time, we had to take a Green Goddess to some godforsaken council estate on the outskirts of Glasgow and show – what did he call them – 'disaffected teenagers' – how they were used during the fire-fighters' strike. Hmm, we showed 'em alright, then they showed us a few ways we hadn't even thought of, and then they stole it. It was found abandoned on some waste ground next morning – none the worse for wear, but we lost a night's sleep looking for the bloody thing and our leave was cancelled to boot. You're not even allowed to give 'em a clip nowadays either. 'Disaffected' must mean they get to do what they like.

Nah, you're best keeping schtum if there's a good cause needing help – whatever it is.

To be honest, this gig sounded like a doddle at first. The

Captain had agreed to help out with some community project called 'Father Figures for the Disadvantaged Child', where we were drafted in to be nice to these single parent families at the community centre for a couple of weekends.

Well, you'd've had a go wouldn't you? It sounded pretty harmless; especially if the choice was between that and square bashing all weekend.

I'll come clean here, I had an ulterior motive. See, I reckoned there'd be a few tasty women around, only too glad of havin' a fit squaddie around. And they'd be grateful for the attention – if you know what I mean.

What I hadn't bargained for was Horace. He's the kid I got meself landed with. I ask you – 'Horace'.

You'd have to go a long way to find a wussier name, wouldn't you? I mean, what sort of mother would give a kid a name like that? It was like she *wanted* him to be bullied, if you know what I mean. Mebbee she heard that daft song – by Johnny Cash or somebody – about this lad who was called Sue. And he turned out hard in the end.

It hadn't worked for Horace, I can tell you that for nowt. He was the kind of kid who had a face you just wanted to smack. One of them pale-faced lads with the look of a rodent. What me mam would've called 'a council-house face' and she should know cos we've always lived in one.

Anyway, Horace's mam, Shaz, took a shine to me. She wasn't bad looking apart from the dyed blonde hair. I hate that, me – with black roots, but intentionally black – like, part of the style. Nice enough face and figure though, and she seemed quite interested in me, so, 'game on,' I thought. I'll befriend the poor kid.

Me an Keeney were put on 'dessert-making' for the afternoon. We'd been spud bashing all morning.

Keeney said it would be a doddle. He was bein' drooled over by this fat lass called Cath who was wearing a tight vesty-thing and a pair of stretchy pink trouser things that showed half a dozen rolls of fat, front, back and bum, but Keeney was never that fussy so he seemed okay with her hangin round him.

His afternoon job was puttin' the jam in the Victoria sponges with a flat palette knife thing, and he'd managed to perfect the single-stroke application, saving enough time for a fag-break every twenty minutes.

Shaz had given me a load of strawberry jellies to make up for the trifles. First time I'd ever made a jelly. The instructions were pretty vague I must say, but I was doin' okay 'til Horace offered to help. Every time I thought I'd made enough, he'd run out, dash back again and say, "Me mam said you 'ave to make more."

Well, there was no more, was there? I'd used fourteen packets, and now the bowl was full.

When I told Horace, he disappeared for a bit then sort of minced in carrying a bag full of assorted flavours and said, "They want you to use these as well." I didn't ask who 'they' were. I just set to with Horace pulling the cubes apart, then I went to look for a bigger container. I don't mind telling you, the sickly smell was making me want to puke, so, rather than mess about making loads of different flavours, I stuck 'em all in this big white enamel bucket I'd found; shoved a load of boiling water on 'em, put a lid on and left it under the table to set. It was a funny reddy/pucey colour but smelt okay. Shaz took me off to ice the fairy cakes at that point so I never thought any more about it.

The Sarge really annoyed me that day. He'd spent most of it in the caretaker's room having cups of tea and sneaky fags. I think the pair of 'em were playing cards. Course, I couldn't say owt, but it grated on me all the same.

Just as I was getting into this fairycake lark, I spotted Horace over by the completed trays of iced cake, stickin' his fingers in the butter icing and lickin' them.

I itched to clout him but under the circs I couldn't, could I? Two hours work up the Swanee. They'd all have to be redone now. I was sick as a parrot.

However, fate took a hand at that point. The Sarge came stormin' over and dragged me into the corridor. "What's goin' on, Private Judson?" he bawled. "Why haven't you been guardin' them jellies?"

'Well, I've heard it all now,' I thought. Jelly-guarding duty! Before I could say a word he was draggin' me into the smokehole that was the caretaker's office. The old bloke in charge was like a wiry, bald version of David Jason. He was eatin' a jar of cockles usin' a pair of tweezers. Made me feel a bit queasy, to tell the truth. And what happened next didn't help either.

At a nod from the Sarge, David Jason wiped his vinegary fingers on his hankie and played some CCTV footage. There, bold as brass, stood Horace, knees bent, relieving himself into my jelly.

Imagine how mad I was. I tell you, I was all for doin' the little sod over outside, but the Sarge had a better idea. And it was a corker!

Ten minutes later I was back at me post, making a vat of pink blancmange. Horace was 'helping'.

In walks the Sarge, looking mad as hell. Horace gaped from one of us to the other.

"Not PINK, Judson, CHOCOLATE!" he yelled, throwing his fag end into the blancmange. I got mad then, and cursed under me breath.

The Sarge and I faced each other for ages. "Watch it!" he spat out, then, "and that's a warning not a threat." He certainly made it sound like one. He stood there a bit longer, looking all sinister and scowly.

I swore again when he looked away for a second, but louder this time, watching the white-face of the frightened kid beside me.

I deliberately moved Horace behind the Sarge at that point, so his view of what happened next was restricted by the Sarge's broad back. "Stay there, Horace," I hissed.

With a nod to me, the Sarge grabbed Keeney's jammy palette knife and raised it above his head, bringing it down with a clatter on the table.

I bent down with a convincing yell of pain, grabbed a handful of the gore-coloured, semi-set, pissy jelly, smeared it over me shirt and raised a 'bloodied' arm in the air.

Horace, hysterical by now, slid to the floor and hid his head in his hands, sobbing. All the women gathered round him and clucked in sympathy. Me and the Sarge wrapped my arm in tea-towels and took ourselves off sharpish before anyone realised what had really happened. Shaz watched, dumbstruck, as we rushed out. I can still picture her, holding the cucumber she'd been slicing in one hand as she knelt to comfort Horace with the other.

I think we *deffo* gave something back to the community that day. But I'm not sure what.

MELISSA

The monk thought for a moment and then said, "Nothing happens by accident."

"So, you believe in predestination then? This choice of career, if I may so call it, was never a choice for you was it? You had to take the path laid out for you. How very passive of you, Brother Marcus."

The monk sighed. "What do *you* believe in then, Brother James?"

"Nothing much. The here and now, perhaps."

'How odd to be called 'Brother James',' he thought.

He looked slowly around at the sparse surroundings. Or maybe this was predestined too? He continued. "I'll tell you what though, I wasn't meant to be here – amongst this lot…" indicating the clinical whiteness of the great hall: the plain oak doors the only relief in the colourless monastery, save for a carved mahogany crucifix taking up the whole of the east wall. The monk remained passive.

Several of the other pilgrims trickled in at this juncture, and stood obediently at the refectory table, awaiting a repast of 'plain fare' as the brochure had promised. How he had ended up here, he had no idea. The monk seemed to suggest that it was meant to be.

'Total bollocks,' he thought. And the morning and the evening were the first day.

The world of the monastery was as deep a contrast to his usual existence as it was possible to be. He'd been in urgent need of a break from the recording studios where he worked. Its mix of ear-shattering sound, self-indulgence and pretentiousness, coupled with a liberal helping of chemicals to get through the days had sickened him.

Botoxed singers, past their best and desperate: and people with little musical talent but big gobs, had become tiresome. He longed for a little purity of air, for clean living and the smell of the countryside, so when Bob had suggested the retreat, he grabbed the opportunity. Meant to be? Maybe in hindsight it was.

By the end of the first week, James was almost converted to the life of contemplation and silence. The only person to intrude on his spiritual retreat was the cleaner, who was allocated to him on the first day.

"James, this is Melissa," said Brother Marcus. "She'll be cleaning your cell when you are at breakfast so as not to disturb the silence of your surroundings. Generally, unless there's something you need to know, she will not speak. We find it works better that way."

Melissa smiled. She wore the white robes of a postulant which, as James couldn't help noticing, might be quite cumbersome when cleaning the toilets, but the girl, slight as she was, looked calm and capable.

In the ensuing days, James' awareness of Melissa grew. Probably because he had so much time for quiet contemplation, which had helped him sort out his 'head and priorities' as he told the Abbott. "This is just what I needed. In fact, it's saved my life, in a way."

The Abbott nodded sagely. "Modern life can do that. You were sent to us in your hour of need." James felt as if he need never think for himself again. God would provide – and that was wonderful.

But then, there was the cleaner. She tended to come in later than expected; straight after breakfast, so inevitably, he'd be there. She moved with the grace of a bird in flight and he was charmed. She spoke only once, to offer lavender oil when his head ached and her hands were small and cool on his forehead.

To his alarm, he found himself thinking about her all the time, instead of spending his days in prayer and contemplation.

He rolled her name around his tongue. 'Melissa.' Even the sound of it was half way between a sigh and a kiss.

He prayed, "Dear God, this place is sending me barmy. Too much spirituality is bad for the soul." Then quickly, 'Am I allowed to even think that?' Just as he'd found some faith, *he* was found wanting. Obviously his needs were not purely of the mind.

It was the penultimate day of the retreat. Fulfilled and cleansed in some ways but sadly lacking in others, he took out some money to donate to the monastery. His bag wasn't yet packed for tomorrow's departure and he was thinking and worrying about his return to the real world. He would be able to cope, now, surely?

He sat on his bed, tired but happy and fell into a sound sleep.

The bell tolled for supper just as the shadows began to lengthen across the monastery lawns.

James was splayed out on his stomach across the bed wearing only a pair of boxers; tee shirt discarded carelessly onto the floor, when Melissa shimmered in. He didn't move, terribly afraid he might scare her off with some sudden, ungainly gesture. He'd almost come to think of her as some shy woodland creature, during the days when she'd cleaned his room. Not many conversations had passed between them it was true, but even so, he knew quite a bit about her life outside the monastery, which sounded, by and large, pretty quiet and boring. Now, here she was, expecting an empty cell and here he was semi-naked. He stayed put, saying only, "I'm sorry. I wasn't expecting anyone. I couldn't cope with any more chanting and prayers today, so I gave it a miss. I'm all prayed out, ha ha."

He had no way of knowing how she'd reacted, as she was at the foot of his bed. He smelled a herb-laden flowery scent and craning his neck, looked to see what it was.

She was holding some sort of unguent in her hand and smiling. "What do you like?"

"What?" He sensed the note of panic in his voice and felt vulnerable for the first time.

"Just wondering, what you liked. In bed, that is?"

And without further ado, she put some oil in her little white hands and rubbed them gently together, releasing more of the scent with the heat of her palms.

Trying to rescue the situation, James stuttered, "What? Liked about what? This place? Not much actually, but it gives you time to think, that's for sure." He still hadn't moved and the small of his back was beginning to hurt.

The shock of the hand slowly ascending his right leg made him jump and made him realise what she was up to. His dream girl – well, for this week at least – was giving him a massage. Had he asked for a massage? Would it be itemised on the bill? Who cared? It was glorious.

Her fingers found the top of his shorts and wiggled under the seam. "Dear God," he panted, then wondered if he was allowed to say stuff like that in this place.

"Do you want me to stop, Brother James?" she asked, breathing gently in his ear.

"Oh, no. Please don't," he begged.

"You know, you're the only good looking man who's been here in ages, and I really fancied a bit of a romp with you before you left. Is that okay?"

Vigorous nodding.

"So. What *do* you like?"

At that, he turned over and she oiled his torso.

'Nothing, nothing like this ever happens to me,' he thought. 'It's like something you see in a film.'

His only regret was; it was almost his last day. This could never happen again – unless...

A sharp rap at the door intruded on the liaison. They froze.

"Brother James? Are you quite well? It's Brother Marcus. I have good news. Father Abbot has decided to accept your application to join our order and he wants to see you as soon as you are able to come."

"I don't feel up to it at the moment, Brother Marcus," he panted.

As he told the lie, Melissa, his pure, dream girl, nodded along the length of his body and whispered, "You definitely are!"

His voice squeaked a response. "Might I see you this afternoon, Brother Marcus? I think there's been some mistake. A monk's life is not for me."

"May I come in?" the monk asked, tentatively, a slight rattle on the doorknob suggesting he expected an affirmative answer.

"NO. No. Please leave me to work things out for myself, Brother. Thanks."

He turned to face Melissa who had removed a couple of layers of fabric. What remained was diaphanous. However, the monk was not to be put off. He spoke through the door.

"You know, Brother James, you came here for a reason, and that reason has been fulfilled. Now is the time to take the next step. I distinctly remember you saying you wanted to give up earthly pleasures and live a cleaner, purer life. The Abbot awaits."

And he was gone.

James remembered the conversation about purity and cleanliness, vividly. Now however, just at the point where he realised what he'd be missing, he regretted ever mentioning the whole 'monk' thing to the Abbott.

'Best beware what you wish for in an unguarded situation,' he thought, remembering his father's wise words. 'It might just come back to bite you on the bum,' which, coincidentally, was what Melissa was doing at that precise moment.

MOONWATCH

An overblown moon
Colourwashed with cream
Squats over the darkening sea,
Above the bobbing light of
The nightfishing boat below.
Where are you?
Trudging through sludge,
on well-trodden midnight paths.
Where is she?

Cruel snowmelt, seeping through thin slippers

The cold – clutching and climbing the
Vein-mapped, bare old shanks.

Silence.
A name called feebly through ancient woodland
In vain.
Time-worn feet feel the slow freeze.

'Come home, Suzie…'
echoes through the forest oaks.
Where can she be?
And where am I?

Nightnavy dressing gown clutched tightly
Across paperthin throatskin.
Too cold here.

Suzie; curled
by the roaring fire,
catstretches;

Strolls stiffly
to the yawning,
wideopen doorway
Sniffs wintry air as the cold creeps and seeps
into the hallway.
The moonwatch almost over.

MUCK

I've always loved muck. No, let me qualify that statement. I don't mean the kind of rubbishy, smelly waste deposited in wheelie bins and stinking of what seasoned bin men call 'maggot juice'. I mean the magic stuff that produces flowers, fruit and vegetables. The alchemy of seeds, tightly closed, dropped randomly in measured rations of earth; which suddenly over-green the surface of earthenware pots in early spring.

I put this love down to childhood days with my dad and Uncle Albert. The latter first introduced me to the pleasure of growing things when he arrived at our tiny street house one May morning and carefully placed an old chipped ceramic sink in the middle of the backyard next to my dad's bike. Nobody was impressed, but I was intrigued.

"What's that for, Uncle Albert?"

He brought the rest of what would nowadays doubtless be termed a 'Home Garden Kit' or some such fancy title, at a posh garden centre. From one voluminous pocket he produced some pieces of broken teacup and gave them to me to cover the plughole, "for drainage," he explained, taking his cap off and wiping his nose on the sleeve of his old khaki mac. Heaps of soft, friable soil were shaken into the sink from an old wicker basket lined with newspaper.

My dad always thought my Uncle Albert, my mam's brother, was a bit slow on the uptake, but I have to defend him here. He realised that a six-year-old wouldn't have the patience to wait for a slow miracle so he'd already done the hard bit.

In came a shallow, wooden box full of greenery. There were lobelias and alyssum enough to fill a dozen sinks. My parents made a frantic search for containers – mainly old crockery, and memorably, a chipped china chamber pot, to house these treasures. I was entranced by the transformation – and by being officially allowed to get my hands in the muck in the cause of planting my little garden.

This wasn't the grey-black muck of the street outside though. (*That* I was very familiar with!) This was brown, composty muck; smelling of the earth and nature – all unknown to me – living as I did in a slummy street, under the looming shadows of the gas tanks.

In the coming weeks the tiny blue and white flowers unfolded, sharing their blossom secrets with us and making a fairyland of the yard. I spent every free second squatting by the sink, observing their progress minutely and wonderingly. Throughout my adult life it has been impossible to recapture the surge of excitement I felt about those ordinary, everyday, little flowers.

My Uncle Albert always brought flowers or veg when he came to visit – wallflowers and Sweet Williams in newspaper bundles, scrunched up and tied with string to the back of his bike; a cabbage or turnip in a brown paper carrier bag streaked with soil. He'd freewheel his way along the cobbles and then tackle the uphill slog back home, where Auntie Vi awaited him.

"And you can get them boots off before you set foot in here!"

Poor man. He was expected to grow the produce and then come home white as a vestal virgin, having thoroughly cleansed himself before he set foot in the house. He even had to wash the potatoes at the allotment tap in all weathers, before bringing them home, Sunday-dinner-ready, for my aunt's razor-eyed scrutiny.

My dad put it down to Auntie Vi being a Roman Catholic. She would go through the house with a flamethrower, tidying, polishing, scouring and scrubbing. If Albert ever stood still too long, I'm sure he too would have been hosed down too. The old, unproven adage about cleanliness and godliness was quoted liberally in Auntie Vi's house.

Meanwhile, we had now moved to a house with a garden. My dad, the other nurturer of the earth, and of me, taught me how to heap up the reddish soil around the lines of green potato shoots at just the right time; and in Autumn, to seek out those hidden treasures for our tea. He cosseted the dahlias – big and round as dinner plates and yellow as egg yolks, lifting the tubers from the garden in autumn and gently cradling them into cardboard sandboxes to weather the winter in the safety of the airing cupboard. (No mystery to me why plant shops are called 'nurseries' after such an apprenticeship.)

We would go out into the six o'clock fields, weekend mornings, me and my dad, searching after mushrooms which we'd cook in the bacon fat for breakfast. Delicious.

You'd expect these two men, united in the soil, to admire and respect each other, and to some extent, they did, but I'm afraid that Albert's lack of backbone in facing up to his fearsome wife diminished him in my dad's eyes.

Years later when my aunt and uncle were long gone, my dad and I were discussing matters horticultural and recalling how pristine the potatoes had to be for Auntie Vi's inspection. "How did he put up with her all that time?" I asked.

My dad didn't criticise her, he simply said, "If your Auntie Vi had been there when they rolled the stone from the tomb, she'd have looked Jesus up and down and said, 'An' you can get that mucky shroud off straight away and let me put it on a boil wash'."

We exchanged an affectionate smile at the truth of it.

This is by way of a tribute to the two gardeners who introduced me to the twin childhood pleasures of muck and magic.

ANYONE FOR TAROT?

What we're buying here is hope; make no mistake about that. There's cynicism at the table and we know it'll cost us, but it's inevitable that a grain; a soupcon of 'what if' has seeped into our collective subconscious.

We hadn't gone into the building to seek out this nonsense at all. We'd gone, primarily, to see some wonderful young musicians; the main act of the day, and we considered ourselves lucky that once a month, our Saturday afternoons could be spent watching live music instead of rootling round the shops in search of the next big thing.

Having equipped ourselves with tea and cake, we sat a while in the café and chatted. Tanya was the first of us to notice that people were going in different directions and wondered what else was going on so we left the others behind, had a wander around and smelt, rather than found, this place. The thick, sickly, seventies smell of joss sticks hung in the air; the fog invading our lungs and making us cough. I was about to 'do a u-ee' and head straight back out and I assumed Tanya was of the same, dismissive turn of mind, but she proved to be surprisingly susceptible and we ended up visiting each stall.

Crystal Healing jostled with runes and psychic readings, competing for our money. Half a dozen home-made-jewellery stalls were dotted around, inevitably run by women with long hair and even longer skirts.

'The Mind, Spirit and Body Fayre' had its share of oddities and it brought to mind an encounter I'd had some years earlier with a woman who claimed to be a 'spirit artist'. She'd collared me and announced that she did portraits of 'souls in the spirit world, and their auras'. Her spirit guide must've been having a day off, or having a laugh choosing me as her mark. She couldn't have picked on a more disillusioned cynic if she'd tried. We stood and looked at each other for a long moment – I, all the while debating on the degree of cruelty I might permit myself to show. I know this mumbo jumbo may seem harmless, but people like this prey on the vulnerable – especially the recently bereaved – and it makes me mad.

I turned to stare at the very bad paintings on display. They looked like something from an old 'Woman's Own' fiction page, circa 1950 – all flowing hair and swirling mists in sapphire and orange skies.

"I wouldn't mind looking like that when I'm dead," I mused as I stood in front of one particularly glam 'ghost'. Only then did I realise I'd said it out loud. The 'artist' looked indignant and was about to speak again when I offered a suggestion. "You could change your strapline to, 'I paint dead people'."

I smiled and nodded encouragingly, taking my tongue out of my cheek temporarily and pretending I didn't think this whole business was bizarre. Foot firmly in mouth, I decided to put the other one in with it. "Like the film... The Sixth Sense," I explained unnecessarily. She gave me a stare laced with icy anger. Ah, well, some fell on stony ground even in the Bible. I wasn't 'feeling the lurve', that's for sure.

Returning to the present, I noticed an anomaly in the gathering. A well-dressed, unbearded man in his mid-forties was in charge of a stall selling books. Tanya had skimmed over him and stopped at another table where a woman was offering Tarot readings. She looked interested but hesitant, and told me she'd never had one before, so the reader pounced; leaning across and introducing herself to Tanya with a warm handshake. "I'm Dulcie."

She ignored me completely.

In an instant, we were seated and Tanya was shuffling a large deck of Tarot cards, but it was immediately made clear that I was not wanted at the reading. "*You* mustn't touch them," she said to me, then, addressing Tanya, "Would you prefer to do this alone?"

I took the hint and made as if to move off, but my friend stopped me.

I wondered why she'd wanted rid. My more gullible side assumed that I must've had a strong Karma. Not that I know *anything* about 'Karmas' or 'auras' but I decided that one or the other was interfering with ley lines or something vaguely 'alternative' like that. I was picking up on the language quite quickly here.

I sat back in my seat beside Tanya and tried to work out what was going on. I looked closely at Dulcie. She was ordinary-smart but with a touch of flamboyance that seemed to be de rigeur for all these people. The clue was in the huge, bright wrap draped across one shoulder and the bejewelled glasses-holder hanging from her neck. Tanya did as she was told. She tried shuffling the pack but the magic cards were rather big and she dropped a few: whereupon Dulcie swiftly swept them up saying, "*I'll* have *them*," as if this clumsy act was somehow 'meant to be'.

She worked quickly, pausing to communicate with the universe for a few minutes as she interpreted the cards. I moved into a more objective mode, listening carefully to what she was saying, but disengaged somehow.

There was to be a new business venture, apparently. It was taking shape even now and would be more successful and satisfying than Tanya's present position. We exchanged glances but Tanya was miles away, so I didn't dare kick her under the table conspiratorially, the way we'd normally do in the presence of the improbable.

A couple of minutes later, the book man ambled over and hovered. He stared intensely at the tarot reader for a minute or two before moving on to the next table.

The cards Dulcie was placing on the table now formed another group. "Are you in a relationship at the moment?" she asked.

"No, no," Tanya said dismissively. Having had a financially ruinous relationship with a dreadful man – father of her two children – Tanya had never even discussed the possibility of a new relationship in all the time I'd known her.

"Ah, well," Dulcie predicted confidently, "there's going to be someone in your life who will help you with your business and he will become your partner eventually… *I* have no influence on what the cards say, you understand," she added, looking above her glasses at me. "I just interpret them. And I can see great happiness coming your way."

The session continued for a while longer and I became convinced that the generality of what was being said applied equally to me and another few thousand women of our age, confirming my long-held belief that this was all illogical trickery.

As we watched the concert later that afternoon, Tanya seemed deep in thought. I didn't say very much but something was troubling me and I lost concentration a few times during the singing, being brought back to the present only when I heard the applause, and realised that the concert was over.

What I had seen as we left the 'Fayre' was an odd exchange between the bookman and Dulcie. He had given her money and had then begun to pack away his stall. What was going on here? I decided it was just my mean-spirited mind playing tricks.

I can sometimes be a bit curmudgeonly.

We collected our coats and bags and were about to leave the room at the end of the event, when the bookman came in and pretended to bump into Tanya, knocking her bag and its contents to the floor. I pushed him out of the way and made sure I gathered everything safely in because I was now convinced that there was some sort of scam going on. Then I looked up and saw that he was deep in conversation with Tanya and she was responding; smiling enthusiastically and looking almost girlish. I thrust the bag into her abdominal area and taking her elbow, tried to lead her away. How gullible she was.

Resisting my efforts she said in a determined voice, "I don't think you know Tom Conway, do you? We go back a long way."

I was aghast. Tanya was flirting with the con-man!

He gave me his best smile. "I suppose you're wondering what happened in there," he said, charm and smarm oozing out of every pore. "Well, I had to slip Aunt Dulcie a tenner before she'd confirm Tanya's name. I didn't want to approach until I was sure it was you," he told Tanya. "Then I messed up by nearly knocking you over."

It turned out they were old flames – had lost touch twenty odd years ago when he'd gone to work in Canada and she wouldn't go with him.

Phone numbers were exchanged. Dates were agreed, and we left.

I still don't believe in serendipity or tarot cards. I still think it's smoke and mirrors, but Tanya reckons it was the best fifteen quid she's ever spent and whatever Dulcie was; whether genuinely deluded or simply making money from fools, Tanya did actually find some happiness – and I have to admit to now reading my horoscope in the paper every week. Just in case.

AUNTIE GERTIE
AND THE FROGS

After the untimely death of my mother, our whole family was in disarray. My father was trying to come to terms with the loss of his beloved wife, and we, the children, simply floundered or pretended that nothing was amiss. I later found out that this was a normal reaction to sudden death – that denial then anger then despair followed a pattern in most bereaved people's lives. However, I had to grow to adulthood before I became fully aware of that pattern.

Most of the time, we all just got on with our lives and accepted the hollowness of our new situations. No counselling for us and little overt sympathy expressed.

As an attempt to make a little haven of normality, though, our family and friends rallied round. My Granny Murphy got two buses to our house to make sure that dad had a cooked dinner every day – usually meat, potatoes and veg – when he came home from his job at Dorman Long, where he toiled in the wire works, taming huge, white-hot rods of steel into differing widths of wire. My sister, still in her teens, went back to work in the packing department of Hintons for a short time, but a consensus of the relatives decided that she should leave her job and take on the task of looking after the house, my dad and me. They didn't think it was a bad choice at the time, but to her it meant the loss of my sister's new-found freedom and any chance of becoming an independent woman with her own income. Of course, all this was lost on me at the time as I was about to go to the Grammar school next year, having passed the 11+ exam, and was only looking forward to the future.

When my mother was alive, we always went away for a week's

holiday in July during the steelworks closure which happened to allow the furnaces to be cooled and cleaned.

Everyone had to take their holidays at the same time, so my parents always opted for a week in Scarborough. We stayed at Auntie Betty's boarding house in Peasholm Avenue, which was luxurious to my mind, having a garden back and front, no sign of gas tanks on the corner, and where the sea air was fresh and I was enchanted because they had gnomes in their garden!

My sister was courting a lad in the army, and she wanted to go away with her best friend later in the season, so that left me and my dad. Luckily, dad's friends stepped in and we went away with them and their daughter who was also my best friend. This pattern continued for a while, but there were other offers from family which were quite exciting too.

Auntie Gertie, my mother's elder sister, had offered to give me dinner each day, because I wasn't eating the dreadful offerings of school. They were all worried about my skinny frame and wanted to make sure I had 'proper' food each day. At that time, the misnamed dinner hour was an hour and a half long – enough time for me to stroll to my auntie's house, eat, get washed and go back for the afternoon session. I loved this arrangement, even though my aunt was somewhat eccentric, combining good and bad points. (She made me a nice new dress but at the same time she insisted on checking my hair for head lice!) I decided not to tell my family about the head lice thing as I didn't think it would go down very well. Picture the scene: You what? She thought you had nits! 'No dad, she was just making sure'… and so on.

This July holiday, my dad informed me, was to be spent with my long-suffering Uncle Will and Auntie Gertie travelling down to the south coast – through Dorset and Devon. Our final destination was to be Torquay. It was doubly exciting to me because we were going to be camping!

My auntie's version of camping was quite odd. We were collected from home that first morning in a tiny black car –I think a Ford Popular – with a double mattress hanging over the sides of the roof.

"Gert thought it was the only way of getting a decent sleep," said my uncle. He was already looking defeated. Auntie Gertie looked triumphant. "We'll be alright, Margaret. I don't want any spiders or stuff crawling on me in the night and I don't want a bad back."

"You mean we're gonna cart that all over the south coast?" This from my horrified father, and I knew he was worried about looking like a weird version of the Clampetts, because so was I.

"Well what I thought was that when we leave, we can give it to someone else who's staying here. I think they'd be glad of it." We all looked at each other, lost for words and made no further protest. She had it all under control.

We made camp on that first night in a field in Tewkesbury and I was running about to stretch my legs when I came across a signpost in the field opposite. "Apparently this is where there was a famous battle, Dad!" I was so excited and we were both suitably impressed as we read about it.

Auntie Gertie however, had discovered a more immediate problem. "Our Margaret, come here!" I hurried back – what now? She was holding the mattress erect on its side on the grass with only her finger and thumb.

"You'll have to go in the tent and get them all out. And I mean all!"

Not being a lover of spiders, I hesitated, but stepped gingerly into the yellowish light inside the tent, to be met by a small army of tiny frogs. "Brilliant!" I shouted, collecting the little creatures and carefully in twos and placing them on the outside of our accommodation.

It took about half an hour to get them all, but in the end, we were frog free. My dad and uncle had a less luxurious tent but didn't complain. I didn't dare ask about their frog situation.

I woke in the early hours, feeling a bit cold and looked across at Auntie Gertie. She was snoring loudly and a froglet was sitting on her cheek. I watched fascinated, not knowing what the etiquette was in such a situation. Finally, I removed it, and the one on her neck and a third from the other side of her open mouth as she was turning over. She narrowly avoided squashing it.

"By that was the best night's sleep I've had in ages, Will," she declared later as we sat by the paraffin stove breathing in the wonderful smell of frying bacon in the open air. "Great breakfast as well," I said, praying she hadn't swallowed any frogs in the night.

AWAY

Here's a question for you: Where's 'away'?

No?

Let me put it another way. When you decide to throw something away, where does it go? Apart, that is, from it no longer being in your vicinity. Out of sight, out of mind. A few weeks ago I was forced to ponder deeply on that same question. I'd been doing a local government survey about waste and recycling in the area and I was shocked at the number of tons of unwanted stuff we throw out. And I asked myself, what is 'out'? Sometimes, we put used unloved stuff into plastic bags and take it to a charity shop (and, we expect the volunteer to *thank* us for the detritus we offload, like we're giving them something useful.)

I've been trying to get rid of a pristine double mattress, Dunlopillo, all safely wrapped in strong plastic left over from my new one, for months now. The council will take it if I give them thirty pounds. I don't begrudge them the money but I hate to think of it being destroyed when someone – a fictional person – would be glad of it. All the charities have refused it because it doesn't have a fire-safety label. So it sits and grumbles at me in one of the spare rooms, feeling abandoned and useless. The fictional person is a man I heard about, who sleeps near a skip by the bus station in Middlesbrough. I'm sure *he'd* welcome my clean mattress. How do I connect him with it though? Such a waste.

My Uncle Leonard, who looks as old as an elephant but is probably only in his mid-seventies, contacted me last week, after many years of being neglected by the family, to tell me he was hoping to get into sheltered accommodation and that he wanted to bequeath his house and contents to me. Apparently, all the other members of the immediate family had either upset him or ignored him for years so were not deemed worthy to have any of his goods and chattels.

This was a mixed blessing. I felt a terrible burden of guilt because my contact with him had been sporadic, to say the least. I'd phoned, probably once a month and I'd reluctantly taken him out for a bit of dinner maybe six times last year. Oh, and I always cooked a Christmas dinner for him. He was always thrilled to see me, compounding my sense of shame at my neglect, and, to be fair, we always had quite a nice time together, because he was so appreciative. The down side was that he was faintly smelly, being unable to get into the shower and living alone. Apparently a 'carer' – and I use the word in its loosest sense – came to help with 'personal hygiene' a couple of times a week. For this, she/he was paid the minimum wage and matched it with the minimum effort as far as I could see.

I always took a present of some air fresheners and a bottle of nice aftershave to slather on his unshaven chin before he came out. This was a selfish gesture on my part because my car is tiny and I have a sensitive nose. Suffice to say that the drive was easier if I didn't have to smell the must of mouse droppings on the journey.

I tend to agree with those who say there's no such thing as altruism. Every time I meet self-sacrifice, I can always see the motive behind it. A kind present-giver? Or someone who needs to be liked? A charitable volunteer – or someone who has too much time on their hands or who deals in second-hand goods and likes to get first pick? Who knows? Is it charitable? I've met both types and it troubles me that I'm the only one who doesn't beatify these people.

We always ate at decent restaurants though, when I took Uncle Leonard out. I wouldn't make him go into a greasy spoon or the like. I was, and am, very fond of him and have a lot of happy memories of childhood trips to the country or the seaside with Uncle Leonard and Auntie Maisie, when my own parents died.

It seems like a pattern for old men that, when their wives die, they let their standards slip. Uncle Leonard wasn't ill as far as I knew, but he just couldn't be bothered, which is far sadder. Also, in a clear-sighted way, he was right. He knew he didn't have long to live so why waste time cleaning and tidying? Leave it to someone else to worry about when he'd gone.

We'd already arranged our latest trip to the seaside, when I had a call from the 'carers' to say that Uncle Leonard needed a new bed – his old one having given up the ghost, so I called him and offered to buy him the base and put my spare mattress on it. You'd think he'd won the lottery, he was so grateful and I was so guilt-ridden. I mean, I didn't know how he was fixed financially but maybe I shouldn't't've offered my cast-offs – it was almost as if he wasn't worthy of better things. However, I reconciled myself to this solution because it was so practical for both of us. (Trying to make myself feel noble, perhaps?)

Anyway, I was to collect my uncle on Wednesday and we would be taking in the sea air, fish and chips, candy floss and ice cream before the day was over. As he only got out of his house when I took him, or the hospital sent an ambulance; when we went out, we had the whole shebang. I usually came home feeling full and slightly queasy with the junk food, but his face was always a picture.

The outing went well until we sat on the sea front eating waffles loaded with strawberries and cream. I could never have imagined the conversation that followed in my wildest dreams.

"You know, I was always very fond of your parents, Debbie."

I turned to him. "Well, of course, Uncle Leonard. You all used to go on holiday together didn't you, with Uncle Jim and Auntie Marlene?"

"Ah, yes," he said. "That was when it happened. Douglas, on the Isle of Man. Beautiful place. It was the year before you were born. June, as I recall; summer anyway. Your mother was a very beautiful woman, Debbie. And I know I'm nothing much to look at now but I was quite dashing in my younger days."

I really didn't want to hear what came next. Well, no one wants to hear the sordid details of the past, do they? Especially about their own family? I wanted to do that 'la-la-la-la' thing with my fingers in my ears, but to no avail. Uncle Leonard was unburdening himself.

"We never spoke about it afterwards," he continued. "It was left in the Isle of Man – quite modern really. 'What happens on holiday stays on holiday', like that film about fighting."

I sat, stunned, watching the glorious sunset for some minutes as the implication set in. Then, the sum total of all the junk food I'd eaten, was regurgitated onto the beach, much to my embarrassment and disgust. I'd just worked it out, you see. Uncle Leonard was suggesting that he might be my father. No wonder he wanted to leave me all his goods and chattels.

I couldn't think straight and, excusing myself, walked away from him and the mess I'd left on the sand. It took me an hour to work out a plan.

Uncle Leonard didn't get much of a chance to drink – I mean alcohol. I needed to know for certain whether he was my dad or not. I decided to take him into the nearest pub and get him a few whiskies. That way, on the drive back, he'd drop off.

I scrabbled in my bag and found a couple of grubby cotton wool balls and the remains of our lolly sticks from earlier. He wouldn't let me throw them away cos he could 'use them as plant markers', apparently.

With my homemade DNA kit I'd be able to know 'THE TRUTH'.

It worked like a dream. Uncle Leonard's mouth flabbed open when we were half way home. I gently brought the car to a halt so as not to wake him – and this was the most disgusting part – pushed the cotton wool swab around his cheek on the end of the lolly stick. Half way through, though, his top dentures clacked forward and nipped my fingers. Horrified, I looked away immediately and pushed them back up as best I could. They'd be at an angle but that couldn't be helped. Job done, I placed the evidence in a little plastic bag and cleaned my hands on a couple of antiseptic wipes, but to no avail. I could still feel the imaginary saliva on them, like some latter-day Lady Macbeth, trying to clean the blood off her hands.

When we arrived back, I woke my uncle up and he adjusted his false teeth without any trouble. 'That must happen a lot,' I thought.

He thanked me again profusely for the mattress, which would only have been thrown 'away,' and for the lovely day out.

"You're a good girl, Debbie," he said, seemingly unaware of our conversation on the beach. Had he forgotten completely, I wondered, or was he once again, pushing the dirt back under the carpet?

"I enjoyed our chat, Uncle Leonard," I said, meaningfully.

"Me too, Debbie." He smiled the smile of the innocent.

I kept the swab of DNA for a month. I always meant to have it analysed, but Uncle Leonard died shortly after our trip out, and somehow it didn't seem worth it then.

'Anyway,' I reasoned, 'I know who my dad was. He was the one who looked after me through all the childhood illnesses and who paid for me to do the school exchange trips and who surprised me every birthday and made sure I had a 'good winter coat' each year.'

I had a painful duty to perform after the funeral, and the stuff I cleared out from Uncle Leonard's house turned out to be quite a haul. Auntie Maisie had owned some valuable pottery and jewellery and the house itself, in a good part of town, was worth a fair bit.

The problem was, I couldn't stop thinking that I'd violated the trust he'd placed in me, when I'd started poking about in his mouth that day. The only way I could think of to atone, was to give away the legacy.

It's called, 'The Leonard Mills Trust Fund,' and it takes oldies on trips to the seaside. Only a local concern, but they're all very grateful for it.

So, does altruism exist? How can it? On the surface I look really generous and good, but *I've* managed to get something out of it too. I've thrown my guilt 'away' and now, at least, I no longer have the awful nightmares about being chased by giant sets of false teeth...

BETTER BY TRAIN

After the uncertainty about the connection from local station to mainline, it is always gratifying when, luggage safely stowed and outer garments folded to fit snugly on the rack above your head, you are installed in your reserved window seat with nothing to do for the next five hours but enjoy the ride.

You have the good fortune to be alone in the seat, so there's no added irritation of a fellow traveller, who would inevitably take up the precious 'spreading out' space you need. A momentary pang of panic, as you squint up at the seat reservation panel above you, subsides when you realise that no one will trouble you until Birmingham, where the other seats will be occupied. Wonderful.

You relax, close your eyes and allow the stress of the morning to leave you as you organise your thoughts. A coffee perhaps, when the trolley comes round, and a kitkat? Maybe. It *is* a sort of holiday after all.

The top button of your trousers begins to pinch a little so you surreptitiously release it from the buttonhole and sigh contentedly, eyes closed, leaning back blissfully in your seat. In an ideal world.

By some miracle, in reality, the connecting train has actually arrived, on the day in question. There have been none of the old familiar excuses for leaving the eight passengers in Saltburn stranded, yet again:

'We were running late so we turned round at Redcar and went back…' 'There's been a suicide off the bridge near York'/signal failure in Darlington…' etc: so today, the original timings of the journey would stand. Hooray.

I am in the quiet carriage. All this means is that we have permission to be irritated any time someone gobby gets on, or a plug-in electronic device beeps too often. Our only means of showing disapproval is a general shifting in our seats accompanied by loudish 'tutting' sounds. I once saw a woman indicate with much hand-waving that the music a gangly youth was enjoying was not being kept to himself but seeping out of his ears; but that was an exception.

Foreign passengers who make noise are tolerated, simply because they are foreign and know no better. We are less tolerant of spoilt children. It's just the way we are, I suppose.

Having planned a space in which to be happy for half a day, imagine my chagrin when a young man flings his rucksack on top of my 'Lovely Homes' magazine – as yet unread – and begins to unload all manner of foodstuffs into a carrier bag. A pungent smell of spices floods the carriage as the transfer takes place, causing an involuntary wrinkling of the nose. I quickly turn my head from him so as not to cause offence if he should see my disgust.

How far down can a heart sink? I do that strange, ineffectual mime of moving a millimetre closer to the window, although there is no way it will distance me from the activity in progress. A pack of huge, doorstep sandwiches wrapped in plastic slide forward and are about to land on my lap. Instinctively, I put out my hand to save them from the floor. The lad grins gratefully as I return them. "Thanks. My mother forced me to bring them." He takes the seat opposite and stretches his long legs out into the aisle.

I feel unaccountably guilty for my bad grace. 'It'll be alright,' I tell myself. He is clean and presentable. I can cope until Birmingham. He tells me his name is Rudi and he's travelling to Oxford.

We settle in comfortably together lulled by the rhythm of the train, and begin to read. I sneak a look at his book – 'Gender Politics'. Hmm. Rightio.

In York, we are joined by Brenda. She flutters and fusses her way into the seat next to me, forcing me to reorganise my stuff into an untidy heap on my quarter of the table. 'This journey is becoming intolerable,' I think – until it strikes me that *I* am the problem. I rearrange my indignant face into a smile. The poor woman has just as much right to her seat as I do.

"Are you going far?" I ask.

"Leamington Spa," she says, still scrabbling around in a giant handbag. "Only for the weekend."

I sneak a better look at Brenda and can't find anything to distinguish her from all the other anonymous looking middle-aged women in the world. She is quite a dun-coloured woman in her beige mac and matching beige countenance. A tiny smattering of pink lipstick differentiates her mouth from the rest of her face, but otherwise, she is unadorned.

I return to 'Lovely Homes', a secret pleasure only indulged when I travel. I look enviously at a converted barn, bought for a song by Catriona and Ben, and lovingly restored using 'junk shop finds'-and her father's building firm. It is now an immaculate show house. A couple of attractive children, Galen and Rowan, smile happily from the sofa ($£2,500$ from 'sofa.com a must-have piece'). I must've dozed off. When I awake, Rudi is still reading and Brenda's finishing a banana. She looks up from her book, dangling the skin helplessly.

"There's a bin at the end of the carriage," I offer. She gives me the semblance of a smile then, as she is rising from her seat, she asks, "So, you like a bit of house porn then?" and carries on to the bin.

Rudi and I stare at each other, then at Brenda.

"No, it's just that I see you're reading, Lovely Homes," she smiles. We don't speak so she continues. "You're shocked cos I called it house porn, aren't you? Well, if you'd had the experience I have, you might understand."

We lean in closer at this; 'Gender Politics' is turned upside down on the table. We are all attention.

She opens a scruffy shopping bag and pulls out an earlier copy of Lovely Homes, a bit the worse for wear.

"When you get to the end of that – thing – you'll see my little house – well, what was left of it after Belinda had finished."

Seemingly, 'country chic' is the latest fad and someone had

told this 'Belinda' – the editor of the magazine – that Brenda's bungalow was worth using as an example.

"She came round and said she loved the concept. I didn't know what she was on about but they offered me good money to take some photos so I said yes. What happened next, though, was horrible. They didn't like the Royal Doulton figurines or my china cabinet so they shifted them out. Well… in the process, they chipped two of my favourites, then they painted the walls a dirty white colour and me cabinet the colour of putty." She pauses and takes a tissue from her pocket. "I probably could've lived with that but then they sanded bits off. It's called 'rustic shabby chic'." Brenda looks at us both, unconvinced. "I hated it. She, this Belinda, said what they wanted was 'not so much a style, but an attitude. A feeling that transcends trends'. I thought she was a bit barmy. In the article she claimed my floral cushions were 'hand crafted in a vintage fabric' because I'd made them meself in 1953. Rustic's a big trend apparently. They trailed in a load of old junk from the shed – still mucky. My aluminium bucket – the outside one – 'distressed by hand for an antique look' apparently. And my gran's old flat iron was stuck on a shelf above the sink – as a 'decorative piece'. The worst bit was, they rummaged around in the airing cupboard and dragged out the ancient tablecloth I use to dry the dog. They creased it and put it on the table with bread and cheese. It was embarrassing. Now all me friends will think I do that. No plates nor nothing."

The buffet trolley hove into view. I got us all a cardboard cup of coffee. We were warming to the subject but by this time Brenda was a bit het up. Rudi asked her why she was going to Leamington Spa. I think he was being kind, changing the subject to calm her down a bit.

"Oh, I'm meeting that Belinda," she says indignantly. "She wants to compensate me for damage done to the house and garden. Taking me to a posh hotel for a night to be pampered. They're terrified I'll sue."

She takes out a packet of fig rolls and offers them round. "I will anyway though." This afterthought is said with a determined gleam. She moves her arthritic old hand until it touches mine and then grasps it tightly for reassurance, jiggling it from side to side. Rudi and I are silent. She continues. "They even changed my name." I gradually ease my hand free, wondering what's coming next.

"What?" asks Rudi.

"Yeah, changed my name. They said 'Brenda' was 'not in keeping with the ethos of the magazine'. A bit too working class."

She reaches for the giant bag and passes around some snaps of her house. It is completely ordinary looking – just like her. Chintzy curtains with frilly valances, a cat on the sofa, and a crocheted blanket over a high-backed old-lady chair. We are bemused that 'Lovely Homes' were interested. Is she just a bit batty? Was it all made up?

In the event, we have no chance to ask any more. The announcer tells everyone leaving the train at Leamington Spa to take all their belongings with them. A flustered Brenda jumps up and panics her way off the train where a tall, botoxed brunette is teetering through the crowds waving and shouting, "Ahoy there, Felicity!" and Brenda, turning briefly to the train window, nods once and is gone.

"Belinda," says Rudi.

"And Felicity," I add.

When Rudi leaves the train at Oxford, having shared his ideas at great length about the roles of men and women in today's society, I am rather sad to see him go. I would have liked to discuss Brenda's story with him but I am too tired to think any more.

Alone at last, drifting off into a daydream, I am disturbed by a smartly dressed businessman. "Sorry, but is this yours?" he asks, handing me Brenda's copy of 'Lovely Homes' which must've fallen to the floor as she left.

It falls open at the right page. There she is.

'Felicity bought this original worker's cottage in the 50s,' it said. And there she was, Brenda, grimacing at the table, elbows resting on the dog's tablecloth, floral china cup in hand. The room was now unrecognisable with bunches of flowers in old jugs on every surface, the replacement furniture all around. 'Felicity' is over made-up and wears an odd assortment of scarves and necklaces. The blurb asserts that the china cabinet – they called it a dresser – was 'Felicity's own'.

A feeling of indescribable sadness floods over me. Is it all true then? Is it all false?

Quickly turning to my brand new copy of the magazine, I re-read the first few pages. 'Warm whites,' it coos at me, 'from soft curd to rich buttermilk, are the building blocks of relaxed elegance.' The veil has lifted. Were we all falling for this load of crap?

A second look at 'Catriona and Ben' reveals them to be interior designers with their own business. The children, Galen and Rowan – or 'accessories' as I now dub them – simply look smug as they pose on the stupidly expensive couch.

I fling it down on the table in disgust. Brenda had been right. House Porn. Those people are all false and ridiculous and Brenda and her house had been violated by them. I stare out of the window for the rest of the journey with the luxury of an almost empty carriage, and wonder if it might be an idea to read 'The Emperor's New Clothes' once more – just to ensure I'll never lose sight of reality again.

'Lovely Homes' goes straight into the designer bin as I step off the train.

DOG ROSE

The dog rose. Its single-layered sweetness opened for me,
petal and sepal newly exposed and frail.
Tissue-thin and lately crumpled in bud,
Now, the petals shake free,
pale and pink as a bridesmaid's dress.
Unselfconsciously delicate, and patient,
It waits,
Exposed to the wild air,
And proffering its blossom to the world.

A dog rose. A 'dog' rose?
A thing, paltry and unworthy.
A throw-away weed
With no value

It waits, insulted and half choking
in the weed-infested dust of a hedgerow.
Pale yellow stamens, upright and proud, encircle its centre.
The strong, honey-sweet scent
At the flowerheart
Enchants me.

I have passed this place a hundred times
and never paused.
Now, I cup its fragrance gently
between gnarled old hands.
Take great care as I
Drink in the exquisite odour,
And feel it charming my senses

Yet still, l am greedily unsated;
And still reluctant to move.

A passer-by
passes by, unmoved,
and takes out his phone.

CAUGHT IN A SHOWER

Last to leave church, still contemplating the message,
And still with the holy dust on my sinner's shoulders,
I stand on the threshold of the porch and muse.
The trees and the lawn wait; postcard -pretty,
staring greenly back;
forever framed in this ancient, stone arch.

Reluctantly now, I wend my slow way home, where nobody awaits.
All Sunday stretches before me – a blank page, languid and lazy.

And so, with the heat of the day
warming sun-blessed shoulders,
I will walk the long way round, in slow motion,
Past cemetery and fields, dog rose and meadowsweet,
God gradually fading into the background.

A sudden greyness in the sky
And then
the pleasing 'plick' of random rainspots as they land,
Remind me how I delight in the changing of the weather;
my weekend ramblings of body and mind,
with nothing to do but
contemplate the world.
God's and mine.
What's he playing at nowadays?
Should we blame him for the wickedness
Or praise him, praise him, for the beauty?

A greywhite cloud looms
As the sky weeps above me.
The raincoat allows trickles of water
Through the thin fabric.
They crawl, insect-like and coldly,
down my neck and spine to my skin.
Too late to turn back,
I hurry onwards,
the thread of goodness unravelling.
Damp penetration complete: scalp saturated
and chilled,
I stand at the door.
Home, now, is the best of places – warm, safe and dry.
Sermon forgotten, I turn the key.
Here endeth the third lesson.

EMPATHY

Charlotte Pendlebury. Even her name was redolent of china teacups and English country gardens. She was obviously slumming it with us. I was jealous, I admit it. She had everything going for her. The only natural blonde I'd ever met, for starters. When all the rest of us were busy doing general maintenance work on our faces and bodies, Charlotte swanned around, slicked a bit of lippy on that perfect cupid's bow of hers and was all ready to go. She didn't even diet, as far as I knew – the cow – and clothes just slid onto her body and caressed it, easefully, without any of the holding your breath or squeezing into various kinds of corsetry that other women have to do.

Why was she here? I'd warned Jeanette, our leader, that if Pendlebury came, Nessie would walk out (which she did) because of all that stuff with Steven Gosling earlier in the year. If any man came within spitting distance of her he was a goner, and Steven was easy meat.

You might imagine she was a simperer, from the way I've described her, which would give us all a reason to hate her; but she wasn't.

I absolutely *hate* simperers. They're usually the most overweight women with silly little girl voices, who lower their double chins and look up through their lashes at men, giggling in feigned admiration of some dire joke. 'Fat kittens', I call 'em. They are delusional if they think this is attractive. And when it fails, they crank up the giggling to almost hysteria level and pray that'll work.

Pendlebury was not one of those. She was clever and looked down on the likes of us, thinking she was something special. Don't know what she did for a living or how she was educated, but someone hinted at a fee-paying school somewhere down south.

That same person also proffered a killer fact about Charlotte. She remembered that at that private secondary school, *her* gym knickers fitted perfectly. Ah, no wonder I hated her. In contrast, my navy blues had faded to an indescribable greyish hue by year eight and could have been pulled up to my armpits very easily had I not discreetly rolled the waist over a couple of times in the school changing rooms.

When she joined the Townswomen's Guild we'd all agreed she was too young and glamorous to fit in, but she charmed most of the others pretty quickly. Tried it with me too at first, but I soon put a stop to that.

When it was my turn to supply the cricket teas, I really pushed the boat out. Sarnies with crusts cut off and everything. My carrot cake with pineapples and walnuts was a triumph. That is, until *she* turned up with proper posh cake covers to protect three of the most enormous Devil's food cakes and a couple of pyramids of 'salambos a l'orange' on matching silver salvers. I was gutted. Never heard of a 'salambo'. Turns out it was an éclair with a wonderful orange cream centre. Delicious, of course.

Then later, when the teams trooped in, someone knocked my only china tea service over and managed to break most of the tea plates. Charlotte fussed around, sweeping the bits up and being really sympathetic then managed to bang her bony elbow into my Lladro figurine – the one my gran gave me before she died. I *know* I shouldn't have used it as a table centre – as all the women pointed out at the time – but I really wanted to outdo her. It was becoming an obsession. Anyway, she couldn't bear to be in the doghouse so Miss Perfect dashes out and buys me another figurine 'as an apology'. I didn't want it. Why didn't she realise that it wasn't the same? You can't always pay to put things right, can you?

After that, I stopped speaking to her. I just couldn't see the point. Life's too short to bother with people you have nowt in common with, isn't it? Funny though; shortly after the cricket tea incident, she stopped coming to the meetings so much. Someone reckoned her husband was back from – ooh, I dunno, somewhere exotic I expect. So, she probably didn't dare come and flirt with our men any more.

I did see her a couple of times in the High Street, shopping in that posh fruit shop near Tesco's the first time, but she hadn't noticed me so I just walked past her. Second time though, she *did* notice me and dashed across the street, all breathless.

"Janice!" she shouted. "How *are* you?" She always emphasised the wrong words. I said I was fine and that me and Bob were going on holiday to Greece shortly.

"How wonderful!" Again, that over-the-top way of talking.

I couldn't help noticing though, that some of the shine had gone off her. Those perfect nails were bitten down and her hair could've done with a wash. She probably thought she didn't need to bother, what with the husband keeping her on a tight rein nowadays. About time too. She'd spent quite enough time with my Bob at the last barbeque. We'd had words afterwards and he's kept his distance since then. Rumour has it that their house is up for sale. Get in!

CHARLOTTE'S STORY

That was Jeanette somebody on the phone. She wanted to welcome me to the village and told me all the little events being held over the summer there. Quite sweet really – having someone interested in one's wellbeing. I do hope she doesn't want to pry though. I need to keep my personal life to myself for the time being.

I've lost so much weight since I left Nick. It's the stress, I suppose. The house is looking better since I had the men in to decorate. All the London furniture has been deposited here but not in the right places, so I'll need a local man to redistribute it soon. Maybe I should go to the Women's Institute or some such thing – they'll have some contacts, I'm sure. I hate being alone. I will call Jeanette and get the details.

That went well. I've been accepted into the group and they've all been very sweet, although I can't cope with anyone gushing – and there was rather a lot of that going on. Two women volunteered their husbands to move the furniture. I have to contact a Steve Gosling, who'll sort it out, apparently.

I quite liked a young woman called Janice. She seemed down-to-earth and very confident. She showed me photographs of her two beautiful children and I felt quite sad. I wonder if she knows how fortunate she is to be able to have children. Before we gave up on the idea, Nick and I were fairly happy, but after so many miscarriages, he began to withdraw from me – as if I could be blamed for such a thing. One thing I do know is – nobody has the right to be violent to another human being. I am so glad I eventually took my courage in both hands and left him. Maybe here, I can make a better life for myself without looking over my shoulder all the time.

Janice has that 'bonny' sort of beauty I admire so much. She has a sort of 'glow' about her and is so positive about everything. She'd had her hair cut when I saw her at the cricket ground today, and I told her how much it suited her – it was in a shortish shiny bob – but she was quite dismissive of me. Maybe she's had a busy day. Anyway, I'd really pushed the boat out with my baking and hoped she'd be pleased. I did my Devil's food cakes: always a sure-fire winner; and some salambos. They were greeted with many 'oohs and aahhs' but seemed to have little effect on Janice. Maybe she's on a diet? She should try living with Nick for a few months – the weight would soon drop off then.

It's about six thirty and I've just returned from the cricket club tea.

I think they all hate me. Well, Janice seems to anyway. It was a catastrophe. Some great hulking idiot broke a heap of tea plates, quite pretty ones too, and as I was helping to clear them up I accidentally knocked a quite ugly ornament onto the floor. What it was doing there I have no idea. It's hardly the sort of thing to grace an afternoon tea-table. Far better to stick with a traditional, small flower arrangement as a centrepiece.

As it was an accident, I thought I'd make it up to Janice and scoured the internet for a replacement. It was a cheaper version of Lladro and I picked up a piece quite easily on an auction site, but she was less than forgiving when I took it round. She didn't even invite me in.

As I left the house it began to drizzle, and I didn't have a coat, so was walking home when a familiar-sounding car horn tooted. Nick had found me.

The beatings have started again. It was fine for weeks until I served the wrong thing for supper. You see, I had forgotten how he liked his lamb and he threw it at the wall. Next time it will be thrown at me.

I have fallen back into the well of depression. My world is so lifeless and dull that I have become lifeless and dull myself. Nick is thriving. He's never away from the cricket club. I have to stay indoors until the visible bruises heal, but today I ventured out and was elated to see Janice at the supermarket when I was buying the last of the late asparagus from Dylan at the fruiterers. I called across to her and she told me of a forthcoming holiday. I hope that when she returns, we will be able to build bridges. I'm desperately in need of a confidante.

ALTRUISM

He should never have listened to Pamela Morton's requests, nor been railroaded by her fragile charm. He knew that *now*, of course, now that it was too late. Looking back on his enthusiastic acceptance of the task he'd been saddled with, he could have kicked himself – and Pamela Morton, for that matter.

"Manipulative bitch." He shocked himself as the words escaped unbidden from his lips. It was the first time he'd thought of her in those terms, having been drawn in numerous times in the past with no reward for his loyalty, nor his labours, yet with a sense of the well-being that comes from having acted kindly, without expectation of gain. There was a word but it escaped him at present. That exact description was summed-up succinctly in just the one word. What was it?

This had been happening quite a bit lately, this scratting around for the expression or phrase that was just beyond his reach. It infuriated him – even more than Pamela Morton – if that can be imagined.

Ah, well, he had fallen in with yet another of her schemes. It was like that Greek bloke who had to do a certain number of labours – the labours of… who was it? And was he Greek or Roman? Anyway, he'd had to do these repetitive things in order to save someone, or himself from a terrible fate or (more likely, this one) to gain the favours of Pamela Morton. Which had been a bit thin on the ground as yet. She did kiss him on the end of his nose once – under the mistletoe and under duress as he recalled.

He was like one of the dogs beneath the table, grateful for any scrap of food, or in his case, affection, that might be thrown his way. Pretty pathetic.

He checked his notice board and found the address he was

meant to go to on this altruistic mission. Ah, that was it – *altruism*. These words usually creep in behind your back when you least expect them. 'ALTRUISM.' He savoured the remembered word and swilled the syllables around his tongue, a few times, planting them firmly back into his brain and almost tasting them.

He suddenly decided he must try to be positive and see this as a mission of mercy rather than a roundabout route to requited love. Keep the Morton out of the question and it might even be pleasant.

The couple he had agreed to help lived in an anonymous-looking bungalow within striking distance of the football ground. He knew nothing much about them – only that they were distantly related to Pamela by marriage and that they'd asked her to get someone ('some mug', he thought, still hanging on to a vestige of bitterness, 'like me for instance') to call round on Saturday 'to help out'.

His precious Saturday. That was the one day in the week when the minutes splayed leisurely before him. The day he simply let the dog go in the garden rather than dash to get the lead to take him and his plastic bag down to the beach. He preferred the beach really because you could coat the dog's doings in sand before you scooped them up and plonked them, held at arm's length between two fingers, into the red bin near the pier.

However, once a week it was good to care less about the dog and more about himself. Stella had called it 'me time'. Did Pamela Morton have 'me time', he wondered, drying the breakfast pots.

Is it 'me time' when your whole life is about you? Oh, Pamela, what have you done to me?

He gazed at the resentful-looking dog who knew there was no beach *and* no walk today and he understood, for the first time, why it had been so annoyed with him when he'd taken it to be neutered.

"I know, Charlie," he said, shaking his head in sympathy and throwing the dog's tennis ball around the kitchen.

"Balls are important to our self esteem. I know now how hard it is to lose them, and I'm very sorry."

In his need to impress Pamela, he had even cleaned the car the night before, so he'd be ready to pick up the couple.

Mavis and Dennis McAndrew. The McAndrews. In their dotage, apparently, and in need of 'a nice day out in the country'. The jobs he was to do by way of 'helping out' were still shrouded in mystery. It was a very vague term, which could mean shifting a hundredweight of coal into a cellar or running a hoover round the downstairs. "Who knows?" he said, defeatist mode having returned.

The bungalow was a clone of all the other bungalows surrounding it. They were built in a neat rectangle with some semblance of a village green in the centre. It had long since become just a patch of grass on which to stand your wheelie bin on a Thursday, there not having been any resident so far, who wanted to graze his cattle or play a game of boules on the common ground. The green had never seen a summer fayre although there had been an ill-fated attempt to organise a Maypole dance by the local Primary school one May day. High winds had soon put paid to that one.

He knocked on the door of number 28 with some trepidation. 'Helping out' was such a nebulous phrase. What would he be expected to do? A thought leapt into his mind unbidden. Surely he would not be expected to do what he remembered was called, 'personal care'? They wouldn't need bathing or – God help us – taking to the toilet, would they? Surely Pamela wouldn't...

The door was opened and a large dog jumped up at his knees and thighs, the nails snagging his new trousers in its delight to see him.

"Come in, come in," called the hearty voice. "You must be..." They sped down a narrow passageway into a neat, old-fashioned living room. There was a stale-ish, leftover-Sunday-dinner smell to the whole house.

"This is Mavis and I'm Dennis McAndrew." They looked at each other for a few moments too long, Dennis smiling broadly and Stuart looking silly, until Dennis raising one eyebrow prompted, "And you must be..."

"Yes, yes," he said hastily remembering his manners. He introduced himself and added, "Look, I have no idea what you'd like me to do in the way of helping but I'm not very good with…" He trailed off, not knowing how to approach the subject.

"Arsewiping and such? No need to worry on that score, son. We're both in complete control of our bodily functions, thanks very much."

He didn't look affronted but there was an edge to Dennis's voice as he finished the sentence. He pointed to an armchair, gesturing to Stuart to sit down. It was only then that Stuart had the chance to really look at them.

She, white-haired in regulation shapeless cardi and he, tanned, and well-preserved in a neatly, pressed shirt and jumper, with something of a military air about him. They looked a generation apart but had been described to Stuart as husband and wife. They offered tea and plain biscuits and settled into what he guessed to be their usual places; he on the right hand side of the sofa and she on the left. They sipped the too-hot tea, Stuart afraid of giving offence if he left it too long, but he needn't have concerned himself, as they sat, coffee table in front of them, answering their phones in synchronised carelessness, their conversation constantly interrupted by persons unknown, who were, nevertheless, more important than Stuart was.

To be perfectly honest, he was becoming a little irritated by their twin self-sufficiency. Why was he there? Should he, in turn, take out *his* phone and contact somebody? Should he contact Miss Pamela Whatsername and complain that this was a ridiculous idea?

He was in the middle of composing an imaginary text to her – and her surname had gone temporarily – when Dennis slammed his phone down onto the glass coffee table and said, decisively, "Right. Down to business. The reason we asked Pammy to find us some help was that we need someone to track down where the smell's coming from."

"The smell?"

He sniffed the air tentatively and could find nothing offensive – simply the aftermath of a few midday meals.

"No, no." Dennis wasn't a man to be trifled with. "Not in here. In the kitchen."

Dennis seemed to be losing patience with him, which was a bit much given that he'd only been in the house for about ten minutes.

Stuart took his cue from Dennis and became decisive.

"Could we perhaps go in and check it out? Then we can decide what's to be done."

Mavis looked up as if she were trying to work out who he was. "Yes, do take him in, Dennis. Has he got his equipment with him?"

"What sort of equipment?"

"Your specialist equipment," she said. "Pammy told us you'd be used to doing this sort of thing."

"Er, well, if I just go in and have a look first?" he asked, realising he could cheerfully throttle 'Pammy' for pushing him into this bizarre situation.

What had she promised them? What specialist knowledge might he need for this assignment? How bad was the smell?

The kitchen, when Dennis eventually opened the door, stank to high heaven. He gagged and stepped back instinctively, as did they.

The smell was most certainly of something dead – and long-dead at that. He hadn't known what to expect but it was how he imagined someone's granny, three-weeks gone-and-only-now–discovered, might smell.

It seemed to be coming from an old-fashioned larder in the left-hand corner of the room. Trouble was, there was an enormous chest of drawers blocking the way. Obviously the larder was not in use because there was no access to it and it was clear to Stuart that he'd never be able to shift the chest alone.

"Do you need to go to the car?" asked Mavis in an almost girlish treble. She then saw his uncomprehending frown, "…to get your suit and stuff?"

"Well," he said, "I don't have anything in my car. I'm not a specialist in anything like this. I thought you wanted a couple of light jobs doing and a bit of a run out so I brought rugs and bottles of water."

They stared at each other.

"Well, that's no use, is it?" Dennis, on his high horse, was getting quite shirty. He sprung into action. "Come on, give me a hand to shift this chest first, before we go scuttling off on a jaunt. And put your back into it."

He did. Well, he put his back *out*, actually. It was agony. He would need physio and pain killers for weeks after.

It turned out that the smell was from a dead rat, rotting in the corner of the larder-thing. Mavis was quite put out when he asked for a pair of rubber gloves and a plastic bag, "so as to dispose of it without exposing myself to the possibility of catching the bubonic plague." Mavis reluctantly supplied them from the topmost kitchen cupboard, "where I keep my dusters."

She burbled on for ages afterwards, still under the impression that he was a specialist 'from the council' who'd ruined a perfectly good pair of her Marigolds.

"Where you taking us then?" asked Dennis after Stuart'd cleaned himself and the larder thoroughly, and still retching because of the lingering dead-rat smell in his nostrils.

He knew they were hoping for a couple of ice-creams at the seaside and afternoon tea at the very least.

There was a word for what he decided to do next but it had gone, momentarily. It wasn't altruism though, he knew that much.

"Let's go to Pammy's," he said – now using the diminutive employed by the McAndrews. She could look after them from now on. He'd had enough.

The rat was inside two plastic bags and a cardboard box with 'Congratulations!' in garish primary colours scrawled across it, that he kept in the boot of the car, just in case. He reckoned the smell wouldn't permeate through that lot for at least two weeks. He *could* take it directly to the council tip… or leave it with Pamela Morton. It all depended on the answer she gave to his very rude suggestion as to what they might do later that evening.

Oh, and now he remembered the Greek lad who did those

labours, 'the labours of Sisyphus'. And he wondered what reward *he'd* got at the end of that lot. 'What was that word again?' he thought. 'Ah, yes, altruism?'

His memory was improving, and with it, the realisation that altruism doesn't exist. There *always* has to be a reward. "Nobody can have something for nothing, not even Pamela Morton," he told himself decisively as he rang her doorbell – the box held tightly in his hands.

COMING ON CHRISTMAS...

Coming on Christmas. All the signs are there. I'm stuck in traffic on Apple Orchard Bank and have just noticed a couple of off-white geese grubbing around on a patch of muddy ground in the garden centre over the road – unconsciously self-fattening for the forthcoming feast, no doubt. People seem increasingly unable to accept the extra few minutes of waiting for others these days. There's a horse box ahead of me and of course that slows progress minimally, but a blaring car horn is sounded – the owner in no doubt that this will inspire all of us –the more patient and accepting ones – to lift ourselves up into the sky and jump out of his way simply to facilitate his need to continue on his journey toute d'suite.

I find it all dismal and depressing. I can't remember the last time I saw a crib scene in a shop window. They were once the focal point of any Christmas display, and yes, it was corny and sentimental, but at least there was no attempt to sell us the plaster figures in the stable at discount prices inside. Everything nowadays is about greed instead of Jesus.

It's not that I find people – I mean ordinary folk just doing their best to get by – to be meaner or greedier than they used to be. Not at all. People are generally very kind in this country. We all want to get on together. If our paths cross and we brush against each other by accident, it's a rare human who doesn't say, "Sorry," and smile. In queues we bemoan the crowds and talk of how tiring 'all this' is, but we smile at each other as we tell our tales of woe.

I still enjoy the Christmas lights going on in town centres. I don't even mind those monuments to bad taste in residential streets whose residents are determined to make it a colourful season with nightmarish figures and signs reading, 'Santa stop here'. I just assume they have young children who are as enchanted as I used to be with our crepe paper ceiling decorations when I was a little girl.

Not a full-blown curmudgeon then, just a little jaded.

The great day arrives at last and I am a guest at my daughter and son-in-law's newly-refurbished and tarted-up house. Rooms have been added. New seating has been arranged to good effect and all looks clean and festive.

In the mistaken belief that I will wish to be 'looked after' for once, I am sho'oed into the sitting room to – well, to sit – and am not allowed to take an active part in the preparations or serving out of the Christmas feast. They are being so kind and are so pleased that I do not interfere or behave like those WI ladies who vie with each other for the privilege of doing the washing up or providing the biggest quiches for the cricket teas.

I stand on the edges of their life and observe the comings and goings. Is this what old age is? Is this why maiden aunts cause such a fuss – because they'd like to claim a little of the action? "Let me help, dear," comes to me as an echo from times past when older women got in the way. Now, at last, I understand them. I am one of them.

And yet… there's surely so much more than this, isn't there?

I seek out my grand-daughter, as one equally redundant but at the better end of the age scale.

We have a new Trivial Pursuit game, and I have time to spare. We quickly scan the rules and then decide to ignore most of them. We can please ourselves and do what we like. It's a good thing to chat to the young sometimes. Our subjects and interests don't always converge, but having taken her to see Horrible Histories in the West End last month and having recommended 'Cinemaniacs' which she loves, we pass the time amicably with conversation and minimal cheating until the others arrive, flustered and hot, to clear the table. Our offer of help is rejected once more. "No, we'll sort this out. It's all done now anyway." (Did I detect a note of resentment in there somewhere or is my paranoia peeping over the parapet again?)

Stacks of food and Christmas telly numb our minds sufficiently to see out the day without any actual murders being committed.

Boxing Day looms into our lives with the prospect of *his* family descending upon us in droves. After the politenesses have been observed come cursory questions about what's in store next year for everyone:

"So, when are you going travelling then, Zoe?" Zoe's itinerary is recited ad infinitum, almost word for word, "Then Cambodia and on to Australia..." We hear for the sixth time how convenient are these towels they have nowadays that you can use to shower: shake and wring them out and put them across your neck and they'll dry out in minutes. I imagine how smelly they'll get but say nothing. She's so young and confident.'

We marvel at progress and realise what we've missed by being born too soon.

As most of the rellies retreat to their own Boxing Day repasts, we stalwarts are left with his parents – apparently invited earlier to share a buffet of lovely salads and cold meats. Cold turkey is not on the menu. I wonder vaguely whether any of it will appear again but it does not. Probably stashed away in the freezer to make a tasty springtime stew; once the memory of Christmas has faded.

My daughter's in-laws are not inspiring people. Pleasant and amenable, they have few opinions and fewer conversational gambits. However, I feel it incumbent upon me to try out a couple of subjects. I tackle Gerry, the partner of Doreen, my son-in-law's mother. Picture Private Fraser from Dad's Army and you have Gerry. The face, the voice and the doleful manner are exact matches. He's from Kirkcaldy and this year has been delighted – for the first time ever – with his Christmas present from my daughter. It's a beautifully illustrated historic guide to his home town and he would love to be left alone to enjoy it, but realises that he will not be allowed to do this yet. Social niceties have to be adhered to. We do a bit of small talk and it emerges that he used to play in a dance band in the '30s. Surprise, surprise! I look at him with a bit more respect as his eyes slide back to the beautiful photographs on the opened page of his book.

She's another enigma. She seems always to have had a man in tow. Married several times. An assortment of children with various fathers and enjoys ballroom dancing. What can we talk about? I begin with our interest in our grand-daughter. We discuss the recent Christmas concert we went to see. I say how much I enjoyed it. She agrees. Everything I say, she agrees with. Constantly smiling and giving nothing much away, I'm finding it hard to engage with her on any level.

Post-prandial lassitude has set in when I get the idea.

Wonderful. This is a game I can win!

Casually, I introduce it to the assembled group.

"What's the worst Christmas present you or any of your friends have ever had?" I ask, innocently.

They are reluctant at first. This is fraught with potholes and faux pas and they're suspicious.

"What if it's something one of *you* has bought me?" asks my daughter, half-laughing.

I am bold. "Doesn't matter," I say confidently. "We are all forgiven for past mistakes."

Slowly, they confess. "An ironing board," says one. Then adds guiltily, "But to be fair, I'd only been saying I needed one in the November."

We double our efforts to top it.

I throw in, "Well, I did get a pair of lightweight stepladders once but only because I'd asked for them, and they've been *so* useful!"

The floodgates open. A pile of useless articles are thrown onto the pile, as it were. Chocolates for people on diets, inappropriate music and film choices, articles of clothing designed for someone in their twenties; wrong sizes, horribly garish sweaters, a pair of garden chairs for a person who lived in a 2nd floor flat. All very good contenders.

The time had come, though, for me to top this with the most

gloriously awful gift of all. Admittedly it wasn't for me, but a friend of mine, whose ex-husband – a man who played banjo in a country and western band and who modelled himself on Buffalo Bill – beard, moustache, fringed suede jacket et al – had bought his lovely wife... a funeral plan... for Christmas.

They were all aghast. I had to repeat it several times for them to appreciate the enormity of it.

A couple of them simply had to repeat it. "A funeral plan?" After the stunned silence, my daughter spoke.

"Is she still speaking to him?"

"Alas, yes," I say. "Well, she couldn't spoil Christmas, could she?"

A BATTLE OF WILLS

Sometimes in the early morning, I lie abed, idly assessing the chinks of light that appear around the edges of the curtains, and try to sense, by the quality of that light, what the day will bring when I eventually draw back the veil.

Snow is the easiest and most exciting light – whiter and filled with promise. Stormy mornings have both grey and yellow in them, deceiving me into thinking I have woken just before dawn, because the bedroom is still dark. The spring morninglight is not always welcome as it comes too early, bringing the birdsong before I want to be fully awake. Rainbeat seems, oddly enough, to bring a sense of well-being; its rhythmic tapping offers the idea of 'nesting' in the warmth of my bed.

This is not time-wasting or idling, but valuable non-thinking time. I tell myself I will reap the benefits later in the day and feel better for it.

When there is no need for hastening back to daylife, we allow ourselves to luxuriate in speculation about the promise of the day, but if there's work afoot, we must plunge right in, thigh deep, and the business of Monday kick starts us directly into the reality of work.

It was one such working day that caused my downfall. It had begun as an ordinary day – nobody's birthday, no work problems to solve, nothing demanding immediate attention. In short – a day devoted to routine. Even the weather was ordinary. The sky, light grey with a couple of dark grey patches, (which I had predicted). Shower, dress, eat, teeth cleaning and gathering up 'stuff'. Forgetting car keys as usual, I unlocked the front door, dashed in, grabbed them off the hook behind the kitchen door and dashed back out again. It was a regular ritual – I'm not very organised.

A thousand clichés tumbled around the washing-machine of my mind as I got to grips with the business of this day. A brand-new blank sheet of paper. How to use it?

Terri – the head solicitor and my boss – who insists we spell his name with that final, pretentious 'i' rather than a 'y' – causing the staff no end of problems when clients think he's a woman – was busy doing nothing, as usual. I greeted him cheerfully, relaxing in the warmth of the office. The comforting fragrance of buttered toast pervaded the space. Sniffing approvingly, I asked whose breakfast I could smell.

"New company policy," Terri slurred, a half-eaten slice hanging from his greasy mouth. With an elbow, he indicated a stapler in bits on his desk. Was he trying to fill or mend it – or break it? Who knew?

"Here, let me do that," I offered. It makes more sense to stop Terri before he does too much damage.

"You're gonna have to go out again, Jane, sorry." This said as he wiped toast crumbs from his chin onto the papers on my desk. I quickly liberated them from the impending grease spots and gave them a quick rub.

"Toast? Company policy? Have to go out again?" I paused for effect. "Respond in that order please." I may have sounded a bit tetchy but, honestly, he can be a very irritating man.

He only answered the third point, and that answer was not very clear.

"Bloke rang late yesterday. He wants someone qualified to sort out his will, but doesn't feel up to coming into the office so I said you'd go over to do it at his house. He's ancient so there's no danger of... well... danger."

"Why can't you go?" This great day was not going as well as I'd predicted. There was a perfect pair of shoes in John Lewis' that I'd had my eye on for ages. I had hoped to get there in my dinner hour. Fat chance now with this dodderer to see.

"No can do, love. Head Office wants to see me at 11.30. Big chief coming over'"

I hate it when he talks like that – unpunctuated, patronising drivel.

"And when am I due at this old codger's house?"

He looked hurt and feigned shock at the same time. It's a gift.

"I said you'd be there at ten. If you hurry you might get a cuppa and bit of toast before you leave." He slid an envelope across his desk. "There's his address. Get his stuff out of the file and take it to read while you munch."

Dear God, this day was getting worse. It's only when I'm actually with Terri that I remember what a prat he is. Easier to just get out of his sight and get on with the business to hand as a rule.

I found the house without incident, under an ever-darkening sky. The air smelt of impending thunder and his garden drooped under the threat of it. Heavy and fresh, it weighed me down too. I felt dismay when I saw the place. I know it's fashionable to love old houses and coo after character, but I really dislike Victoriana in all its guises. Dark, fussy and dismal, it seems to have the distinctive scent of my granny's kitchen cupboards about it. Cursing my idle boss for sending *me* instead of doing his job himself, I rapped on the brass knocker.

Nothing happened. I knocked again with the same result, then took myself round to the side door – probably the servants' entrance in some bygone age.

It was unlocked. I took a few tentative steps and walked in, at the same time realising I didn't even know this man's name. A frantic scrabble amongst the papers showed Dr J.A. Anderson, so, trying to sound confident, I called his name.

"In here," responded the darkened hall. I walked boldly in. The day was about to become much less ordinary.

"You're late," sang the goat-headed old man in the overstuffed chair seated by a stifling coal fire at the far end of the room. There was no time to refute this because I realised at once that I recognised the man as my grandmother's old 'friend' from years ago. What I didn't recognise was the name. I knew him as Rupert. I also knew that he was the rogue who'd persuaded her to sign over the bulk of her life savings to him as part of a dodgy investment deal some ten years ago, and –

whilst I wasn't sure of the particulars – that sheepy-goaty face was unforgettable.

My inner washing-machine churned anew. I jumped in with both feet. "Rupert?" I asked, tentatively.

His countenance changed immediately but he made an admirable recovery. "James Archibald Anderson. I'm afraid you have the advantage of me, my dear. I am delighted, however to be misidentified by so... interesting... a young woman." On his guard from that moment, I had my work cut out to keep calm and attend to the business in hand.

The will involved some substantial bequests to family and friends, besides ten or more properties held in various countries under several pseudonyms. Dr Anderson wanted to collect them together into one portfolio, under his current name (for I had no way of knowing which of his names was real). He told me he needed to "realise the capital from some investments abroad." Apparently he had debts to pay.

'Too right,' I thought. My poor old Nan's for one.'

After an hour of discussion, he remembered his manners and asked if I'd like tea. I took this opportunity to wander round the room and look at various ornately framed photographs and paintings adorning its grimy walls.

Outside, it was raining hard, with only the odd flash of lightning relieving the inner gloom. I had to think fast. This could be a chance to recoup Nan's losses. Our only chance of vengeance.

Forcing myself to act, and surprised by my nerve, I scoured the documentation on the computer screen to see if there were a miniscule alteration I could make that would help her regain what was hers. I realised of course that it was risky. I was only a trainee after all, but Terri was sloppy and lazy and the old man had trouble with his sight and was ready to be rid of me.

There was a bequest in the will for a Mrs Maisie Beresford – £15,000 'with thanks for services rendered'. Huh! What kind of services were they, then?

When he returned from the kitchen with tea, I offered the screen for his perusal. "Probably easier to read with the light behind it?" I asked, with my head on one side and a sympathetic smile on my lips.

"Very thoughtful, my dear," he crowed.

It took him an age to check it. You'd think he didn't trust me or something. I felt quite indignant.

"Is that all in order, Dr Anderson?" I asked, controlling my trembling hands as best I could.

"Yes, I think so. Ah, this will be a weight off my mind," he sighed.

'Aye, and mine, you old crook.' I thought; almost hugging myself at the thought of putting right an injustice.

"How about a glass of something stronger to celebrate?" he asked, leaving me alone as he went out to the drinks cabinet in the other bleak, dusty parlour.

As soon as he'd gone, I changed the name to 'Mary Beckley', my Nan's name and, heart thumping, I printed off the document on the correct paper and passed it over for him to sign. It worked like a dream.

"To the future, my dear." Our glasses were raised and I quaffed the whisky in record time. I couldn't wait to be out of there.

I glanced at the dirty windows. The rain was still hammering to get in. Packing away my laptop and grabbing papers into an untidy pile, I was heading for the door when a completely unexpected thing happened.

Reaching gnarled hands into a fat wallet, he brought out two £50 notes and pressed them into mine.

"Get a taxi, dear, would you? It wouldn't do to damage the documents at this stage. I may end up in *the other place*," this said indicating the floor, with his goaty grimace and a yellowing index finger, "but maybe a last act of kindness will afford me redemption, eh?"

Two days later, he was dead. Heart attack, apparently. I admit to having felt a twinge of guilt about my trickery, and about Maisie Beresford, but it didn't last long.

Terri took it badly though, which seemed odd until a work colleague whispered that the old man was a distant relative.

Apparently Terri's mother would be a beneficiary. Ah, so that's why I was sent in his stead. I just hoped *she* wasn't Maisie Beresford.

The weather turned, and the morninglight became the shine of summer behind my curtains. Early rising and the air full of promise, I completely forgot about 'Rupert' until he intruded on my consciousness again when I had a phone call from Nan.

How delighted she was that Rupert had, 'done the right thing' by her, as she had always believed he would. It had worked like a dream and nobody suspected a thing.

I felt really clever and smug. That is, until a courier came with a barely legible letter from a Dr J.A. Anderson. He had realised who I was of course; and that *I'd* defrauded *him* this time. He had left letters that would expose me unless I complied with his instructions. Heart sinking, I took a deep breath and looked at the final paragraph.

'Give Maisie her money,' it read. 'I'm half way down the greasy pole by now, and I need a foothold. Say sorry to Mary.' It was simply signed, 'Rupert'.

I looked up and noticed that it was raining heavily again.

WINTER CHURCH SUNDAY

It's sleeting horizontally in fat flat flakes, and I;
emerging from the cold stone shelter of church,
have left the orange umbrella propped in the doorway.
The heavy, old wood of the doors is slammed shut behind me
And I shiver, unnoticed, on the threshold.
Reaching for damp gloves (shoved in a pocket earlier)
I tug them onto unwilling hands – ready-frozen.
Hannah hurries past to the warmth of her kitchen.
Smiles through the hood of the substantial raincoat;
Sunday lunch almost ready.
'Only the puddings to do.'
I return, bent double, to an unheated house,
wrestle with the key in my numb, red fingers
And pick up the bouquet of scarlet roses from the vase.
They have waited three days for the weather to change.
I examine the blooms. They won't last long in this.
Wet, sleety cold penetrates unsuitable shoes.
Then, kettle on, ready for later, I return to the punishing outdoors,
Into the greying daylight, once more hailing the hail,
Slide up my thin hood and walk to the cemetery,
nithering hands holding
Red, blood-spot blossoms
Already wilting
in the wintry weather.

TOWN TWINNING WEEK

I have a kidney infection. This may at first elicit sympathy but wait – not yet. It's a lovely summer's day and the garden looks particularly inviting but I choose to stay in the relative peace and quiet of my bedroom – an insect-free-zone. I *could* wish for a cooler breeze through the dusty sheers at the window, but that would be churlish and besides, I'm happy to languish here on the bed, reading in desultory fashion for an hour or two. The book is undemanding and therefore not particularly engaging and I'm minded to put it to one side and snooze awhile.

She's gone out for the day, my visitor. She's been here since Sunday and today is Thursday and I am free – thanks to my illness – having packed her off on a coach trip with the rest of her group. How do I feel about the turn of events? Well, to tell the truth (and I'm ashamed of this) I'm tired of being nice. My frozen-on smile is scarily permanent nowadays. Even the stuff I don't understand is accorded a smile or nodding approval, which must be bloody annoying for my guest. She's here on a town twinning exchange visit between Oberhausen and Middlesbrough which, remarkably, has been ongoing for thirty-eight years.

I was dragged into this set-up by default – a slight misunderstanding when I said I'd like to see Anna again after fifteen years – perhaps have coffee or take her for dinner. It has ended with me playing mein host; and a more curmudgeonly host it would be hard to find. Look; see what is happening here; German constructs in my writing. This is one of the pitfalls of having a guest who speaks another language living in such close proximity.

I decided early on to talk only about simple things without

being completely inane, but so far we've had her marriage break-up, her hobbies, children, husband, neighbours and the places she's been to in Britain in the past twenty years. She knows very little of me, but that makes it easier.

She's a pleasant enough woman but so energy-sapping. Her speech is punctuated by urgent arm-grabbing and, "Yes, iss normal. Dis iss normal!" or, "I hev, yes, at home, same," as she indicates some kitchen utensil or cushion cover. There seems to be no sense of social space during these disjointed conversations. It's all into my face, and the most mundane of subjects takes on a ridiculous importance. Of course, one can't then say, "Oh, okay," or the equivalent of a teenage, shoulder-shrugging, 'Whatever.' There has to be more nodding (oh, the spondylitis in my cervical spine!) and vigorous agreement, before she accepts that I have indeed understood.

When I get her drift early on and say the correct English word, she refutes it instantly with, "NO," and pillages the dictionary for a word which means exactly the same as the one I've already said. I don't think she even needs me to hold up my side of the discussion. I'm there to nod and smile or nod and frown. Can you believe we spent fifteen minutes on the word 'stencil'? Apparently it's a 'schablone' in German, although we couldn't authenticate this in our school-level dictionaries.

Last night I was called by one of the organisers about yet more changes to timetables. As I put the phone down, my guest told me exactly what had been said. She was wrong but adamant. I cut her off in mid-sentence and asked her to jus*t listen*. You see how it is. I'm losing patience and I still have some days to go.

However, today is my day to be me again. I could watch a television programme later – perhaps lunch on a tray in my room? As long as I drink plenty of water, my condition should improve with the antibiotics. I have five more hours before she returns. It's the first time in the week when I know nobody is taking candid shots of me blinking, gurning or looking miserable. I checked her camera on day four and she'd already taken 2,672 photos. Imagine.

Did I say she smokes? About thirty a day, in my estimation. Makes the up-close thing quite unpleasant, but otherwise it's a bit of a perk. When she's out with her endearing little portable ashtray, I give my features a rest and slap on a bit more Nivea to protect the skin from drying out. However, despite her best efforts, the smoke drifts inevitably in through the opened bathroom window in the mornings. I generally open it to let the steam out after my shower and she times it very badly, that first fag of the day, but it's not intentional, I know.

This experience is not good for my self-esteem and I am becoming aware of my odd little habits and ways of doing things – in short – I'm beginning to realise I'm a bit of a nitpicker. My teenage self would hate me, especially if I were her boss in a small office and wanted the systems I'd put in place to be respected. Lots of tongue-biting going on this week.

On the other hand, I've become adept at nodding in the right places, and explaining-in-slow-motion-with-accompanying-hand-movements. It's quite a skill. She tells me that she can't understand most of the English hosts but that I am *very clear*. It's because I come up with about five different words or phrases to explain everything, but it's utterly exhausting. I really wish she liked television. Even my favourite film – which is in German – was refused yesterday.

Saturday. It is the last full day of the visit and it is unfurling like a blank page. We have no scheduled activities and apart from a leisurely breakfast, I have absolutely no idea what to do with her.

Fortunately, she saves me from further worry by asking if we can go to the beach. Of course. Germany is largely landlocked which is why she's enchanted by my 'veef'. Sorry. This German pronunciation is catching. For the first three days she marvelled and exclaimed about the 'veef'. Beautiful. Wunderbar.

By the fourth day I'd worked it out. It's the view from my back window, which looks spectacularly on to the sea and cliffs. I make no comment about this mispronunciation. Who am I – with my seven simple German sentences – to ever be disparaging about someone else's far superior attempts to communicate in our difficult language? However, view or no view, my kidneys are still playing up, despite being awash with filtered water, and I feel dismayed at the thought of tramping across the sands – all that fresh air – but at least it will take up part of the day. She wants to collect fossils. Great.

As things turn out, the day is fine. We do the beach, then another beach where she finds a couple of fossils and a lump of striated sandstone which she insists on bringing back to sit on my front step. That might be illegal, but neither of us knows the word so I just keep quiet.

We break for doorstep sandwiches chez moi and I take the opportunity to check my sandblasted face before heading off to the second beach, in Saltburn. I am ready for another cuppa at this point so I sit outside a cafe and wait, like a mother watching her child play nice on the sand; I am satisfied with tea and a book.

After all the exertion, we have little time for anything but a quick wash-and-brush-up before it's time to go to the grandly named Farewell Dinner.

This is a strange affair of faux-camaraderie between the warring factions who organised the week, contrasting with the warmth of the relationships that have built up between hosts and guests. The food is predictably bland and there's little elbow room from which to tackle the rubbery Yorkshire puds, but we are all determined to make it work and keep smiling.

Inevitably, some of us are snapped in mid-chomp and feel annoyed, but Anna is unrepentant as ever. "It's my hobby," she explains, endlessly. The photo count must be in the three thousands by now.

As we wave them all off in the car park the next morning, with promises of, "See you next year in Germany." I heave a massive sigh of relief. Some of the German guests have become friends – people I'd be glad to see again but not at close range. I unlock the car and feel happy about having my own company again as the telephone rings. It is my sister telling me that they've organised a family party for my niece's 50th birthday.

Apparently, "Jen's coming. And she wants to see you." This

last, said in a portentous voice – as if to remind me what a very great honour it is. After all, Jen lives near London. "If you can't come, she'll be over to see you... so don't worry." My heart sinks again. My kidneys are complaining. "Great," I say, nodding and smiling as I put the car into first gear.

UNDER THE BRIDGE

"All water under the bridge now," they tell me, but what if you're on the bridge with your stick and you throw it and it never comes through to the other side? What if you're the stick: stuck. How do you move if you can't dislodge yourself?

The world changed forever on 29th November 1957 for me. It was a Friday. I was nine. At approximately 6.30. I woke in my mother's bed where I was snuggled deep in the downy feather mattress with the big, blue silk, padded eiderdown tucked snugly around my skinny kid's body. My father was our early morning wakeman, tired and stiff after a steelworks nightshift in Dorman Long, where he was a wiredrawer. I didn't know what a wiredrawer was until I was grown up and at college, when I read a line in The Duchess of Malfi. Delio is warning Bosola that he's 'like a wire drawer'. I immediately asked my dad about it, of course. It was the first time I'd genuinely showed an interest in his job.

Every day, summer heat and winter cold, he stood in a massive shed – open to the elements at each end – and converted thick steel rods into varying sizes of wire. Sometimes the wire would snap, white-hot from the furnace and the backlash would catch my dad's bare arms and cause the painful raw burns he accepted as part of his life.

On the morning of the 29th, he came upstairs as usual, with a cup of tea and a slice of bread and butter for my mother. Since I didn't normally sleep with her, I thought it would be a good joke to slide under the covers and surprise him, but she was taking her time in waking up, so, impatient to be discovered, I nudged her under the covers to prompt the return to consciousness.

When nothing happened, I looked out at him and started to laugh anxious not to lose the moment of surprise, but his face was white. All I remember was the unearthly animal sound from my father as he heaved my mother up from the pillow, turned her to face him, and tried to rouse her.

Shocked to the core, I scrambled out onto the freezing lino and ran to the far side of the room, looking for some shelter from the horror of what was happening. My older sister came in from our bedroom, terrified by the sounds of grief coming from our dad. She ran to me and held me as he began to call our mother's name. I cannot write it, even now, decades later, but it is also my sister's name, and of course it was she who responded, misunderstanding.

"Dad? What's happening?"

His anger was palpable. "Not you!" he shouted as though he hated her. "Not you!"

Somehow we must have got downstairs and my sister must have woken the neighbours and asked for help. I don't remember. All I can recall is sitting numbly by the unlit fire, bare feet resting on the beige 1950's tiles of the fireplace, unaware of the seeping cold and staring at the grey powdery ashes of last night's fire in the grate. I have no idea how long I sat there or what was happening in the house.

I expect there was tea being made – that old stalwart we fall back on when we don't know what else to do; when we can't make it right again.

After some time our kindly neighbour roused me from my numbness and told me to go next door to her house. She felt my thin calves and feet with her plump, red hands. "You're freezing. Go and get your dressing gown," she said. "Is it upstairs?"

I knew where it was; my lovely red dressing gown with the ladybird buttons. It was in my mam and dad's bedroom, hanging on the wardrobe key. The wardrobe had a long mirror in the central panel. It was next to the bed where my mother's body still lay.

I felt a pang of panic. My stomach made a fist. However, nobody was aware of any of this. They assumed I'd slept in the other room with my sister as usual. Anyway, I was the least of their concerns. My Granny Murphy, who had bustled in by this time, was instructing my sister to get the bus to town, go to all our relatives' houses, and tell them the news. It was as though none of this was anything to do with either of us – as though we were in the way. Hegemony ruled.

Rather than cause any fuss, I duly made my way up the stairs.

'If I don't look anywhere but at the wardrobe key, and grab the dressing gown quickly, I won't have to see her,' I thought.

It was trickier than I thought, disentangling the 'Ladybird' label quickly from the fancy metallic design of the wardrobe key. As I wrestled clumsily with it, my hands too cold to be efficient, it dropped to the floor. 'Just don't turn round,' I told myself.

I bent to pick it up and found myself facing the dressing table in the corner of the room, with its triple mirrors reflecting the bed and three images of my mother, still lying there, her arms bent at the elbow covering her face. Three images. I turned quickly back to the wardrobe and saw, reflected in that mirror, the dressing table triptych. Horror-struck, my whole body stiff, I darted out and stood stock still on the landing, hardly daring to breathe. Someone was calling my name. It echoed hollowly up the stairs. I was about to go down but turned back first to close the door carefully behind me.

But the door is still open.

The stick is still stuck under the bridge.

SNOBS?

The smell of stale fag-ends pervades the space directly outside the supermarket. It is damp and cold, and what's more, I've positioned myself in our designated meeting place, beside a dirty metal bin, and that makes it worse. I have no idea at present, why we are meeting outside this shop. We usually wait inside a, shall we say, more salubrious, coffee shop, where at least one is able to sit in some comfort to wait for the latecomer.

Some people are always late, or dead on time and breathless with excuses for their tardiness. I am the opposite. Too punctual, in fact. It wastes a great deal of my time but it's an obsession with me.

I wait several minutes, then move to a relatively more pleasant position, out from under the canopy. Not-exactly-fresh air hits my nostrils but it's somewhat sweeter than binsmell. However the relief of breathing cleaner air is short lived.

A family of five bounds noisily across to await a taxi. They appear to be dressed down for the weekly nightmare of the 'big shop'. A pot-pourri of odours hangs around them, nudging me to the left as I try to escape. I wonder if they've noticed this shift. I don't like to offend them, but then, they're offending me.

These people seem to be typical of shoppers nowadays, judging by the folks who are filing in and out of the revolving entrance doors. Most of the children wear thin, garish t-shirts with either a cartoon character on the front in pink and yellow or some monster in blacks and greens, scowling from their thin chests, bearing aggressive slogans which threaten mankind.

The mother is all fleeced up. The fleece looks to have anonymous stains down the front and the zip is open, revealing what must have been a party blouse about five years ago but whose sequins

189

have all but given up the ghost. It must have been white once, but settled, exhausted, for grimy grey after the polyester fibres stopped battling with a 'coloureds only' wash some time ago. The garment is what many people refer to as a 'shove-on'; meaning it'll do for the supermarket where nobody of note will see it. The woman has dry, pale yellow skin and wears no make-up, but her hair has been over dyed to a straw-like texture and there's a great deal of it. I think she may have been pretty once.

I am fully aware of being judgemental and superior in my attitude towards this family. I do not claim to be otherwise. Perhaps I would have shown more kindness had the smell of dried-in urine not followed the woman around; her every movement, punctuated by a waft of public toilet, hasn't endeared her to me.

The children carry a scent of school dinner halls and stale sweetness which is marginally preferable, but they are loud and spitting out profanities as they chase each other in the never-ending loop of the door in an attempt to cope with their boredom. Each one, inevitably, has sweets or chocolate of some kind. The lollipops the younger two are holding, stray perilously close to my new coat several times, so I shift further along to protect it from the sugar and slaver. Monica would call me 'too fastidious'. Hmm. If she'd been here on time, I mean.

It is coming on to drizzle and I've been forced out of the protection of the overhead canopy, so will not be afforded even the slightest cover. I now know what will happen. My freshly-washed hair, only half dry when I set out this morning – so as not to be late – will slowly revert to its natural cavewoman frizz in approximately three minutes. It's curly and has a mind of its own. I call it my 'wicked-witch-of-the -west' look – the one which precedes the madwoman-in-the-attic, and is followed by the universal droop. The latter is where the hair skilfully plasters itself to the head until dry air touches it and brings it back to flat and curly again. Isn't nature wonderful? What's more, some of the droplets have got together to form a stream. This is slowly meandering down my neck, and yes, forming some sort of oxbow-lake effect in a loop of my new woollen scarf. I reach round in an attempt to halt the unbearably slow procession to my spine; pressing on hard where I think it might be, only to dislodge it and send it on its merry way, waistwards.

Then, to my horror, one of the urchins approaches. He's about three and seems bent on engaging with me. Horror-struck, I freeze. It's too late to walk away, and anyway, his mother is watching, head on one side and with a smile of approval on her face. I wonder if I've missed something as I battled with the drizzle?

The child holds out a really filthy hand and offers me something. Oh, dear God, it's a half eaten piece of Dairy Milk chocolate. What to do, what to do? Glancing sideways at his mother – still watching – I try a gracious smile and shake my head.

"Oh, no. Thank you, but I've just eaten."

He stares and smiles. "So've we."

The hand stretches upwards, wobbling a bit in his attempt to reach me.

"Well, I try not to eat between meals," I explain, more to the mother than the child, whose hand is still reaching for my face. I force a tight smile.

Uncomprehendingly, she half smiles back at my spurious excuse, "We-ell, if you can't let your hair down at Christmas, when can you?" she asks, as though giving me permission to indulge myself in an unaccustomed treat. I am rather surprised at the woman's voice. It is pleasant and the accent is not local.

At this juncture, we are distracted by a man pushing a baby buggy. The child inside is fast asleep and clutching a bottle with some brown-coloured liquid inside. I dread to think what it is but as the child is so dead to the world, I hazard a guess. Morphine?

All the children run to him shouting excitedly. This must be 'dad'. Dad wears only tracksuit bottoms and a t-shirt. It is red and sports the slogan, 'What's the worst thing that could happen?' The words are distorted by the size of the man's beer belly, part of which remains uncovered by his three-sizes-too-small outfit.

I want to laugh out loud, or shout, 'I think it already has, mate.' But I don't. That might be rather too coarse.

Taking my phone out, I tap in Monica's number. Outrageous that she's now fifteen minutes late. The woman is beckoning me back to the shelter of the canopy and I can see why. Real rain is falling now and I'm going to be soaked if I stay where I am. There's nothing for it but to comply.

The man is busily dismantling the buggy. It's obvious he's done it many times before. The taxi draws up and shouts a name and the children cluster around the doors, jostling for position. They jump in and he lifts the baby in with surprising tenderness, and lays it on the seat, sliding the buggy into the space beneath. He says his goodbyes to the woman with great affection, telling her to enjoy herself then jumps in beside the buggy and the taxi pulls away.

Where? I wonder. What's she up to? Pub crawl? In her best blouse? Perhaps?

I have no more time to speculate because, in the distance, I can see Monica, going hell-for-leather from her car to our meeting place. She's excited and apologetic.

"So very sorry," she pants, "problems with a flat tyre. Got the AA out. Took ages."

It is only now that I realise she's addressing, not just me, but the woman in the grey blouse too.

Oh no! I hope she doesn't think this is a friend of mine. How mortifying! She's such a snob. She'll make a meal of it for certain, when she gets back to the office.

Suddenly, the woman and Monica are embracing. Monica clearly doesn't smell the wee. Oh, hang on though, she's holding her at arm's length now.

"Annabel, I can't believe how well you look. Sally, this is my little sister, Annabel – black sheep of the family. I hope you don't mind if she joins us?" And Annabel is embracing me enthusiastically as the rain slides down my neck in torrents.

ALL THE WORLD'S A SNOWY STAGE

Used to the usual, dun-coloured sludge of 'outside;'
the glow of snow at the margins of window blinds
is a morning gift.

Inviting the light into his living space,
He carefully lifts the safety curtain,
Revealing the stage beneath.
Tiny figures, variously garbed in shiny snow-suits
Trudge purposefully across;
Their entrances and exits timed to perfection.
Thickly falling flakes obscure his view –
a temporary transmission fault
interfering with the screening of the drama
unfolding beneath him.
First, grey against the white sky,
Then pale and pure,
they hit the ground below
With balletic grace.

It is bin day.
He hears it first,
The waste disposal truck.
Men in orange suits, quick and intent
Pull out dustbins ready for the hoist.
Leaving squares of green and brown in their wake.
Orange lights flash in time to the tempo
Of the 'reverse' warning sound.
They never miss a beat.

He must go down of course,
But the second act is about to begin.

Curtain and beginners.
Madeleine is there
Dragging at the snow-burdened recycling box.
Inappropriate in fluffy mules and thin nightgown,
She coos at the cat
Who, paws poised, sits atop the pile of papers,
Claws flexed and ears a-twitch. Ready for anything.
Shivering, Madeleine slips and slides as she hastens indoors.
He has missed his chance!

Something stirs in his muddied brain
He pulls on drab, brown overcoat,
Laces up the Doc Marten's
Breathes…
And joins the panto.

Three storeys below, the bin-men lift their arms
to receive the empty bins.
Fling them back, any-old-how now:
unconcern etched on weatherworn faces.
"Am I too late?" he asks.
Nobody speaks. The final straw and the final bin.
"They hate me."
But he smiles in gratitude.
Madeleine, towel enveloping the mewling cat,
Waits in the lobby.
Looks up.
Coffee?
He smiles and nods.

A BRUSH WITH
THE LAW

The policeman had been quite odd. Not exactly stand-offish, he nevertheless exuded an air of suspicion, with, "What have we here then?" in his facial expression and his body language. I felt as if he might pull out a cartoon truncheon at any moment, simultaneously flexing his knees, fingers hooked in breast pockets.

He hadn't come to see *me*, you understand. He wanted to speak to my parents about the latest mysterious disappearance of my sister Charlotte – their favourite.

I wanted to laugh out loud when he took out his sitcom-style notebook. 'Any moment now,' I said to myself, 'he'll take out the stub of pencil that's fastened to it and lick it exaggeratedly, readying himself to take down their evidence.'

The best strategy for me, I decided, was to sit quietly at the end of the sofa and stay silent.

When we were kids, Char was constantly disappearing or storming out, an eight year old who couldn't have her own way. She managed to look pathetic when she allowed herself to be 'found' wandering; or she turned up at a neighbour's house, crying pitifully and claiming to have been ill-used by one or all of us. We of course, were expected to be ecstatic – 'that which was lost is found' style – and though my mother sobbed over her regularly, I, being of an age and well aware of her tricks, saw through the gossamer-thin thread of these dramatics. I used to say, "Silly cow," under my breath but I don't bother nowadays cos I end up being the baddie if I say owt.

"Oh, Petra, how could you?" A pause for my reaction. Then, when none came, "Look, now you've made her cry again."

"Just get out of my sight," my dad would say in his stern-parent voice. And I'd go to my room. When I was half way there, I'd hear Char shout, "and stay there!" with some venom in that Veruca Salt voice of hers.

A different policeman came on the fourth day; a detective. He was a watercolour of a man, this one; pale and pastel. In stark contrast with the defined darkness of his clothes, his skin had a transparent pallor which might, in a woman, be called 'ethereal'. I liked him better than the comedy policeman and co-operated in the questioning.

No, she didn't mention where she was going. No, she wouldn't tell me her secrets. No, we are not close (I nearly laughed out loud at that one.) and no, to be honest, I wasn't worried about what he called her 'continuing absence'.

Why? Because I don't like her, I wanted to say, but knew that would make me a suspect so I just looked blankly back and shrugged my shoulders. "You could ask James." It was an afterthought to get them off my back, and it worked. His sidekick made more notes and they left.

I must say I was surprised that Char had stayed away so long this time. Usually it was only a day or two – or until she ran out of money. She was probably staying at some dodgy friend's house this time. Realising I'd just dropped James in it, I phoned him to confess. Poor sod didn't need any more hassle, he gets enough at home.

"…so I accidentally mentioned your name, sorry." I could feel him thinking along the phone line. "Just tell the truth. They don't seem very bright," I lied. That pale one had hidden depths, I reckoned. "I could meet you from work this aft… fill you in on the details?"

His worried voice filled up with relief. "That would be great but we'd better make it somewhere less public."

Dad heard the end of the conversation and raised an eyebrow.

"Oh, just one of the lads from college," I explained, trying to sound breezy and smiley as I grabbed my coat and left.

The grass had been left to grow wild and there was an acrid smell around the river path which I usually avoided, but it cut at least fifteen mins from my journey and I was late. Today it was deserted. I held my breath and my nerve and ploughed on. I must admit the silence unnerved me. What if, this time something bad had happened to my sister? I walked closer to the water to avoid the cloud of midges that danced near the waste bin when I noticed a bright green leather sandal… same style as my new ones. It was half-floating on the weedy margins of the water, partly in shadow, part sunlight. I was well past the spot when some instinct tugged me back. I remembered Char had borrowed those sandals, even before I'd worn them. We'd rowed about it until my dad told me not to be so selfish, and she'd carried them off. Did I get them back? I couldn't remember. 'If she's thrown them in the river out of spite…' the thought began.

I looked at it. The shoe couldn't have been there long because the colour was still bright. Curious now and emboldened, I reached across and picked it out, drying my hand on my coat. It *looked* like mine – the left one, but ruined. I spotted another patch of green, deeper in, entangled in the grass and weeds. This rescue was tricky, but I managed to pull it towards me using a stick, with a hankie over my hand (you never know what bitey thing's lurking in the water do you?). It was the right sandal but as I bent forward to feel, I touched something hard. The sandal had a cold foot in it.

Revulsion overcame me and I squatted against a tree trunk and vomited. The world hadn't stopped turning but it must have tilted a little. It was like staring at a distorted image in a fairground hall of mirrors.

What happened next surprised me and even now I can't account for it. I suppose it was shock. I shoved 'the thing' further into the weeds, wiped my wet fingers and, head reeling but refusing to think about it any more, I carried on to my meeting. It was quite weird, actually, the way I'd switched to automatic pilot.

'Let someone else find her,' was all I could think.

I have no memory of what happened next. I just remember going home and sleeping a lot. Just numbness, I suppose. The cold, hard imprint of the leg was still on my fingers and like some latter-day Lady Macbeth, I couldn't wash away the sensation, try as I might.

As the days passed and James was interviewed fruitlessly by the watercolour man, ('He belongs in the river, a river sprite,' I thought), it seemed like the whole affair was happening to someone else, not us.

We tried for normality. We ate, we drank, went to work in a daze. It was like someone else was in charge of my limbs. The weeks passed and the police seemed to lose interest until one evening, I was watching the six o'clock news, when I saw Charlotte's ghost on the High Street. She was wearing her usual dark blue jacket and jeans and carrying a few Asda shopping bags. My parents were not in the room and I was too shocked to call them. "Mam, our Charlotte's ghost's on the telly." Imagine.

Confusion and fear gripped me in equal measure. Nothing made sense. They'd already dragged the river, done 'fingertip' searches and still not found the body.

Convincing myself that it was some lookalike on the TV was not possible. It would've been easier that way but I could no longer live with the guilt. It was getting dark but I had to go back to the scene of the crime – like in the novels.

At the spot where I'd seen 'the thing' I grabbed a tree branch and poked about in the murk. Nothing. Digging deeper, and sliding about on the mud, I wondered how they could have missed her. Why was I seeing apparitions? It must've been the guilt. It was dusk when I gave up the search and walked slowly to the police station in a state of dread.

The pastel-coloured policeman was very accommodating. His eyes stayed serious but his mouth smiled.

"Oh, you find all kinds of crap in the water," he said dismissively, "except what you're looking for. Now, take your sister. At the start of that case we were convinced she'd just taken off with some lad. Turns out she just needed to get away from the family for a bit – mainly you. Went to stay with your gran."

I stared dumbfounded at him.

"Yeah, and when you had your illness, your mother thought it was for the best, keeping it from you – just 'til you were more yourself again."

As an afterthought he changed his expression to 'here's an interesting titbit'. "As it turns out, we managed to solve another case when we dragged the river, so that was good. We found Caroline in the weeds."

Oh dear God! Another woman! It was *another murdered woman*. And I'd shoved her further in! My knees buckled and I must've gone deathly pale, because he scraped a chair across to catch me before I fell. "Are you alright, Petra?"

I nodded. Why were they all being so matter-of-fact about everything?

"Who's Caroline?" I managed to ask.

"Not who – what?" He looked smug as he explained. "Theft of clothes from Freemans. The gang took the stuff away in a shopping trolley. One of their women must've taken a fancy to the clothes on the dummy in the window cos they pinched that as well in their hurry to escape. It had nowt much on when we dragged it out. Thought it was a body at first. We called it 'Caroline' when we recovered it. For a laugh. Anyway, she scrubbed up a treat. Back in the window now. You alright, love?"

Someone brought me a glass of water.

I walked home in a daze, having refused a lift from the watercolour man under the pretext that I needed some fresh air, but I went straight to Freeman's window to see their display. There she was. "A dummy on the outside, looking at the dummy on the inside," I said to myself as I stared at what I'd thought was a body. I suddenly shivered, remembering the feeling of that sandalled foot in my hand by the riverside.

At home I found my green sandals in the back of Charlotte's wardrobe, and wondered whether my sister would ever come home again to claim them. I hoped she would.

I feel now as if I owe someone an apology but I don't know who.

CLASS

"And will you tell me what the others won't say, Mr Horohan?"

"That's a somewhat intrusive question, sir."

"All I'm asking for here is the truth. Is that too much to hope for?"

'Yes', thought Hannah. 'Yes, it bloody well is.'

Jeff contemplated his feet. He had nowhere to go from here, Hannah knew. The turmoil he must be suffering was almost palpable.

She was sitting in the squashy chair, squeezing her body tightly into its soft cushions, and wishing she could disappear completely through the upholstery but-where exactly could she go? Where was safe, now?

The atmosphere in the sitting room was electric. Every nerve on edge. Every body taut with tension.

'I should speak,' she thought. 'In a way, it's my fault it happened. I instigated it, because I was bored. That's the truth of it. Why don't I just tell them all?'

Even as she was thinking this, even as the words formed themselves into sentences in her brain and her mouth opened to speak them, she knew she wasn't going to save him. That was a sacrifice too far. If he just kept quiet – just refused to say anything else – it would soon be over and they could all go on as before.

A quietly deferential tap at the door broke the atmosphere, closely followed by Jane, with a tray of tea.

'How very English,' thought Hannah. 'The universal panacea of tea.'

Mr Morton indicated a small table close to the door. "Thank you, Jane." Mr Morton said dismissively, to the woman he'd been secretly sleeping with for the last six months. "We'll help ourselves."

Turning to the rest of the assembled cast he said, "There are too many anomalies of time and place that will not bear close scrutiny in this case. However, I shall have plenty of opportunity to check stories and examine alibis, and believe me when I tell you I'll be thorough and exacting in my questioning over the next few weeks."

They all recognised the speech from the play they were currently rehearsing for the traditional 'Morton Players' event but no one smiled in recognition.

When he left the room, everyone breathed out and busied themselves with trivia. Jeff, however, seemed glued to the spot. Hannah touched his elbow. "Come out to the garden."

"If only everyone would stop lying," Mrs Morton complained. She was a fretful woman, thin and dissatisfied with life. Susan suggested that maybe she should be in the vanguard with the truth. After all, she was at the centre of this fracas. She was the one who witnessed the kiss that tumbled the house that Jack built, so to speak.

The lies had been piling up steadily over the course of play. These events often became quite incestuous, with former and present lovers exchanging positions and partners on a regular basis. Who was Susan with nowadays anyway? Who was her latest little bit on the side that nobody but everybody knew about? It was so easy to be confused by partners – official and un. One had to be alert to the backstage politics and keep up.

Hannah had begun it as a game. She saw Jeff as an innocent and underestimated the degree of passion with which he lived his life. Earthy and easy in his manner, his honesty had impressed them all. He would do the job in the extensive grounds of the hall and be modestly paid for his hard work. A perfect arrangement for the Mortons.

Hannah, finding him engaging, had flirted outrageously and once she realised that he knew how to play that particular game, continued to hang around, offering opinions and advice about where to cut back and where to leave well alone in the gardens.

She was enjoying the game so much, she was startled one afternoon when he came to the door, ostensibly to ask for advice and with a look that said, 'we both know this has to happen', he took her in his arms, in the tradition of the most trite romantic novels, and suddenly his tongue filled her mouth and instead of the powdery cheek-kisses she was used to from the ancient aunts, she had an overwhelming sensation of being taken over. It was a mixture of fear, pleasure and danger. She loved it, yet backed away without knowing why.

Unfortunately, Mrs Morton, Hannah's mother, having seen the kiss, hurried to disapprove and to make a major incident of it. "Get rid of that young man," she'd commanded.

The task fell immediately to Susan, the elder sister who was mightily sorry about it. She knew Jeff to be a kind and decent man who – by the way – had done a magnificent job for minimal remuneration. He was trying to make some money, to set himself up in business, too. He'd told her as much when she hired him: and now, to pull the rug from under him? Well, she just wouldn't do it.

In the garden, Mr Horohan was looking and feeling a little annoyed. Had he now lost himself the easiest job he'd had in ages, and just because he'd been provoked into kissing that annoying little creature?

Yeah, he could do banter, he thought, but usually the playing field was level, This lot were different. They could turn on you in an instant – and being rich, they had all the cards. Apparently this was an annual event – 'a house party, and theatricals' they called it. Well, on his estate they called it something worse, but at least his people were honest about what they were doing. This lot were despicable.

"I didn't think you were like the rest of them," he eventually managed to say aloud to Hannah. "But…"

'Aw yeah, come over all breathy and innocent now', he thought, spitefully, as Hannah apologised.

"It was all my fault. I see that now. I just thought you were nice…" The rest of the sentence tailed off as she looked at his expression.

"Do you hate me?" she asked.

"No," he lied. "But I bloody hate them."

"Them, who?" The innocence in her voice made him furious. "Who do you think? The lot of them. Mean and sly. Bedding each other – like magic tricks. Now you see it, now you don't. How can you bear them? Two faced and… sly." He used the word again, assuming that she'd despise him for his lack of education, but instead she coloured up and looked embarrassed.

"You're worth ten of 'em," she said stoutly. "They want to sack you. And for something that was my fault. Entirely mine."

"Yeah, well, just forget it. I'll go and get my pay and cards from the old witch."

Hannah almost said, 'Hey, that's my mother you're talking about', but she didn't. She wandered miserably behind him into the sitting room where the cast were still sitting, looking at their lines or practising their moves. Mrs Morton was writing a letter. Probably Jeff's reference. "I hope you gave him a good one."

Mrs Morton looked startled for a few moments and then gathered herself and said, "Well, yes, Hannah. His work has been excellent. I just didn't want him interfering with my daughter. He is a liability."

Jeff stood there in front of her and had to listen to that speech as if he didn't exist. 'That's how they treat us all,' he thought. 'No manners.' Then, to Mrs Morton, "And will I be getting my bonus?"

Hannah expected a haughty put-down, but her mother was surprisingly placatory.

"I hope I know how to treat my staff fairly, Mr Horohan." She reached into a small compartment in her handbag and brought out a brown envelope. He went closer to take it and there was a second's hesitation before it was relinquished. The young man made a show of folding it, unchecked, and stuffing it carelessly into his shirt pocket before he strode off in the direction of the servants' room, with Hannah following, like a lapdog.

"Jeff, I can't tell you how bad I feel..." she began, when he took a firm hold on her wrist and said with some urgency, "Where's your room?"

"Umm, off the main corridor, why?"

He took her hand and marched her up the stairs.

Some time later, Mr Horohan emerged from the massive double doors of Morton Hall, with the beginnings of a smile on his face. He had some justification for feeling smug. After all, he'd managed to seduce Mrs Morton; Susan Morton, her sister; Jane, the maid; Sophie, the under-maid and now, Hannah, the daughter of the house. What's more, Mrs Morton had paid handsomely for the privilege. He checked the crumpled envelope. 500 quid. Not as much as Susan, but then her old man was likely to withhold a lot of money if he found out about this particular lover. The upper classes like to keep their seductions between themselves.

'Probably because they're no bloody good at it,' he laughed to himself as he got into his car and put the envelope under the seat with a pile of others.

WAITING FOR THE BLUE LIGHT

I noticed the swallows perched along the guttering this morning, the mist balancing lightly on their shoulders.... hang on... do swallows have shoulders? Probably not aerodynamically sound, so 'no' is the answer to that one.

It made me sad that they're planning to leave us so early this year. It also reminded me that *I'm* still here, despite my best intentions. I'm trying to remember the date the light will turn blue again but I'm still feeling confused after my last experience. I did everything right, you see, but *still* that damn red light was on every time I tried to slip back through to the other side.

This time I have to get it right because I've had enough. I've done what I wanted, seen who I wanted to see and I'm definitely ready this time. God knows I don't want to stay for the winter again. No fun, that one. I haven't got the resistance, you see. Cold enough at the height of the summer, let alone the snow and sleet. I also seem to have run out of options – who to see, who to listen to – or – and this is more likely – who to be disappointed by next.

'If only they knew,' I think to myself, 'about all those heroes. All the people we admire most in the world.'

"If you could see them with their guard down," I told Lucy the other day, "or how dirty some of their fingernails are, you wouldn't be praising their prose or going all gooey if you happened to meet one."

There, you see, I'm getting bitter and I swore I wouldn't.

The ordinary ones are okay but deadly dull. They just want to see their rellies again or check up on whoever inherited to see if they really were worthy or if they'd just wasted the inheritance. I try to keep away from them most of the time, although I do meet up with Lucy every now and then. As I said, the famous ones have feet of clay so it's best to give 'em a wide berth mostly. There are some exceptions, of course, but then it's probably like meeting Obama – all those high hopes about him were dashed when he turned out to be Mr Cool and a great mover, when they needed a wise politician. Lucy's hero as well, he is. Aw…

You always need to be prepared for disappointment.

Take Shakespeare, for example. He didn't have a lot to say for himself. And, honestly, I was so thrilled to meet him – thought at first he might write me a little something, but when I asked, he was pretty lukewarm. I was on the train to Cambridge and sat next to him. With it being a long journey, I tried something else; just to fill in the silence, you know.

"Which ones did we lose then, of your plays? We haven't got 'em all, you know."

He just shrugged. He was hard work. I tried a different tac. "Which one was your fave? I loved Othello, especially that speech where he's just landed and he sees her again and calls her, 'my soul's joy'." I wish someone had called me, 'my soul's joy', I thought, feeling quite pensive.

He looked at me for ages and just said, "You have lovely white teeth." Obsessed with teeth he was. That's why he stayed so long and kept on coming back to meet me.

"It's so clean here. The streets stink where I come from – even with a nosegay under your neb." He actually said, 'neb'! Liked the new slang, apparently. And it was one of mine. I felt really proud that I'd taught William Shakespeare a new word. Wow.

"Read me something then," I said. "That would be such a thrill." And I expected a romantic bit, from the sonnets, you know.

"That's what the public would ask for," I told him. But no. Starts going on about 'Don't mourn for me when I'm dead. As soon as that funeral bell packs in – forget us.' *He* put it better, like. Well, you'd expect that, wouldn't you?

I've asked him loads of questions since then: Who is the dark lady? What was going on with Mr W. H… all that, but all he wanted to say was, "Look, if you get a chance, tell the critics that no, I would never have 'written for the telly.' It infuriates me when they say that. I'd still have written for the theatre. It's my first love, you see." I didn't believe him though. He'd soon have changed his mind if he'd found out just how much money he would have earned at the BBC.

We were in Binns department store at the time, trying out different aftershaves. He's really into toiletries and cosmetics nowadays.

Most of the dead people I meet are not famous. I find it's better in the long run. Nobody notices you if you just look ordinary, but with Will, he insists on wearing this long cloak thing; and he stands out. He stands out a bit too much if you ask me, and you feel daft if you're with him.

They – the living – all assume we're from a theatre group or we're advertising something. I suppose that's why I chose, as my 'coming home' outfit, this hi-viz jacket.

Ironically, when you're wearing a hi-viz thing you become invisible. Nobody gives you a second glance. It's like you are the coat – you don't have any distinguishing marks, or personality. You are a workman/woman and that's the end of it. I've been all over and just putting a hard hat on with the jacket gives you access to anything. It's like you're legally allowed into places.

Tell you who I met last Wednesday – and this made my day… Fred Astaire. I know, I know. I was dead excited. But then, you see, when the excitement subsides, and you've asked him to twirl you round the dance floor and he says he doesn't dance these days, what've you got? An old man, that's what.

Although, I will say this for Fred, he has loads of stories about all the stars in Hollywood in the '30s and '40s. The veil was truly lifted on that lot – what with the drug taking and smutty little affairs and all. Did you know, for example, the only way he could do the kissing in his films was if they did a take and then slowed it down – yes – slow motion so it looked on screen as if the lip action was twice as long. That was cos his wife watched him like a hawk on set, especially with Rita Hayworth, who he *really* fancied. I felt a bit sorry for him, to tell the truth. All that glamour and not one decent snog. To be fair, he didn't complain about any of that – his wife's controlling ways or his unfulfilled lust. Nice fella, especially if you got him talking about musicians and jazz. Brilliant then!

Funny though, how he clammed up when I asked him about the Fatty Arbuckle scandal. They all do. Clark Gable and Marlene Dietrich were the same. I don't get it. It's not as if anyone can prosecute anyone. After all, they're dead. I tried again, "Do you fear retribution beyond the grave? Is that why you won't dish the scandal?" He gave a wan smile at that, head on one side, and he tried to whirl me round and do a timestep, but it didn't feel right. I haven't seen him again since then.

There's a definite nip in the air today. I wish I had a fleece, but it was summer when I had to choose. I might have a wander round the Costa Brava, where it's a bit warmer, or maybe take a train journey somewhere.

There is one place I daren't go though. I left my daughter behind – that was decades ago when she was just a sprog – and I'm afraid to find out what happened to her. How odd, you must think. After all, that was the only reason I came over this side and I've done nothing about it. I know where she is, and that she has a little child, but if I go, then I'll know, won't I, what sort of deal she got out of life. And I'm terrified. It might be truly horrible. Then I'll blame myself, even though mine was a quick and unexpected accidental death.

Will's on the train. In one of his moods. He told me ages ago that Coriolanus was his biggest mistake. Wanted to do a rewrite and get rid of the gore, but he never got round to it.

I soon found his carriage – you could smell him a mile away – all that deodorant. "Hello beauty," he said. I'm not, by the way – a beauty, that is. It's just that he thinks anyone with good teeth and skin is beautiful. So used to the pockmarks filled in with white lead that were the norm in his old life. I suppose everyone was so scrofulous in his day that we all look like models to him. Told me he's "still enchanted by 21st century people – their good diets, and clean habits." Aw, it's quite canny really isn't it? He's a man out of his time, bless him.

"Will, I need some advice," I said, and sat beside him. It was one of those four-seater places in the middle of the carriage. "Sorry to interrupt, by the way."

I hadn't noticed the papery copy of Coriolanus on the table next to him. "Still on the old rewrite then?" I asked sympathetically.

"Almost finished." He smiled and I couldn't help noticing his brand new teeth. Must've cost him a packet cos they looked like implants. "You look nice," I said, smiling back.

I dunno where he got it from but on a closer inspection, I could see he was using a quill pen and the paper was a bit crinkly.

"Here, use this, it's easier." I'd nicked a writing pad and biro from Smith's earlier that day, hoping to write a note to leave for my daughter before I left. The pad now lay between us, untouched. He looked at me with scorn. "Oh, I don't like these new-fangled gadgets."

I think every one of us is a bit scared of the latest fads, whichever century we're from. But we're all still 'on a mission', so to speak. Unfinished business, and all that stuff. Why else would we return?

It was then it came to me.

"Hey, is that stuff you're using kosher?" Incomprehension. "I mean, Can'st thou be writing with 16th century materials?" I corrected, for a laugh.

He nodded. "Hidden about my person in the cloak pockets." How exciting!

"So, you'll want it to be discovered then?"

That was when the plan began to form in my mind.

•

I waited until it was dark before I approached the farmhouse. There was an edge of frost in the air but it was bearable.

Jenny, the child, was asleep in the front bedroom. I got to see her lovely face in the light of the full moon. The whole place was a bit shabby but nice and clean. Her mother, my daughter Jane, was in the back room, propped up on pillows and reading. I didn't want to scare her – we all get a bit gaunt and shadowy when we come back. Blowing her a kiss, I tiptoed out.

Making my way up to the loft, I tried to be silent, and scouted around for a hiding place. I'd have to cause a bit of damage to the roof of course. That way, they'd be forced to repair it quickly and find the precious document.

I'd made Will blot the manuscript so he'd leave a fingerprint. Then, if they were to authenticate the thing, nobody could dispute its provenance. Squeezing the bundle of ancient paper into a crack between the roofspace and the tiles, I loosened a couple of them and threw them into the guttering, making a loud crack. Then I dashed down the stairs and watched and waited. A job well done, I thought.

As dawn broke, and the lovely 'green' smell of the morning was all around, the little family came to the windows to watch a flock of Canada geese flying overhead. 'Ah, it's time,' I thought.

I was chilled to the bone when I finally reached the portal but I hardly felt it. I knelt down and peered along the narrow beam of pale blue light. *Blue*. I could go home. Divesting myself of that horrible, sweaty nylon jacket, I began to laugh to myself about the hoo-ha that would ensue when the manuscript was found. The TV coverage, the shedloads of money for my family and the amazement of all the scholars – truly a miracle. 'Coriolanus Rewritten!' I could imagine the headlines. I also managed a chuckle at the number of modern idioms and slang words he'd managed to include in the new version. I'd counted at least seven 'nebs'. What a genius.

ON THE TELLY

Well, I watched the first part of The Musketeers but was very confused. Everyone's after a fight with d'Artagnan, for no good reason. The loud, grunty fight sequences last for at least 60% of each episode. Everyone gets incredibly mucky. Knives are thrust horizontally up to exposed throats and an occasional wench casts secret, lustful glances at our heroes. What's going on?

Then, slowly, the mists began to clear. I've seen this before …

A dimly lit vault (disused factory/multi-storey car park): a group of bandits (the Mitchell brothers?) our hero, beaten but unbowed, threatened with unspeakable torture, joins the Bandit Leader and plays a game of double-bluff.

A trusty minion ("I'd've given my life for you") ends up dead. Tough women offer their services and nobody means what they say.

The jokey dialogue shows how cool the guys are.

("God, I love that in a woman," says one of the heroes, rubbing his cheek after being punched in the face. "What?" asks his mate. "Violence," he responds, after a meaningful pause. The lads respond.) *Now* I get it. The Musketeers *is* Old Style EastEnders! I'm just hoping for the following dialogue before I give up on it altogether.

"D'ya want me to cut him, Boss?"

"He ain't worf it Phil/Vadim/whoever. Anyway, I trust him."

Sharon/Queen walks in on Aramis/any given Mitchell (she's undressed him in her head already) and gets up close. He looks around nervously.

"Ere, leave it out treacle. You're Grant's/King Louis' missus. I don' want no trouble."

She snogs him anyway, then stares directly to camera over his manly back, looking troubled. Bom bom bom bom bom...

I can't wait...

BROWING THE HILL

When you reach the hill and look to the summit
Man and machine fused together in a mad determination,
There's an indescribable challenge in the air. You love it.
You versus nature. You against yourself.

Thighs flexed and body taut, the ascent begins.
Nobody thinks about the end. You wait and see.
What will you see? What will there be, when you
Brow this hill?
And what do you hope for?

The best hills are the toughest and steepest.
You leave the ordinary behind
And seek out the glorious lack of humankind. There's only
the wide expanse of wild country,
And you.
You are a god
with no time for the paltry; the everyday-humdrum.
You are intrepid, expunging what has gone before;
blotting out the past
With only the internal rhythm of the wheels
dictating to mind and body.
You reach your limits; the fire still inside you;
The waiting, and the wanting ended.
Life rushes at you like a sudden gust
'So, this is what lies ahead', you think, as
Your future unfolds
Over the brow

WHY IS IT THAT THE POETS TELL SO LITTLE OF THE SENSE OF SMELL?

The first two lines of this poem, vaguely recalled from years ago, prompted me to muse on whether an acute sense of smell is a blessing or a curse. I constantly irritate people by asking, "Can you smell *that*?" only to be met with blank uncomprehending stares or – worse still – that grimace with the corners of the mouth turned down as they shake their heads at what they assume is just my colourful imagination. Someone once told me I was looking for an excuse not to eat some beef that smelled suspiciously 'off', but later found, to their cost, that it was foolish to ignore their very own 'oracle of the odours'. Montezuma's revenge was swift and not too sweet on that occasion and, 'I told you so' was in my eyes but never uttered to the other guests thereafter. I'm not mean-spirited when I'm right, just smug.

My sense of smell is such that I can equate the scent of newspaper with that of the old-fashioned borax cream used to guard against nappy rash in the fifties and I can taste the scent of icicles on certain breads – most often on the panini sold in a certain supermarket. I really love icicle bread; it has a hint of coal fires which reminds me of my childhood: breaking icicles from the washhouse roof and sucking on them. (How did we survive pre-Health and Safety legislation?)

I once fancied being a 'nose'. That is what they call people who create new perfumes; who can detect the ephemeral nuances of scent underlying the top notes. "There," I grumble to anyone

214

who'll listen, "my skill would be appreciated and I'd be lauded instead of being ridiculed."

As things stand, I tend to annoy people by insisting on sniffing at the thresholds of fish and chip shops and cafes to determine the quality of the oil they use. Beef dripping is, of course, king in fish frying but alas a rarity nowadays, since we've been scared off by 'good and bad cholesterol' campaigns. However, the cheap palm oil used in many a greasy spoon is much worse for us *and* tastes disgusting.

By now you think I'm really odd, don't you? It can't be helped. I've tried grinning and bearing it through many a tortured lunch with friends but then I can smell the grease on my clothes long after the fresh air has hit me and I'm just miserable until I can get them into the washing machine.

In public places such as theatres or cinemas I seem always to be seated beside someone whose hair smells or whose coat is impregnated with long-standing doses of perfume wafting stalely into my uber-sensitive nasal passages for the duration of the performance.

One method I employ to overcome my distaste is the 'half-nostril cover-up'. You lean an elbow on the near-side seat and press gently on one side of the nose, eliminating most of the offending odour. It's not perfect, but I commend it to the house as a survival skill, deployed most successfully during a recent performance of Waiting for Godot at the Newcastle Theatre Royal.

A discussion of body odour is usually taboo, but as a youngster, I was once the subject of an embarrassing and hurtful campaign by an older work colleague during my time on the switchboard of a bakery in Middlesbrough.

Sandra was in a position of slight authority: the worst kind. The tiny amount of power had gone to her head: "Go and have your break now, Linda, and don't be too long. You'll have to wait, Margaret. The rat catcher's coming and he'll need help."

She didn't look like a bully. She was what I would term 'handsome', blonde, blue eyed with straight white teeth and simple make-up, and I thought she was my friend. She used to complain to me about the other girls and I was naive enough to believe that this gave me some sort of immunity from persecution.

At sixteen, and with no mother to guide me, I was experimenting with beauty products. The latest was 'Veet', claiming to remove underarm hair with miraculous speed. My sister had bought some. Sandra probably didn't need to worry about such a thing. Her blondness probably meant that she could whisk a tiny razor across her armpits and 'Hey Presto', but being dark, I needed more help.

Initially, the Veet process had seemed to work, but then I began to have some difficulty in raising my right arm, so my dad sent me to see the doctor.

"It's a boil. Lift your arm up and I'll lance it." (Great bedside manner.)

"What? Now?"

"Have you been using anything under there?"

"Well, yes, to get rid of the hair."

"It's blocked your pores and caused this." Scalpel in hand and working as he spoke. "There you are. Don't use any more of that stuff. Keep it clean."

With that I was dismissed. Two weeks later, I found more underarm swelling. This time my dad took control. "That Doctor Arthur's an idiot. Here, I'll sort it out. Granny Murphy's poultice will get rid of that."

Granny Murphy's poultice, as remembered by my dad, was a mixture of green soap and sugar, heated up on a piece of lint and slapped onto the offending area then taped in place with a few giant Elastoplasts. I had a bit of a scream as it went on, but I dutifully wore it for a few days thereafter, even though it made me round-shouldered and uncomfortable at work.

Sensing a weakness, Sandra went in for the kill. I had been unable to use any scented products and I imagine the blue nylon shirtwaister overall we had to wear wasn't helping the poultice to breathe. I smelt like the boil wash my granny did in the poss tub every Thursday.

"Isn't it your birthday next week, Margaret?"

Sandra smiled innocently and a couple of the girls giggled nervously. I told her the date, hunching over the telephone exchange to avoid further armpit discomfort.

"Oh, we'll have to get you a 'sweet seventeen' present."

The next day, a parcel was left on my desk. Soaps and talc in a presentation set.

It took me a week to realise the implications and the spiteful intent behind it.

Meanwhile, things were changing in the abscess department. The folk-remedy had failed. A return visit to a different doctor landed me in A&E, having seven abscesses removed under local anaesthetic. It worked, but the lingering embarrassment at work was not so swiftly expunged.

Having watched Sandra's bullying escalate to include several other younger workmates and realising I'd got off lightly, I changed jobs and went to work in the steelworks offices, where the knives were blunter.

I was so happy there! I was on the central exchange board and answered calls from everyone in the building. People popped in and out all day and my fellow telephonist was a married Methodist called Pam who spent much of her free time knitting.

When Pam left, her replacement was a girl called Elise. She had a name like a melody but seemed a bit odd. Her first request, when it was my turn to get the bacon buns at the café, was, could I get her some 'Slippery Elm'? We all had a good laugh about that one – but out of earshot. She was clearly ahead of her time and was into health food shops.

Eventually though, I realised that it was too easy to ridicule the girl. It bordered on bullying and I was wise to that now, so I kept her at arm's length.

I was also more than happy to keep my distance because a new, more troublesome problem had raised its ugly head. Poor Elise had an odour problem. This wasn't just me and my nose. Everyone commented on it. Our tiny cubicle seemed some days to be coloured by the strange smell of her and I tried to keep the windows wide open to counteract it. And, because I'd been there longer, it fell to me to speak to her about it. Mr Morris, my boss, had taken me to one side. Apparently some of the draughtsmen had complained that the corridors smelled bad after she'd walked down them. "Of course, I can't say anything…" (Why not?) "…but a young lass like you would be the ideal person to tackle the problem." Thanks, Mr Morris.

It took me a week to speak to her. I spent part of that week trying to work out what the smell was. It was almost animal-like in its muskiness. She didn't *look* dirty but there was no mistaking when she was round the corner. It was the Ready Brek glow of smells. But how to tackle it? I immediately ruled out the Sandra method… too cruel, and besides, I still had to work with this girl afterwards.

The Teesside Bridge offices had one of those old-fashioned lifts where you had to pull two heavy metal doors across to close it. I asked Elise to come to the top floor with me. I wondered if she could sense my heartbeat because it was drumming into my head. In between floors, I opened the first one a tad, to stop the lift. I had a fleeting thought that any of the office staff would be able to see right up our skirts should they happen to be passing, but I bravely shrugged it off.

"I'm sorry to do this, Elise," I began, going red, "but it's better to say it to your face than behind your back. The thing is, sometimes you don't smell very nice and people are complaining." I took a deep breath. I didn't look at her face so I couldn't tell how she'd taken it.

There was a long silence, then she simply said, "Oh."

"Sorry," I said again. "Maybe you could just put a bit of perfume on before you come in to work or something?" My voice trailed off.

And of course I knew it wouldn't solve the problem but I had to get back down to the ground floor without any more silences. "I hope you don't mind me saying. It's a bit embarrassing for both of us, I know."

She sprang into action. "No, no. Thank you," she said, leaving the lift. "I'll get some stuff tonight."

I stood in the empty lift awhile, thankful it was over. I waited till the corridor was empty, then I sprayed a little 4711 eau de cologne around to disperse the smell.

Well, I didn't want anyone thinking it was me.

RONNIE

Ronnie was a caretaker, and as caretakers went, he was a good one. A dapper little man in a neatly pressed khaki coat over immaculate shirt and tie, he was out of step with a changing world. He took the same strict pride in his surroundings as in his dress, keeping the wooden benches of his office in excellent order, with a place for everything. Tools lined the walls, each in its designated station, hanging inside its inked-on outline – knowing its place.

As a somewhat rigid man, Ronnie's choice of companion was surprising. Perhaps opposites really do attract? Ronnie's partner – a cheery woman, round and comforting as a dumpling, always looked happily unkempt. She wore too much jewellery and loved shopping for flamboyant outfits, most of which were unfortunate choices on such a tiny, tubby frame.

Her latest acquisition was a black silk kimono, decorated with embroidered dragons front and back, which breathed fire from the Dumpling's bosoms down to her dimpled knees. Ronnie was charmed but disapproving in equal measure when she twirled for his approval.

Her greatest pleasure was to go to what she termed, 'The West End Shows' by which she meant musicals from London, when there was a touring company in the district, although she never knew where she was going. The coaches disgorged their cargo at the theatres and babied them back safely to the mid-priced hotels. No geography was involved, and no culture was accidentally absorbed along the way.

Coach trips to London with entertainment thrown in were the Dumpling's favourite way of spending a weekend. "Good value for all-inclusive!" she'd say to Ronnie, as he struggled to eat the bland pensioner-food served up by another very average hotel chain.

Ronnie was philosophical about this. He bore it with his usual calm. Given his own way, he would have made a bee-line for the National Theatre, or to Stratford. He was the exception that proved the rule – a cultured caretaker. He would spout the occasional quotation from Shelley or a Shakespearean sonnet, but as it hit the brick wall of her understanding and fell in a heap at his feet, he would simply smile and return to his crossword.

Thus it was and their lives would have continued smoothly were it not for the apprentices.

Ronnie had been chosen to oversee a new apprentice scheme at work. Six young men had been recruited to learn from him, with a view to sending them out into the world with some kind of qualification.

He didn't know his life was to change forever. These young men might have been an alien species for all he and the Dumpling knew of their upbringings. One boy in particular, a well-educated, arrogant lad, seemed determined to make him miserable.

And where he led, the other sheep followed.

The problem was that, as a methodical man, Ronnie had his routines – which were anathema to the young.

Each day their irritation grew, particularly during breaks and lunchtimes. Ron's tea was always made in a white enamel mug with blue edging. He always brought two small 'Vaseline' jars to work; in one of which he carried leaf tea and in the other, condensed milk. The sweet, strong brew they created was very much to his taste, but the lads found it so old-fashioned as to be offensive. None of them had ever seen leaf tea before, and instead of taking an interest, they began to take umbrage. Their coke cans littered the benches at the end of the working day, and they left Ron to clear their detritus.

At the end of the second week, Ron found his jars had been emptied out into a cupboard. The viscous mess took most of his lunchtime to clean up. When asked if they'd seen the culprit, the apprentices became loud and belligerent, so he backed off.

The next day, when he brought in replacement Tupperware containers, their glee was unconfined. The smallest lad suggested that someone had done him a favour and dragged him into the 21st century.

At lunchtime that same day, when he reached for his mug, he found it had been screwed to the workbench. The next day, one of the legs on his stool was sawn in half. By nobody, of course.

The boys did so many cruel things that by the end of the month, Ronnie was at the end of his tether. He became jumpy and wary and the change in his behaviour was noticed by the Dumpling, who decided to act. His reaction was to 'spout a bit of verse' as she called it.

"We need to teach them a lesson in respect," she told him, clasping her pudgy, be-ringed hands over his gnarled, scarred ones. "I'll come in and sort 'em out for you. With a carrot and a stick," was all she would say.

The next morning, before they all arrived, the Dumpling had set up the office as a tearoom. She had arranged freshly baked scones, butter, jam and cream on trays hoping to tempt the boys, who shuffled suspiciously into their usual places, whispering profanities and nudging each other but not daring to address her directly.

The singing began at 9.30. First she did selections from South Pacific, followed by the whole of the Rodgers and Hammerstein canon. Her voice was somewhat wobbly and strident. And rather loud. Nobody, not even Ronnie knew what to do. The lads looked sideways at each other, wondering who would break first, but they were all a bit unnerved. So they just pretended it wasn't happening.

Coffee break was at 10.30. The smells of hot coffee and warmed scones filled the air, alongside the heavenly silence. The Dumpling renewed her scarlet lipstick and smiled. "Come on now, lads, help yourselves!" she purred.

The young men stared, not sure how Ronnie would react. He simply nodded and spouted a few lines of appropriate verse, which they took as permission.

"There's lemon curd, strawberry and bramble jam or treacle," she trilled.

The main man, afraid that she'd won the others round, looked her up and down, noting the gaudy outfit, and sneered, "It's called blackberry jam, actually. The bramble is the plant but the fruit is a blackberry."

She fixed angry eyes on him but addressed Ronnie. "You like a bit of verse, don't you Ron? Well here's an impromptu one for smartarse." She pushed her face so close to the boy that he could smell her stale face powder. In a sing-song voice she began to recite her own poetry:

"I know it's not called bramble jam
But when I was a kid,
nobody else said 'blackberry'
And so *I* never did.'

There yer are – that's poetic license. Now bugger off back to work."

The others began to laugh. The boy was defeated. More might have been said but the Dumpling had already begun on Rodgers and Hart, to be followed by West Side Story. "I like a bit of Leonard Bernstein," she explained.

I Feel Pretty was her favourite, so she treated them to several encores and by the end of the day, there wasn't a nerve unfrayed in the whole workshop. The youngsters vowed never to provoke the wrath of the Dumpling again. The trouble stopped.

However, over the next month, and despite the apprentices having been tamed, Ronnie became increasingly morose. He would panic on his way to work each morning and was wrung out like a dishcloth on his return home. Ten more years of this would kill him.

The Dumpling was at a loss as to what to do. He hinted at selling his house to fund an earlier-than-intended retirement, and she agreed it was for the best.

Then the magic happened. Ronnie had a win on the lottery. It wasn't silly money as it was shared with a few other winners, but it would allow him to retire and live in comfort. He calmly watched the numbers come up on TV, and when it sank in, he found her in the kitchen making tea. She was wearing the black silk number.

"Fancy a month in London, love? I've won the lottery." It was the first time he'd smiled in ages.

The kimono quivered. The Dumpling beamed all over, the embroidered dragons trembling from neck to nether regions.

"All them West End Shows!" she bellowed, burying him in her vast bosom.

The next morning, instead of going to work, Ronnie went shopping. He bought six small boxes and six white enamel mugs with blue rims. Beneath each one, he sellotaped a £50 note. He had them wrapped, and labelled with the words 'Good luck, lads,' and sent them to his office.

Of course, Ronnie's absence hadn't gone unnoticed by the firm, but by then, the apprentices were able to carry on without him, now they were almost skilled. However, the place was never the same again. Filled with regret, they all wished he'd come back, but the postcard he sent, months later, bearing a quotation from Shakespeare, made it clear that would never happen. 'To thine own self be true,' it read, 'and it must follow, as the night, the day, thou canst not then be false to any man.' And he added, 'And if all else fails, *bring in the wife.*'

The gifts were unwrapped. In the bottom of each mug there was a number. The six numbers that had changed his life. 'They'll work it out eventually,' he thought.

Ronnie was a caretaker and as caretakers go – he went.

THE CHICKEN
THAT BLINKED

I once lived in Somerset for a year. It was an idyllic spot with uninterrupted views of the Mendip Hills from my tiny one-bedroomed bungalow. That year proved to me that despite my fierce northern loyalty, the south west would definitely win on climate, being milder and wetter than my part of the world. The wildness of the north Yorkshire Moors and the dales are matchless in their beauty, but I definitely didn't miss the cutting, biting Nor'easterlies blustering in straight off the sea.

I'd relocated to this part of the country on a stupid whim really. The head honcho at work was a vain and shallow man (and I need to say in all fairness here, that I do share those particular vices, but to a much lesser degree). This was the man who walked around for a couple of days displaying the lining of his new work suit, with the 'Armani' label in full view, so the world and his wife would see it. For those who missed his peacock-display, he called a staff meeting, emphasising his initial point by removing his jacket and hanging it over his arm, label-upwards as he spouted. Sadly, he believed that would convince the workers what a splendid fellow he was. Pathetic.

Moreover, he had taken an unwelcome shine to me – more to my physical appearance than my personality, which was a bit too much for him – and he would find reasons to stare at my bosom (not spectacular) and make comments about the exact shade of my eyes. "Look, they're not dark brown. They're more of a chestnut colour, close-up," he muttered to a male member of staff, much to our mutual embarrassment. On another occasion, he took me by the arm to the opposite side of the staff room where a friend of mine was standing at the notice board. "Jane, there's a hair, just there," pointing to the aforementioned bosom, "and *I* can't remove it, obviously." Then he'd watch to make sure she did it properly. Very offensive.

Sadly, none of this 'admiration' translated to promotion, even though I was good at my job. Having convinced me to apply for a tiny step up the ladder, he rather enjoyed kicking me back down again. One particularly humiliating interview comes to mind, but I'd prefer to draw a veil over that one. His behaviour got to me so much that I became a virtual prisoner in my room rather than have him stalking me around the building.

I hated having no control over my situation and finally applied, in a state of high dudgeon, for the next job that came up, "Wherever it might be. At least I'll get a morning off for the interview," I told sympathisers naively.

Bluff called, I found myself on a train bound for North Somerset – a place I'd only ever travelled through on the way to somewhere else. Ah well, eating buffet cart chicken sandwiches and enjoying a short respite from the boss was great! Further bluff called, though, when I was offered the job and at a higher salary and with more prospects than my present one. And thus I found myself living by the Mendips, close to the Cheddar Gorge.

After the first couple of months, I began to settle in to my new surroundings. Indeed, so many members of the family came down for short breaks that I was never lonely, and the charm of living in the hamlet – for it could hardly be called a village – compensated for the paucity of social life.

I tentatively made a few friends in my cul de sac, and was invited to the Harvest Supper. "Don't forget to bring a torch," my neighbour Graham said. "We have no street lights. We were offered them but we voted against." I decided it must be a safe place to live in that case, and found I could happily relax and feel comfortable there.

I'd brought my old push-bike from home and with the country lanes in the Somerset levels being, well, level, it was a daily pleasure to ride around watching the seasons change. It was also a novel experience for a townie to socialise with the farming community.

Nobody I knew had even met a farmer and because of this, I saw them as quite glamorous – a bit James Herriot-like; bluff but kindly.

Jill and Bob, who had the farm up at the end of Biddisham Lane, were archetypal salt-of-the-earth types, and Jill had decided to take me under her wing. She fed me up and showed me how to plan my garden to get the best displays of sweet peas and roses. She also suggested that nobody would care if I took apples from the garden of the empty house next door. "They'll only go to waste, my dear, if you leave 'em."

One very lovely morning as I cycled along the lane, I noticed Bob, usually so hard at work, leaning on his farm gate, staring into space. I waved as I passed but he didn't acknowledge me.

On my return, I noticed that he hadn't moved. He was still idling away the time, with the same expression on his face. Slowing down, and putting one foot on the ground, I asked if he was okay.

"Just waitin' for the chicks." The Somerset burr was soft and could have been taken for an American accent. For a split second it was as if I'd strayed into an early Elvis film. 'Waitin' for the chicks' was a bit more suited to a leather-jacketed youth with upturned collar and a ciggy dangling from a sulky mouth.

In contrast, there was Bob; a short, thick-set man in his middle years with a farmer's tan – face, neck and forearms burnished to the colour of a nicely-grilled sausage, in contrast to the whiteness of the upper arms which rarely saw the sunlight.

It turned out that he was expecting twenty thousand week-old chicks. His job today was to unload them from the lorry and from then to nurture them for six weeks, eventually sending them on to 'the next stage', he called it but I knew what he meant.

I felt excited to see the tiny creatures, but horrified that this nice man was involved with factory farming. I was pushing the bike into the lane, when he spoke again. "Fancy helping?" We looked at each other. Did *I* fancy helping? How could I do that? "Jill'll be here in a minute," he went on, to clarify the situation.

'Oh', I thought, 'he thinks I don't want to do it cos I'd be on my own with him.' With every fibre of my being I revolted against the situation, but I couldn't see a way out of it without causing offence.

"We need all the 'elp we can get." Jill was standing behind me. "You'll have to wear something very light though. It's hot in the sheds."

It was a fait accompli. I left the bike, took off my jumper and let my heart sink down to my boots as I walked robot-like to the farm buildings.

A few minutes later, a massive, blue lorry filled the lane, blocking the other traffic. It was packed to the gunnels with blue trays – like those used for carrying bread – but the cargo was living. We had no time to talk. The trays were heavy and we were expected to unload the chicks quickly and efficiently and empty them into the safety of the sheds. At first I picked them up in twos and threes, taking care not to hurt their tiny feet and thin legs, as I placed each one carefully in a space, but there were so many. I watched Jill tipping the trays at one corner, close to the straw-filled ground. The chicks were okay. They clucked, righted themselves, and walked off, no harm done.

Hours later, the sheds were filled. It was difficult to move because of the yellow chicken-carpet, but the little fluffballs instinctively kept away from our giant footsteps and went in search of food.

There was no cruelty in those sheds. It was spotlessly clean. Gas jets above kept the temperature constant and there was plenty of light, food and water. Nevertheless, despite feeling half-reassured, I also felt treacherous. How could you nurture something then send it off to its death? The hypocritical townie's eternal dilemma. Exhausted, and dehydrated, I dragged my rosy-faced carcass over to the bike to wheel it back home.

The farmers were very grateful. They invited me to dinner but luckily, they didn't serve chicken.

About a month later, I was watching a TV programme about factory farms. It was like an animal concentration camp There were rotating machines at eye level and the workers were picking up fully-grown hens by their legs, which they crossed over at the ankle and pushed neatly into slots upside down, so they were powerless to move, held as they were by a sort of manacle. As the machine rotated, other workers slit the chickens' throats and a third group of workers unhitched them and sent the bodies off to be plucked.

I knew. I knew how this worked, so why was I shocked? It's an odd thing, but I was alright until the camera gave us a close-up of the chickens' upside down heads as they rotated, combs shaking in alarm, But then, one of the chickens looked directly into the camera and blinked.

It broke my heart. The awareness of that particular bird will always be there in my head because it was an almost human reaction. Seconds before death, it blinked.

I didn't sleep that night. I was haunted by that tiny moment. I kept thinking, I want to do something – at least for one of those birds now living 200 yards from my house. Surely I could rescue one or even two and keep them from that fate. The fate I'd helped get them into. But how?

I found my torch easily, and emptying the laundry bag, I dragged on my old, hooded coat. It was not yet midnight so the outer door to the sheds hadn't been locked. Inside, it was no warmer than in the lane, the gas jets having been turned off. I steadied myself and took a moment to catch my breath. What now? No plan had been formed, just a desperate emotional response to a situation beyond my control. Grabbing the two hens nearest the door, I stuffed them in the laundry bag and made my escape.

What do hens eat? I wondered. I gave them bread and milk, my own personal 'Tamworth Two'. It became clear at once that I'd taken on more than I could handle. How could I keep them secret? I named them Gert and Daisy and decided that country life was a bit too rich for my liking. Leaving two months rent and the price of the two hens on the kitchen table and a thank you note to everyone for their kindness, I arranged the move back north again.

Gert and Daisy continue to thrive. I might get a cockerel

to keep them company. Oh, and I've become vegetarian. It's a lifestyle choice.

Nothing much had changed at my old job. They took me back but in a different department. The new girl – my replacement – had a magnificent bosom, so that would keep the old lech happy… or so I thought. We were chatting in the Ladies one day and I asked if she'd had any trouble from him.

"Nah, he was a bit touchy-feely at first," she said, "but I think he felt intimidated after I bought these." She reached into her bra and fished out two odd-looking gel-filled half-moon shapes. I must've looked horrified.

"He only seems to like boyish lasses," she confided.

"What are those things?" I asked, aghast as she replaced the false breasts. "I think they call them chicken fillets," she said. "Anyway, I'm leaving in a month. Moving south west. Isn't that where you used to live?" She twirled a strand of curly hair between finger and thumb, smiling at herself in the mirror as she applied fresh lipstick. "I quite fancy marrying a farm lad. You know, all fresh air, good food and muscles. " I smiled, indulgently. "Yeah, right," I said. "Just make sure it's not chicken farming."

THE EAST WIND

The east wind was the worst. The new red pantiles on the side of the house rattled and crashed as if a careless burglar were slamming into them with a sledgehammer, unaware of the damage he was doing.

She'd had the builder back twice. No joy there, though. He'd put a few token tacks into the first line of tiles and left it at that.

"Nowt we can do, I'm afraid; short of taking the whole lot off and starting again." He'd laughed at such a preposterous suggestion and, packing up his tools, went gaily off down the driveway, dismissing her from his mind and anticipating his next job.

She wanted to call him back, tell him it was a great idea and to do it at once. That way, the newly-created loft space in her tiny bungalow could be enjoyed in all weathers. As it was, how could she have family or guests to stay?

She cut a forlorn little figure, standing in the garden, buffeted by what felt like a force 9 gale. Stray hair whipped across her cheeks and eyes making her squint against the harshness of the light

'Yet how lucky I am to live here,' she thought, 'the envy of my friends and family. Is it churlish to complain about what is, after all, such a small drawback?'

It was true. One could put up with many tiny inconveniences when one had the privilege of living in such a beautiful place. She had the drama of the cliffs, the sea, the tiny railway which seemed to hang suspended above the line of the hawthorn hedge, and above all – oh yes, more than anything else – she had the sea. It was the fulfillment of all her dreams – a sea view!

But the wind. The damn wind was relentless. She recalled a

poem about the wind. Was it Ted Hughes? 'This house has been out at sea all night'. That was the first line. And that was how she felt now. At sea. Not just looking at it.

"The thing is," she explained to Elaine over tea at the community centre, "the builder doesn't have to put up with the noise. I swear I didn't close my eyes all night on Sunday. There must be something else he can do with the tiles, surely?"

Elaine was not very forthcoming. She loved the place and went into raptures at every visit. What was it last time? Oh yes, the 'fine field of yellow rapeseed flowering amidst a green and blue Elysium.' Very fanciful. But then, Elaine had tendencies.

When she'd first seen the view she'd exclaimed (she was prone to exclaiming), "Oh Jenny, you live in the sky!"

Ah, yes, she remembered now – a flock of seagulls had wheeled and screamed around the balcony as Elaine was speaking. That was why she'd been so captivated.

Of course, the birds were nice enough, but they did make an awful racket first thing on a spring morning when one wanted to sleep. Elaine could always go home to her sheltered little terrace and rearrange her beautiful potted plants in the still heat of the greenhouse.

'Not me. I'm stuck with the whistling of the banshee wind and the bone-rattling doors. And the cold!' This last as an afterthought.

'There's no shelter here. That's what they all forget when they tell me how lucky I am! It's draughts and blankets and frozen feet all winter for me.' The tiles clattered rhythmically on the new roof.

Moving to the relative comfort of the kitchen, she set out a second plate of fondant fancies for Mary and Mel who were paying her a late afternoon visit. Both were on constant, unnecessary diets so she took particular pleasure in tempting them. "Silly women!" she cawed, anticipating their inevitable succumbing to the well-stocked tea table.

The windows shuddered slightly as she pictured the scene…

They'd both be resplendent in pastel-coloured dresses and a

tasteful touch of lipstick. There would be numerous references to 'being naughty' throughout the cholesterol-fuelled feast and the ladies would moan about the wind playing havoc with their hairdos and it would all be a bit of a pain. She began to wonder why she'd allowed them to invite themselves, yet again.

The wind complained in the eucalyptus tree.

In the event, the tea was somewhat more brutal than she'd anticipated. Just as she'd started to complain about the direction of the wind, Mary had knocked it out of her sails.

"Why don't you just move house?" she demanded tartly.

After a protracted pause during which many significant looks were exchanged, Jenny muttered, bemused, "Move? But I love it here."

The wind fluttered the nets at the rear windows.

"Well, clearly you don't," responded Mary. "You spend your life complaining about it."

She looked seawards. The best thing about windy days is how the sea, too, is blown so that tiny rivulets of white foam dance about in it. There they were; those sea-riders; those mini-surfers, bobbing on the edges of the waves. How she loved them.

"Anyway," she blustered, "it's the wrong time of the year to be selling – and the market's weak at present."

"Oh, you don't have to worry about market forces. Not with a view like this," Mary answered, triumphally.

They were both very helpful. The next few weeks were a whirlwind of activity. Mel called the estate agency. Mary took room measurements; wrote the prototype advert – including Jenny's curtains and carpets in the sale without permission, and Elaine offered to find her 'a more suitable, sheltered house' on the nearby estate – "so you won't even have to leave the village." Hm, did she detect a spiteful glint in those small, pale eyes?

The wind had subsided.

Looking out of the window as the usual early morning sea fret retreated, Jenny could see that not even one leaf of the eucalyptus tree was ruffled. From the balcony, she heard a curlew crying overhead as it wheeled silently in a forget-me-not-blue sky. The still air was heavy with the scent of early May blossom and the promise of summer. To her left, tucked semi-discreetly in a corner of the garden, the 'For Sale' sign declaimed its message in blue and gold.

A sudden gust of wind unsettled the peace of the day. She shivered slightly. Ah well, Mary had offered her a decent price for the bungalow. She couldn't complain really. She glanced at her watch. Lots of packing to do today. No time for dawdling. Contracts were about to be exchanged shortly. She sighed sadly.

It shouldn't have taken her by surprise really. She'd googled the weather forecast that evening and prepared for a bad night's sleep; but this was more terrible than even she could've imagined. Storm-tossed and shipwrecked, she lay wide awake, staring at the one pointer she could see on the old clock. Three something-or-other. It didn't matter.

Tiles were clacking. She imagined burglars hacking their way in. Guy ropes were needed to hold the place in place. 'Close your eyes,' she told herself, 'It'll soon be morning.'

After a fitful half-sleep, she roused herself and switched on the radio. 'The worst storms since records began,' it announced. She looked out to review the damage. Tiles were scattered randomly across the garden. There must be a sizeable hole in the roof. There was no sign of the sign. It must've been uprooted overnight and flung to some distant part of the planet. The sea was dancing some sort of final dervish-dance, to the rhythmic whistling of the wind.

By the afternoon the winds had subsided.

Unable to keep the smile out of her voice, she phoned the agent.

"I'm afraid nobody will buy it in this state," she said regretfully. "I'm going to have to take it off the market."

Outside, a breeze flirted with the wallflowers.

STEEL MEN

The ghost of my dead father, flat-capped,
searches the high-ceilinged sheds
His arms still-scarred from the white-hot whiplash of steel slabs
transformed by the wire-drawer's skill,
with unerring precision
to each exact specification
Shipped off to build the Sydney Harbour Bridge
Shipped off to build the Severn Bridge
Shipped around the world
from Teesside

A tall, wiry figure in steel-toecapped boots;
walking past
now-stilled furnaces and empty air.
A man who once flexed steel-hard biceps
beneath his khaki workshirt
– survivor of a greater conflict-
to entertain his children.
A tentative touch… awestruck they ask,
"Don't they hurt, dad?"

Still searching; through the newly-silent sheds
Tapping out his strides with the metal segs in his workboots,
Past one final load of grey, steel slabs
Finds his grandson
And with a sigh that holds the sadness of two lifetimes
Leads him into the fresh evening air. Into idleness
Away from a century of history
Followed by seventeen hundred strong
Out of the sheds at the end of the final shift.

THE LEG

"…but take care how you show him that room at the top of the house." I knew what she meant. Keep your mouth shut and if you have to say something, be positive. All well and good but what about the truth? Where does that come in?

I forced myself through the hallway to the stairs.

It was never pleasant, mounting those stairs. Too narrow and dusty. I'd left well alone for a few years now and even though she claimed she'd "done a bit of a makeover" on the room, I couldn't imagine it would amount to much. If the rest of the house was anything to go by, there'd just be a thinner layer of dust on the surfaces – and she may have put a few cheap ornaments on the windowsill – hardly up to Llewellyn-Bowen standard.

'Can you feel your blood pressure going up?' I wondered. Mine must've been sky high by now. I pictured a cartoon thermometer with the red shooting up to the top – with a cartoon zoomy noise. Woosh! Red cheeks flushed, 3D-like, back at me in the ancient mirror on the stairs as I started upwards.

I took the stairs very slowly and at every step my dread was in my mouth, a sort of drying up of juices and a taste of something unpleasant adhering to my clamped tongue. I licked parched lips and wished there was a bathroom on this floor so I could slake my sudden thirst.

The familiar charity-shop smell misted around me when I finally reached the topmost landing. It was the opposite of an air-freshener. What would you call that?

An air stale-ifier? Ha. Not much of a market for one of them, I thought.

Reaching the top was inevitable of course, and I knew that when I applied even the lightest of touches to the door handle,

I'd hear the noise again in my head. Uncertainty gripped me. Blood pressure boiled over.

As a child, I hardly slept because I was scared all the time in that room. At this point it needs to be said that at that age, I was an inveterate embroiderer of the truth, which could be such good fun. Even when people were laughing, knowing the lie, they accepted each tall tale because, wouldn't it be great if it were true? I never let on that this particular piece of fancywork was a true story. I was simply making capital out of painful childhood terrors in a vain hope that it would diminish their impact on me. It worked for a while too, this attempted exorcism. It was the one about my uncle, whose leg had been shot off in the war. He was fitted with a monstrous false one made out of god knows what. It was disgusting and had a dirty padded bit where the knee would have been. When he eventually died, the leg – now considered a sacred family relic – was hung up behind the door in what was to become my room. Every time I closed the door at night the leg clonked malevolently against it, slowing gradually to a quieter scraping sound until it stilled.

All was well until my mother climbed the stairs to bed, when the leg would move, like a restless sleeper turning over to escape a bad dream. It was not to be touched at any time, mother warned, oblivious to my fears.

I tried various methods of silencing the leg over time – first was a cushion underneath (as if it were troubled by the gout and needed nurturing). That lasted a day before the silkiness of the fabric caused it to slide gradually floorwards. I recall waking with a start, believing the sound to be a ghostly manifestation of my uncle, searching for his missing limb.

Once, in desperation, I'd slipped one of my grandmother's lisle stockings on the leg. I almost laughed as I watched it swaying slightly on the back of the door. It looked incongruous and strangely coquettish, but of course, a stocking would scarcely succeed in muffling the sound.

I even stole bandages from Aunt Lily's cupboard one Sunday and did a competent job of wrapping them round the stockinged leg, in the hope of hiding the theft from my mother, who'd shown signs of irritation when she could only find one of a pair.

"Well, someone's bloody moved it!" she glowered in my direction.

The upshot of this latest attempt was that the weight of the swaddling, on the stocking, on the leg, caused it to sidle slowly downwards a la Norah Batty. Very elegant.

But still the clonk persisted.

After that I put my faith in the power of prayer, begging the Lord Jesus Christ to forgive my sins and while he was about it, to stop the leg from penduluming to and fro in the dark of the night. Oh, and then there was the time I draped a rosary around it, which made the clonk sound somehow holier and less threatening. The holy stuff seems a bit childish in retrospect, but at the time I believed that at least the ghost of the auld sod, whose leg-substitute it had been, wouldn't haunt me from beyond the grave in an attempt to retrieve it.

"What you doing up there? I've told you the room's all sorted."

Hm, those 'dulcet tones' – as my second cousin Tim used to call them. There was something about mother's voice – it was as if a cheese grater had been applied to her vocal chords when she was young and nubile. It might have sounded sexy then, but now it was plain raucous and rasping. I sat on the top stair and took several deep breaths, hoping to slow down my heart, which was racing like one of dad's pigeons.

How would our new lodger take to us this time around, I wondered… I never dreamed I'd see Tim again after what had happened all those years ago.

Mother was calling him a 'paying guest' as if we were middle class and he were a stranger. She'd managed to make the rent high *and* to keep the rest of the family in the dark, so far. A good example of greed overcoming dislike, I thought. I breathed deeply. My mother was one of those people who could suck all the air out of a room.

"Please don't let it be too horrible," I begged as I reached out and for the first time in years, grabbed the handle – a battered brass knob, dull from lack of care. I gave it a peremptory rub. Unable to find an excuse for further hesitation, I ventured in; heart in mouth.

Well, if I'd thought the landing unpleasant, I was now about to sink further into despair. The old dark brown bedstead was still there – and made up with bedding left over from the Second World War by the look of it. I recognised the counterpane from childhood – but this was a faded, worn version of it. The green was paler where the sun had blanched it and the floral pattern had given up long ago. The rest of the furniture was as bad, but, to give mother her due, she *had* polished it and the beeswax smell, though 'churchy', was better than the smell of the landing.

At the foot of the bed, laid with the careless nonchalance, typical of my mother, was a messy pile of thin towels. 'Oh no', I thought with a sinking heart, 'she's let the cat in.'

In the centre of the towel stack was a darkened area, thick with at least three weeks' worth of hair and animal detritus.

Heart plummeting, I now forced myself to close the door and look behind it.

There was the nail. Dear God, there was the nail it used to hang on! Below it, there was evidence of damaged paintwork, scratched off in a wide semicircle. Would Tim remember?

Surely we *must* still share a mutual memory of that fateful night when he'd heard my night-time weeping and knocked on my door (causing a gentle leg-clonking?). He'd peered into the room to discover the origins of the noise and after quieting my distress took a firm grip on the swaddled, bestockinged object and angrily flung it through the open window into the garden.

Of course, mother's mean little mind assumed there was something 'going on' between us. A massive row ensued and she banished him 'forever' – well, fifty years as it turned out.

It was with deep satisfaction that we'd eyed up the naked hook on the back of the door the following morning.

"Hooray, your room's legless!" he'd laughed defiantly as he'd carried his belongings downstairs for the last time.

I was jolted back to the present by the thought of the grubby mess he was coming into today. I dragged my brain away from all the childhood pain the room once held, and determined, at the very least, to put the cat-hair problem right.

Taking the stairs two at a time, and checking the clock in case I'd left it too late, I headed for the kitchen. Cloths and sweet-smelling cleaning products would soon wipe away all traces of old-fashioned beeswax.

An hour later, jobs done, I grabbed my coat and headed down the road to the supermarket to buy nice towels, pillows and a duvet and sheet set. I *would* make him welcome despite the best efforts of my mother – and to hell with the recriminations it would cause. It was sheer vanity on my part, I know, but I suddenly wanted him to feel comfortable here. I was tired of being ashamed. I found a few flowers that weren't past their best in the garden and arranged them in a vase on the newly-scrubbed windowsill. I couldn't shoo the ghosts away but maybe Tim could? Dipping my hand into the supermarket carrier, I brought out a padded heart-shaped sign, and hung it on the nail behind the door. 'WELCOME' it said. And he would be.

I thought about how long I'd hoped for him to come back; how impressed I always was whenever I heard about his achievements and how – yes, how proud I was to be even the tiniest bit connected with him. I felt sorry that I'd let him down – that I'd let them disown him because of that stupid incident and that I hadn't spoken up in his defence – however useless that would have been.

Tim, a few years older than me, and quite famous and probably rich nowadays, was my childhood hero. When he was invited to make a documentary about his origins, he'd asked to stay with us, and my mother, sensing money, had agreed (at a disproportionately inflated price, of course.) Feeling almost scared, I now wondered what he would be thinking, as I watched him park his shiny new car in our shabby street.

A smell of cologne wafted in with him. Greetings were exchanged – cool on mother's part, enthusiastic on mine. She went to make tea as I took his luggage and indicated the staircase.

Half way up, he took the cases and, putting them on the stair, turned me to face the old mirror. In the worn silvering we stared at our 50-year-old selves.

"Look how we've survived." I smiled then, deciding that in order to carry on surviving, I'd have to leave this house and start living properly, instead of being stifled. I wanted a better future.

Then, "Did they ever retrieve the leg?" he whispered, a smile in his voice.

Relief flooded through me. I laughed and continued up the stairs, "You'll have to see for yourself."

GETTING IT WRONG

The very serious upturned face of the small child had been watching me impassively for some time now. It was disconcerting. I had already tried twinkling – or at least, I'd tried my version of twinkling, which consisted solely of attempting a non-surgical facelift raising every muscle to the limit – brow, nostrils and lips grimacing foolishly in the direction of this unresponsive being.

She was almost scary for all her clear-eyed prettiness.

The chubby hands clutched a doll with implausibly dull yellow hair, whose expression echoed her own.

"That's a nice dolly," I smiled, filled with self-loathing at the patronising tone I'd adopted.

I leaned over the short wooden gate of her garden and made as if to caress the matted-looking doll-hair but the child pulled it closer to her chest in one deft movement of ownership.

"Where's Mummy?" I asked, the grin immovable now.

Before I'd launched into this one-sided conversation, she'd been animated enough. I'd observed her for some time, playing in her front garden with an assortment of soft toys. The game seemed to consist of pouring water from a pink plastic teapot into tiny plastic cups and placing them in front of each of the playmates. In an assertive voice she addressed them in turn: "Sit up nicely!"

The cups soon acquired a sprinkling of detritus from the lawn and then the child tipped the water down their fronts and scolded them again:

"Now then, drink your tea and don't make a mess on my nice clean floor."

"Timmy Thomas, you naughty boy!" Thwack.

The orange bear was thrown headlong into a toy shopping trolley for committing some imaginary sin. "Now sit there and don't move!"

Timmy didn't.

I reckoned the child must've been about four, although that estimate could be wildly inaccurate as I have about as much experience of small children as I have of Martians.

The little girl suddenly pointed to the house behind her without taking her eyes off me for a moment.

'Hooray, progress,' I thought.

The house was an end-of-terrace with a low wooden fence surrounding it. The garden wrapped itself protectively around the front and side and in the right hand corner was a green, wooden gate.

I began to walk slowly over to this gate, still smiling and attempting another opening gambit.

"So, what's she called then, your dolly?"

'Despicable and transparent,' I scolded inwardly. 'I wouldn't answer, never mind her.'

Surprisingly, she was sucked in.

"Peachley Parsenby."

I was silenced. I'd expected… well, I don't know what I'd expected but it wasn't something double-barrelled, that's for sure.

Her face was still a mask of passivity.

I had another go.

"I used to have a doll called Wendy when I was a little girl," I confided. "She used to say Mama when I tipped her up."

By this time we'd both reached the gate – she on the inside, I on the street side. There had been no response to the Wendy revelation, disappointingly. Obviously, technology had moved on and the toy of choice was more sophisticated nowadays. I was well out of the loop.

Moreover, a new complication had thrown itself into the mix.

The gate had been tied up with some sort of grey-looking fabric, possibly from an old t-shirt. It looked as if it had been in situ for some months and the weather had tightened it into the

Gordian knot. Short of hacking at it with a machete, it seemed unassailable.

My temper was beginning to fray.

"How does the postman deliver your letters?" I asked, grin tightening into a rictus.

She was defiantly twisting a lock of the doll's strawy hair. Peachley Parsenby stared blankly back at me, oblivious to this ill-treatment.

The child pointed at an American-style post-box attached to the fence. Embossed on it in gold was the house number and incongruously enough, a painted robin perched on a snow-covered fence at the top. It was mid-June.

"What about parcels?" I countered, triumphantly. A small but mean-spirited victory. I didn't like myself much.

This kid was the queen of cool. Not even bothering to answer, she trotted off to the side of the house, Peachley in tow, and swinging, I noticed, by one golden plait.

"Hey!" I yelled. "Tell your mother I need to speak to her."

But my speech had already acquired that hopeless, upturned ending that signalled 'loser'. I heard that last word echoing in my defeated ears, and swore under my breath.

What to do now? I stood a while, hoping someone would come. This mission had begun in a blaze of righteous anger when my worst fears had been realised earlier in the day.

Something duplicitous had been going on for months and I now had evidence. The receipts in my husband's breast pocket proved it. They all came from an upmarket hotel with 'Sal' marked neatly on them in red ink and they seemed to show where the money had been filtering out to since last January. My husband was guilty as hell. I knew that now and I wanted to confront the other woman, this scarlet 'Sal', whilst I was in the first throes of anger.

To then be deflated by a four-year-old with a doll whose name sounded like a Dickensian heroine, was more than I could bear.

As I turned away, a slim, dark haired woman appeared from the back of the house. She was wiping her hands on a tea towel and was being shadowed by a scruffy grey lurcher.

"Can I help you?" The face was expressionless. Presumably a genetic trait.

"I'm looking for Sal. This is the right address, isn't it?" The stonewalling of her face made me uncertain about the arrangement of my own features. I decided against any more smiling.

"What do you want?"

The child came from the side of the house carrying a piece of toast which the dog began to lick at. She used her doll to bat it out of the way and continued eating, but 'Sal' hadn't noticed any of this.

Time for the denouement, I decided. Might as well do it now I'm here.

"Oh, I just wanted to have a look at the woman who's been on the receiving end of my generosity all these months," I spat out with some bitterness. "Yes, it was me who paid for those expensive dinners and hotels. And I've seen all the receipts so don't deny it." This all said with an air of self-righteous pomposity and an upturned chin.

Identical tiny frowns had appeared on the woman and the child. They tipped their heads to one side in a synchronised gesture of incomprehension. I could see I'd have to spell it out more clearly. It was brazen, this 'innocent' act.

Before I could continue, she said, "You want Sal?" It was my turn to misunderstand. "Yes." I began to waver. "Who are you?" I demanded.

"I'm his wife. My husband is Sal – Salvatore. It's Italian."

She paused to let me take it in. Dear God! My John's gay and he's having an affair with some gigolo? It was worse than even I could've imagined. I started to imagine there and then. Aagh!

The woman shook her head in a gesture of despair and sighed deeply. I managed to calm the teeming set of images in my head long enough to look embarrassed and apologise for getting it all wrong.

"Sal's an agent for them Christmas club things. He does it through the hotel. He's the manager there. If people save up all year they get a couple of cheap weekends whenever it's quiet.

Only, clever bugger puts it through the hotel's books, doesn't he? It's a bit dodgy cos it looks like they've been using the facilities instead of saving up. Keeps Head Office out of the way, apparently. He promised me he wouldn't do it any more after last year's near miss." She went quiet for a few minutes before rallying. "Anyway, sounds like you're in for a Christmas treat this year, eh? But you've spoiled his surprise." Throughout this speech, the woman barely smiled.

Very slowly, and trying to keep my dignity, I smiled back – a genuine smile this time. She was the betrayed woman, not me. And did she care? She looked too tired to care.

I thanked her, apologised again and walked away. The child waved gravely at me as I left. The lurcher had grabbed Peachley Parsenby by the chest and was shaking her vigorously to and fro so that the strawy golden plaits were beginning to unravel, but her expression remained as gently passive as ever.

THE LIGHT FROM
THE CANDLE

Here we are, then… tea no sugar, wasn't it? I'll just settle meself and we can begin. Ooh, nothing like a good hot cup of tea I always say. Mind if I take these shoes off? Oh, what a relief. Right then, where to begin?

We were out singing the other evening, Thursday, I think it was, when I noticed that the light from the candle suddenly made the softened features of the choir seem grotesque. I looked across at Dennis belting out 'God Rest Ye Merry, Gentlemen'. All his bad points had been exaggerated by the uplighter; the overbite giving him a look of Muttley, the cartoon dog. His sincerity was unquestionable, of course, but he was hardly aesthetically matched with the lyric he was expressing. Anyway, back to your question. You were asking about the choir members?

Well, Carole, here, this one in the red sweater and black coat, looked much older in the candle light; see the make-up collecting in the wrinkles at the corners of her eyes? The immaculately applied lipstick bleeding into the tiny vertical lines around the mouth didn't do her any favours either, I thought.

Carole's voice, however, rang out as pure and sweet as ever in the evening air. It has been known to bring tears to the eyes of many audiences once upon a time, you know. She was quite famous, I believe, in her younger days and, as with many talented children, she was so pampered and cosseted, it spoiled her for adulthood. She still sits and waits (on the rare occasions when we go to the pub together), for some man or other to get the drinks in or put her chair away for her after rehearsal. Some women are like that, aren't they?

Is this what you want, by the way? Just general observations about before the news broke? Well, as I was saying, poor Carole…

I think it's just that she doesn't know how to be any different now. Jill has a go at her every now and then – prompting her to buy a round or help out a bit more with clearing things away – but with Carole, great star that she is in her own mind, it feels like an imposition.

By this time we had moved on to the finale of the first set and were changing to more solemn mode with a few verses of, 'See Amid the Winter Snow', when Mr Seldon, our latest recruit, arrived in great haste, carrying several packages along with his trombone, and took his place in the brass section – such as it was.

John Withers stood beside him momentarily, to light up his tealight and affix it to his music stand. He had a supercilious look on his face, like he'd stepped in something nasty – but that was par for the course with John.

Mrs Bexford called him 'Withering Withers' on account of that very look, and he seemed to have adopted it as his fallback position these days.

I noticed as we moved along to the cul-de-sac (that's where we usually have the mulled wine served to us by Norah, in the corner house) that Carole had slid along out of formation and placed herself next to Mr Seldon, whom she insisted on referring to as , 'the mysterious,' as in, 'the mysterious Mr Seldon'.

A spurious title as far as I could see because there was nothing in the least mysterious about him.

True, he didn't hang about much after rehearsal, but, as he'd explained to Dennis, his wife was an invalid, so I could see that he'd have to get back to her as soon as he could.

If it comes to that, a few other choir and band members had pretty shady home lives too. Ted breeds boxer dogs and he's constantly falling out with the neighbours on account of their barking at all hours. He'd had a falling out with Dennis too, over not bringing the biscuits when it was his turn. Petty, I call it, but you have to take people as you find them, don't you?

I was glad they'd made it up, in the end, cos Ted has a lovely, mellow, tenor voice that blends in well with the baritones.

I personally haven't had much to do with Mr Seldon, yet, but I know Carole has always tried to push him into joining our fundraising activities. At one point, in a moment of weakness I suppose, he *did* work with her at Sainsbury's – you know, where the volunteers stand at the end of the checkout packing your bags in the hope of a donation, but there was a complaint, apparently.

Not about Mr Seldon, but one of the women had been making comments about the items in some woman's bag. Something to do with her being too fat and buying all the wrong stuff – I don't know the details, but anyway, we're all banned now.

I reckon it was Madge who did it. She's too thin and keeps quoting that Wallis Simpson thing about you can never be too thin or too rich. "Yes you can!" I told her when she said it. "This is not personal, but you're too thin when your head looks too big to be supported by your body!"

She just walked off but I've noticed her clocking how many biscuits I eat at breaktime in the hope of getting her own back on me. 'Good luck with that,' I thought.

Anyway, to get back to Carole; I think she's always fancied Mr Seldon… and… come to think of it, he *is* quite fit actually, even in the bad light from our candles.

Well anyway, that's how *I* saw it all, until yesterday – just after *you* phoned me, actually.

All this stuff is news to me. It's funny how you think you know someone…

You know, you work alongside them for all these concerts and rehearsals, and you never find out their terrible…

I suppose, someone who's, like, a monster, you'd expect to be able to see it in their face, wouldn't you? I mean, the Nazis and that. I've looked at pictures of Goebbels and Hitler and there's definitely something wrong there – but that Josef Mengele who did all those experiments on people – looking at him, you think, 'Well, he's so handsome, he couldn't do anything bad, could he?' But you'd be wrong.

You know, if I'd seen him on a dating website, I might've connected with him. Not Mengele – Mr Seldon, I mean. Although, who knows… But *this*… and in the middle of the day, an' all.

All this time, sharing our music together. Eee… It's truly terrible… terrible.

Another biscuit? Oh, right. I'll just leave them there in case you change your mind.

I expect the choir will have to break up now. Well, we can't carry on, can we? Nobody will donate next Christmas, will they? Not now, with this scandal hanging over us. And none of us knew he had a wife anyway, let alone… well, enough said about *that*.

Have you switched that thing off now?

No, no, I really don't mind talking to the press, actually. From the horse's mouth, as it were, eh? *Someone* should tell the real story. Not often you come across a real life murderer. Or a few body parts wrapped up like a couple of Christmas turkeys. Well, not in this town – and 'specially not carried round with the carol singers! His poor wife, eh?

Payment?

Oh, even better. No, that's great, thanks. Very generous. Hang on a minute though. If you're going to take a photo, I'll need me lippy on. Bit of colour, you know. Can't look like Marley's ghost in the paper, can I?

Shall I top up your tea first? Oh, right, of course you must be busy. I'll just go and get my bank details. Won't be a minute. Have a look on the mantelpiece while you're waiting. There's a photo of us all performing at the community hall last summer. *He's* there look, smiling his angelic smile. The swine.

THE MEETING

The last thing anyone wants at the end of the working week is a staff meeting. It's the worst possible thing to inflict on anyone – especially on a hot Friday afternoon when the kids have been sweating into their acrylic-clad armpits and plastic trainers since Monday. All a man wants on a Friday afternoon is a quick yomp through moorland or a trek up the gentler slopes of Roseberry Topping to clear the lungs of schoolsmell.

The kids felt it too. Listening to their whoops and cries in the playground, that blissful escape from captivity, he was reminded of the joyful release of homing pigeons from their containers when the groups of fanciers finally open the cramped wicker baskets.

No such release for Tom. He stared out of the dirty staff room windows and prayed that the end would come quickly and that Mr Phipps would steer clear of 'targets and boys progress' today.

The room was rapidly filling up and noise levels were rising. The younger and livelier members of staff – who still had plenty of energy left for their weekend pursuits – chattered and confirmed half-made plans for the weekend. He listened sporadically. *His* plan was to get a few pints down him then head to the fish shop and collapse on the sofa as the expected indigestion hit home. As usual.

Molly, a kindred spirit, indicated a couple of seats near the door (quick escape) and plonked her ample bottom on one. 'Thank God for Molly,' he thought. At least he had a fellow conspirator who would share the odd satirical aside when the Head got too pompous.

"Just had a run-in with Kyle Campbell," she sighed.

Not surprised by this, he made sympathetic noises.

"He knows how to wind me up, that kid. But then he is from the shallow end of the gene pool."

The Head coughed expectantly. "If we could make a start, ladies and gentlemen," he intoned in what he thought was the voice of authority, "it *is* Friday afternoon and I'm sure we all want to get home as soon as possible." The smile of the viper slid across his thin features.

"Have you noticed how all our troublemakers are called Kyle?" Molly observed casually, ignoring the head's background drone, "but this one's Kyle factor is supercharged."

He nodded and leaned across, conspiratorially. "I reckon his dad spat on a wall, and when the sun came out, he hatched."

Sharp intake of breath and choking noises as Molly enjoyed the audacity of the insult. She grinned broadly at the whole room as the staff turned, as one, to see who was disturbing the peace.

Nobody noticed Annabel Lacey sashay into the room. Seeing that there were no chairs available, she perched next to the Head of Geography on a table opposite Molly and the business of the afternoon began.

Tom, a big, easygoing, affable sort of man, had an avuncular way with the students. He was sharp and witty and full of good sense, which endeared him to both pupils and staff. Past his sexual prime, he was happy to spend time with the wife and kids on a variety of harmless hobbies, but today as the meeting progressed, he became aware of the proximity of Annabel Lacey's body to his. His eye level was at her crotch level. She was wearing a disconcertingly tight-fitting black skirt which had ridden up slightly as she'd hoisted herself onto the table, exposing a fair length of thigh. Interesting. Or it would have been if he'd been sitting in Molly's seat.

The Head droned on. The room was stuffy and hot. His eyes were magnetised by a side view of the thighs.

If he were to shuffle *minutely* to the right – not even moving his chair, but sliding his body across imperceptibly, he would be able to see – well – more.

Molly nudged him. "I've heard two 'tick all the boxes' and

one 'thinking outside the box' so far," she urged. "Are you playing?"

He was brought to earth with a jolt. Ah yes. Wankers' Bingo. It was a game they played when edu-speak became too horribly irritating. You ticked off the meaningless, ridiculous expressions as the Head trotted them out. Tom had heard two, 'blue-sky-thinking's and a 'moving forward' in one memorable session last Easter. He nudged her back and nodding at Molly, wrote, "Five 'robusts' and a couple of 'ball park figures'!" on the flyleaf of his diary. He passed it to Molly, still preoccupied.

'Control yourself, man!' his subconscious urged as his eyes went unbidden back to the forbidden.

He didn't even fancy Annabel Lacey. Too much make-up and a Tory to boot. She also had a habit of standing in the doorway having conversations and not budging –even when she could see you behind her, struggling with sets of books, unable to get past.

And yet, here he was, trying to get a glimpse of her crotch. And he would too, if he moved a little more to the right and put his weight on his right thigh.

The Head of Geography, a small, round woman, was blushing and responding to a criticism. Something about exam results? Who cared?

However, this gave Tom a legitimate reason to stare in their direction, just as Annabel was shifting slightly, the better to hear her.

'Ah, that makes it a bit easier,' he thought.

Stopping himself and looking at the situation logically, he realised what he was doing.

If he succeeded in the business at hand, what would he achieve? He'd see a triangle of cloth. That's all. A private triangle of cloth. And although he was disgusted with himself, he couldn't stop.

Molly handed him a note. These distractions were usually diverting but he felt a little impatient today. His need was becoming all-consuming. He dropped the note on the floor unread and lurched to his right, ostensibly to retrieve it.

Annabel's now-crossed legs had lifted the skirt slightly, allowing tantalisingly-easy access to his goal.

In a split second he saw the pale triangle of her knickers. Annabel Lacey wore cream silk underwear!

But his triumph was short-lived. Losing control of his own body, he toppled to the floor, banging his head on the sharp edge of a coffee table. Annabel jumped down at once and rushed to help him. She squatted at his feet, heedless of the acres of underwear now on display for his exclusive perusal. Alas, they had lost their charm. He was aware only of the throbbing in his head and the pain in his jaw. He realised he'd have a black eye tomorrow.

A plastic cup of tepid, chlorine-tasting water was thrust to his lips and spilled down the front of his shirt as he shifted his ungainly bulk to avoid Annabel's opened knees.

Molly lifted him bodily and plonked him back on his chair, his last shred of dignity gone.

"I'm fine," he assured them all, with a grimace that tried to be a smile.

He read the note later that night, a couple of pints to the good. He took it from his trouser pocket and uncrumpled it.

'Wanna swap seats?' it asked. 'La Lacey is exposing herself to me and it's not a pretty sight.'

REMEMBRANCE DAY

Barriers in place, the road closed off, robed choristers troop
down the path from church,
Line up,
respectful, in the bright, November air.
Before us, the stone column to the village dead, gleams gray.
'Sunny this year, at least,' a nearby voice mutters.
We are bathed in the sun's light
And blinded by it, as we silently honour the carved names
Read them aloud, one by one,
Village lads; tradesman, labourer and landowner,
Farmer and fisherman
Standing safe in the middle of the road,
We think of their short lives,
The ones who shall not grow old.
The familiar words, a catechism every year on this day,
Repeated again: lest we forget.
At The Last Post, we fall silent, as the guns of war fell silent.
But today there is no silence.
The traffic still revs in the distance,
The gulls wheel and scream overhead, careless of our solemnity.
Nearby, crows caw from rooftops,
discordant above the bugle's call.
Behind us, a child runs amok, rubber boots beating out
arhythmically on the tarmac'd road.
The dead – used to screams and tramping boots – don't mind.
This is, after all, what they fought for.

One young soldier, immaculate and dignified,
Stands proud, salutes,
And breaks my heart.

ISAAC

Isaac fell into deep silence. I dared not breathe. A while later, he looked up and smiled.

Having once held a loose connection with 'theatricals' and indeed, having once been paid for small parts in what he termed 'the film industry', Isaac could be forgiven for being self-absorbed.

Flamboyant and ego-driven, he lived up to his name, having a whiff of the Old Testament about him in his speech and his way of thinking, which must have arisen from his theatrical past. I think we forgive him because we all love him, although I did find him distinctly odd at first.

He certainly has us all in his thrall nowadays, being in the habit of making melodramatic pronouncements from time to time just to keep us on our toes.

None of us have any idea where this self-aggrandisement originated. It wasn't passed down from a moneyed family. His origins were humble and his relatives were, without exception, pretty uncouth. I imagine that's where the disconnect is and why he seems free – floating just above reality most of the time.

Apparently, in his younger days he'd had bit parts in several (un-named) films and had rubbed shoulders with – to quote him – 'some of the greats'. Nobody ever found out which 'great' he'd spent more than a couple of minutes with but, since that was more than any of us had done, nobody cared to question any of his yarns.

Even though he eventually admitted to not knowing Richard Attenborough, he always referred to him as 'Dickie', as if they'd been on intimate terms. I loved him for it. I think it was this naive vulnerability that charmed me. How easy it would have been to call his bluff, should any of us be cruel enough to do so. But we weren't.

Isaac is in the pub, writing a poem. It is, as always, addressed to the assistant in the newsagent's where he buys his paper every morning. His preoccupation with her began some years ago when he was in his artistic phase. At first he tried to paint her from photos he'd secretly taken using his new toy, a camera with a telescopic lens. I'm pretty sure that's illegal, actually, unless you get permission. I'm not up to speed on these things. You'll have to ask Monty if you want to know how he managed that one.

I know, I know, it sounds creepy, about the photos, but Isaac is such a child when it comes to his passions. He's quite pure in heart. You think that sounds like an excuse? It isn't. Ask any of them, they'll confirm it. Everyone loves him.

Anyway, the portrait was hardly a success. He threw away countless sketches and a few canvasses before he gave up. Now he's attempting to 'capture her in words'. I'm not sure she knows about this... could you call it a crush? She just treats him like any other customer, so he has to keep the worshipping to a minimum when he's in the shop. Such admirable self-restraint.

Of course he knows he hasn't a hope in hell of his affection being returned.

There's the way he's dressed, for a start – those, shall we say, 'pungent' sandals he's been wearing all summer, well, until we had a word about them anyway. His unruly mop of hair, his random passions for odd ideas and odder people, his dietary whims, going on and off certain foods until you never knew what to cook if he were coming for dinner. Locusts and wild honey, anyone?

Sometimes, he would lose heart, though, and he'd steal yours in the process. We had to coax him to re-enter the world when he was unhappy. Those days when his grand schemes came to nothing and the scales fell from his eyes were almost too painful to watch. We usually gave him the alcohol cure, then he loved us all again, and then he loved himself again and jumped back onto the switchback of his life and we paid our fares and rode along with him once more.

This poetry writing was something new, however.

"Go on then, Isaac, read it out to us," said Benny on the night of the pub quiz.

He turned horrified eyes to us. "What? Let some of the pismires in on the work of the Gods? This is about an angel. The angel with the Good News."

We laughed, getting the biblical reference, and he was satisfied.

"Come off it, mate. She works in the paper shop," Benny laughed.

He left then, muse intact and still private. "I'll do a reading though, when I'm happy with it," he promised, pausing at the door to make an exit; but we weren't satisfied and plotted the evening away, working out ways to get to see the poem. How we would come to regret it.

I didn't see much of Isaac in the weeks that followed. He must have been labouring away at his redrafting in between shifts at the steel mill where he worked. Once I caught him as his shift finished but he waved away any suggestion of coffee or food, and I laughed as he indicated a scrubby old pencil behind his right ear.

Benny, in the meantime, had managed to penetrate Isaac's inner sanctum – being the only one who lived in his block of flats and therefore the only one with a key. Having made such a fuss about it beforehand, he was strangely quiet once the deed was done. We all thought the poem must be a disaster and decided to speak no more about it, even to each other.

It was the evening of Isaac's birthday when he finally graced us with his presence at the pub quiz.

"Hooray!" we all shouted in unison when he made his entrance, flapping a piece of paper like a politician with portentous news.

Benny stood at once, agitated and anxious. "Nah, mate. You don't have to read it to us. As you said, it's private."

"S'okay. The world is now ready for this, I think."

Benny took Isaac gently by the arm and led him to the corner of the room. They talked for some moments, with us as bemused onlookers, then Isaac turned on his heel and left.

Benny returned to our table and explained. He had photocopied Isaac's poem and sent it to the girl in the newsagent's shop.

"Well, he'd never do it, would he – left to his own devices." Benny sounded worried and unsure.

The group was split. Everybody had an opinion and we all thought differently. Was there a breach of trust? Was it a good thing – in the long run? Would he ever speak to us again? Did he think we were all involved?

Benny threw the crumpled copy of Isaac's poem onto the table. It immediately absorbed a small spillage of beer before I could snatch it up and wipe it on my sleeve.

Should we read it? Would that compound the problem? How do we get back from this?

I took the moral high ground at first, and said on no account should we look at it but Monty reminded us that Isaac had come intending to read it to us, so it must be okay, right?

Somehow it fell to me to read it to the gang. Taking a deep breath, I began:

"The face without a flaw.
I look at the lips
Neglecting the rest –
I hate perfection.
Greedily, now, I take in lashes, pupils,
that half-smile in the eyes.
Is it echoed in the lips? Now? And now?
I slide my eyes down
To trace the mouth again.
Sulky
And more interesting?
Perfect until…
Unsated, I gaze at the face complete.
How can it be so perfect?

How can skin be smoothly sandblasted into living marble?
I need the flaw.
And at last, I find it.
A tiny scar above the sculpted eyebrow
A laughter line along the lips.
And I say, 'Thank you, God.'
It's only in our flaws that we are lovable.
It is movement, the voice, the not-quite-perfection that
Defines us as human.
A stray curl or frown line,
the clothes that glide uneasily across the body.
Details that relieve us of our fear
that we cannot measure up."

As I reached the last line, Isaac was suddenly there again, in the silence. I dared not breathe. Then he smiled, and I read:

"It's the flaw that gives me leave to love her."

A hush followed my reading. Then Benny said, "That was bloody rubbish!" and Monty said, "Wow." And in the silence that followed, I was left with a sad sort of homesickness.

PLAYING WITH THE PROFESSIONALS

A buttery sun struggled through the early morning mist and in through the window of 36, Acacia Avenue.

Bernice, noticing the time and ignoring the morning light, hurried through the house, picking up randomly-strewn documents from floor and furniture, and doing a bit of desultory tidying as she went.

It was a ten minute walk to the station so she'd have plenty of time to make sandwiches for the journey and be there with a little time to spare if she got a move on.

The dog barked at the rattle of the letterbox and she dashed to head him off before the post or the postman or both were destroyed. He was a rescue dog, and quite unpredictable. Now, having done the rescuing – which had been the easy bit – Bernice was in the process of training him a bit. Trouble was, they hadn't agreed yet about what was good behaviour and she was resorting to bribery-by-food now, after an attempt at 'strict commands' and 'tugging-at-his-lead' had been abject failures. Bernice sighed. Perhaps she should have accepted that she was really a cat person.

The licking had been a bit of a shock at first. "Cats don't lick," she'd told him during the strict phase.

"Oh, well," she said to him, ever the philosopher, "maybe we'll come to some arrangement when you grow up a bit."

Sending a text message to Mrs Wilmslow, her neighbour of thirty years standing, she listed the times and needs of the dog's walks and feeds. Slipping the spare key into an envelope, she hurried to the neighbour's back door and shouted, "You-hooo."

A tiny woman in jogging bottoms and a t-shirt came smiling to the door.

"Oh, hello, Mrs Watkins. Is this the key?"

"Yes, I'm afraid I'm running a bit late, Mrs Wilmslow. The instructions were texted from here," indicating her phone, "and thank you so much for looking after him. I'm trying to get control of the licking but I'm afraid you'd better prepare for the worst. I've got packets of wipes all over the place so please feel free to make use of them," then, glancing at her watch and hoping she wasn't seen doing it, she waved a cheery, final goodbye before she hurried away, back to the chaos of her own house. Although the two women had been friends for so long, they somehow never got round to the familiar first name terms that usually mark out long term friendships. Both of them seemed to have got used to the status quo by this time and could see no reason to change.

'And,' she thought, returning to the dog vs cat argument playing out in her head, 'at least cats don't make the house smell of dog.' Then, laughing at her own stupid observation, she did a final quick check of herself.

Make-up, okay. Hair, too unruly as usual, despite that new mousse stuff her daughter had bought her. Clothes... 'Hmm, not sure about this new dress but it's too late now. Just teeth to clean and lippy to reapply and I'm all set.'

On her walk to the station she *did* notice the weather, which had changed to a diamond-bright sunlight in a blue sky, now that the morning haze had burned off. It reminded Bernice, as these days always did, of the first day of Autumn term when she would walk to Secondary School. There was the customary nip in the air after the lazy summer and she, in her stiff new uniform, too big as yet, could sense the promise of the future. The weather meant business, and so did she.

Today, though, there would be no rowdy teenage reunions as old school friends hallooed greetings, regaling each other with news of holidays, romances and disasters. Today it was up to her. Today was very important and would decide her fate.

The city, greyer than Bernice's small town, looked grand and proud. Beautiful architecture and huge public fountains and green spaces made Bernice feel small and insignificant, as people ignored and pushed at her. Feeling slightly ill-at-ease with it all and clutching her document case close to her chest, she struggled with her handbag – trying to pull the long straps over her head and across her body for extra security.

"So many people," she said, then wondered if anyone had heard her. Not that it mattered. There were plenty of odd people in strange-looking garb passing by. It was unnerving.

At last she saw a taxi and hailed it successfully. It was the third one. Two others had sailed by.

It was only when a young man told her, "They only stop when their light isn't on," that she understood the code. So much to learn.

"Please would you take me here?" she asked, handing a crumpled piece of paper to the driver, who called her 'love'.

"No problem, love."

She wondered what he called the men. 'Mate' probably. 'No problem, mate.'

"Written a best-seller then, love?" he asked, laughing.

"Well, as a matter of fact, I have."

He craned his neck then, to look at her properly. She knew what he was thinking. 'Old Biddy like that, writing a best-seller? Pull the other one.'

"They want to buy the rights for a film company. I'm here to speak to them about the changes they want to make."

That shut him up.

After a long journey, which Bernice suspected had been the long way round, or the 'scenic route' as Jim used to call it, they drew up beside the flashy front of the publisher's head office. She'd never been anywhere like this before and her jaw dropped at the size and height of the building.

The driver relented at the last, shaking her hand and wishing her luck, so she tipped him extravagantly before walking in through the grand entrance.

Suzie and Annabelle were there to meet her. This would be a lucrative deal for them both and they meant to 'help' as much as possible to ensure a smooth negotiation.

"Now, Bernie," said Suzie, in the sort of patronising voice she generally used for junior clerks, "Dom has been so-o-o busy lately that he's been unavoidably delayed, so *we'll* outline the plan until he arrives, if that's alright?"

"Oh, where's he coming from today?" she asked.

"Oh, er, no idea, but the traffic in London, as you know...'"

"Well, I *don't* know, as a matter of fact. It's eleven o'clock and I've been travelling for three hours to be here – on time."

They exchanged knowing looks. The knowingness was how to deal with the likes of Bernice. They must have done it many times before.

"Oh, Bernie, darling!" cooed Suzie in mock-sympathy, "Annabelle, get Seth to bring some food will you? As quickly as possible. You poor love, you must be absolutely starving."

Bernice smiled. "I don't need food. I do, however need good manners and 'Dom', whoever he is, is not showing me any courtesy by being late."

"Oh, but we have all the proposals here!" said Suzie, gluing on a smile.

"I've read them."

It was Anabelle's turn to gush. "Of course you have. So... are we ready to move this along?"

"No. I don't want you to take Mrs Wilmslow out of the story. After all, she's the one who helped bury the body."

"Hi there!" shouted a voice from the doorway.

"DOM!" exclaimed the two women.

Dom, a fat, brash American, booled into the room and was embraced by first Suzie and then Annabelle. He then turned his attention to Bernice, and turning his ultra-white teeth on her exclaimed, "And you must be Bernice! Glad to meet ya, Bernice," and to prove it, he enveloped her in a massive, rather damp embrace and kissed her on both cheeks. The excessive use of his rather pungent cologne clung to Bernice's new dress and drowned out her own, milder, perfume for ages after.

"Sorry about the lateness, ladies. Traffic, ya know."

Suzie broke the news to him. "Dom, Bernice doesn't want Mrs Wilmslow to be cut from the screenplay."

"Well, now, Bernice, our thinking on that score wasn't that we'd take the Wilmslow character out, ya know. We just thought we'd give her a bit more glamour, a bit of 'pazzaz' with a makeover. It'll be great because if 'Mary' and this Wilmslow were in their twennies, the whole thing would be sexier. I mean, ya godda admit, Bernice, it lacks sex right now."

Taken aback somewhat, Bernice gathered herself.

"You know what, Dom, it took me years to write this book, and a bit longer to do the screenplay. Now don't get me wrong, the money would come in very handy, but you can't just sweep in here with your dollars and add things that didn't happen. These are ladies – shall we say, of a certain age. What they lack in sex-appeal they more than make up for in ingenuity and wisdom. No flibbertygibbet could have planned and executed this murder. That's what made the book such a best-seller."

Annabelle interjected anxiously, "And it's *wonderful*, darling – positively grisly! But now it's time to let the experts sort out the screenplay. Sex sells, you know."

"You bet," nodded Dom, re-inflating his ego. "So, that's sorted then?"

They all stared at Bernice, confident and happy about what they thought they'd won.

"Well, no, actually. That's not how it happened. The disposing of the body and the aftermath were exhausting. If a couple of girls did it, most of the effort and the grimness would go. You'd probably let the camera linger on their bodies wouldn't you – a few arse shots and heaving bosoms with designer mud placed strategically, yet lipstick still in place – and that's not me nor Mrs Wilmslow at all."

Suddenly, Bernice saw the futility of it all. And suddenly, she fancied a cigarette. She'd given up 25 years ago, but now, all of a sudden, it seemed a good idea.

The girls scrabbled around for an ashtray, but Bernice just used a saucer from the best china coffee service on the table.

She looked at Dom's copy of the new 'improved' script on the table, pristine but adulterated, on the clinically clean surface of the desk.

After that, it was easy really. She simply put the match to it and it smouldered for a second before it took. Then in just a few moments, there was a small greyish-black mound of ashes, still definable as paper but thinner than tissue. Bernice was fascinated by the way the leaves kept their shape as they burned.

Suzie, in panic mode, reached for the fire extinguisher, yelling.

'A bit of an extreme reaction,' thought Bernice, 'but typical of her.'

Annabelle took a more measured approach. "What the f..." She stopped in mid-sentence, watching Bernice sip the last mouthful of the executive coffee before gathering up her document case, handbag and coat.

"Well, it's been interesting," she said, "but a complete waste of time." She smiled serenely. "If you don't like true crime thrillers, maybe you should get someone else to create a fictional version?"

Pulling herself up to her full height, she raised her voice slightly, as if ready to make a declaration. "Me and Enid Wilmslow are proud of how we bumped off my Jim and no simpering teenager is going to steal our thunder on screen. I put up with years of abuse from that little worm. If you change your mind, and get a couple of OAPs to play us instead, Dom, I'm in the phone book."

Later in the afternoon, emerging from the railway station into an orange-coloured sunset, she strolled happily back to her quiet little home. She would enjoy telling Mrs Wilmslow about her day in the big city and how she'd left them all open-mouthed. They would never work out whether she was telling the truth about the murder. She was really such an ordinary-looking woman, after all.

The dog was there to meet her at the door of Acacia Avenue, waggy and slobbery in his joy to see her home.

"I think you need a name if you're staying," she said. "I think I'll call you Dom."